Bad Press

Maureen Carter

*For Joyce
With love and affection
Maureen
x*

CREME DE LA CRIME

Praise for Maureen Carter's gritty Bev Morriss series:

Many writers would sell their first born for the ability to create such a distinctive voice in a main character.
- Sharon Wheeler, Reviewing the Evidence

Complex, chilling and absorbing... confirms Carter's place among the new generation of crime writers.
- Julia Wallis Martin, author of *The Bird Yard*

Imagine Bridget Jones meets Cracker... gritty, pacy, realistic and... televisual. When's the TV adaptation going to hit our screens?
- Amazon

Fast moving, with a well realised character in... Bev Morriss.
- Mystery Lovers

a cracking story that zips along...
- Sarah Rayne, author of *Tower of Silence*

British hard-boiled crime at its best.
- *Deadly Pleasures* Year's Best Mysteries 2007 (USA)

... a first-rate book... Carter did an excellent job of showing the pressures... I have ordered the first books in this series!
- Maddy Van Hertbruggen, *I Love a Mystery* Newsletter

... it is good to see a publisher investing in fresh work that, although definitely contemporary in mood and content, falls four-square within the genre's traditions.
- Martin Edwards, author of the highly acclaimed Harry Devlin Mysteries

Crème de la Crime... so far have not put a foot wrong.
- Reviewing the Evidence

First published in 2008
by Crème de la Crime
P O Box 523, Chesterfield, S40 9AT

Typesetting by Yvette Warren
Cover design by Yvette Warren
Front cover image by Peter Roman

ISBN 978-0-9557078-3-4
A CIP catalogue reference for this book is available from
the British Library

Printed and bound in Poland EU, produced by Polskabook

www.cremedelacrime.com

About the author:
Maureen Carter has worked extensively in the media. She lives in Birmingham with her husband and daughter. Visit her website:

www.maureencarter.co.uk

I am again hugely indebted to Lynne Patrick and her inspirational team at Crème de la Crime. Many thanks also to Lesley Horton for her editorial skill and insight. For their help in my research I thank the *Birmingham Mail*'s women's editor Diane Parkes and the crime correspondent Mark Cowan. Being back in a newsroom was great fun, though of course the journalists in *Bad Press* are fictional creations. Like Bev I became an 'instant expert' on the UK comedy circuit thanks to stand-up comedian Caimh McDonnell who shared his knowledge and expertise so generously.

As I've said before, writing would be a lonelier place without the support of some special people. For 'being there' even when they're sometimes miles away, my love and affection go to: Sophie Shannon, Peter Shannon, Veronique Shannon, Corby and Stephen Young, Paula and Charles Morris, Suzanne Lee, Helen and Alan Mackay, Frances Lally, Jane Howell, Henrietta Lockhart, Anne Hamilton and Bridget Wood.

Finally, my thanks to readers everywhere – as always, this is for you.

For Douglas Hill
in fondest memory
1935–2007

For a man who'd be dead in five hours, Adam Graves looked remarkably good. He couldn't see that – or anything else – right now. The bathroom was like a sauna; it was difficult to detect the aquiline nose in front of his face through a mirror wreathed in grey mist.

Adam wiped away the condensation, then stood back and took a long detached look. He was fit, and knew it. A deep tan enhanced the defined muscle tone. He was in better shape, ironically, than most men half his age. The thick black hair was definitely, defiantly, too long for his forty-four years, but women liked it. A bitter smile ghosted his lips: the thought no longer gave him pleasure. He snatched a jade silk dressing gown from the back of the door and tied the cord tightly round his waist.

Fastidious about his appearance, he took even greater pains this morning. What was that movie? *Looking Good Dead*. He scowled. Sick joke. Not funny. Momentarily overcome, Graves lunged at the basin and gagged.

Deep breaths helped regain superficial control. He flicked on the radio, ignored *Today*'s running order, willed himself through his own early morning agenda. Shave. Teeth. Hair. Shave. Teeth. Hair…

As he lathered his chin, the smell of almond cream mingled with those of the espresso and croissants Madeleine was fixing downstairs. The thought of food turned a stomach that was already churning. Not that he'd breakfast at home. Not on a Wednesday. It wasn't part of their domestic routine.

Adam expertly ran the razor along his taut jaw-line. For a nanosecond, he imagined slicing the jugular, ending it here and now. He stilled the blade over the artery; observed, clinically almost, the pulse flicker, then closed his eyes, could almost taste blood. No. Stick to the plan. Shave. Teeth. Hair. Shave...

Carefully, he drew the blade down the plane of his cheek, chiselled features once more impassive, long sensitive fingers steady. The mauve smudges under his grey eyes talked of broken sleep, not shattered lives. These things he noted coolly, dispassionately.

A neighbour would later tell police that Doctor Graves always looked the same: like a man who didn't have a care in the world. The observation would have pleased Adam. It was what he wanted people to think.

A shiny scarlet bead oozed as the blade nicked his skin. He winced, pressed tissue to the tiny wound, uttered a sotto voce, "Damn." The unwitting irony provoked laughter bordering on hysteria, both immediately stifled. More deep breaths. Shave. Teeth. Hair...

He'd agonised for weeks about what to do; the thinking time was over. It was the first of August – the last day of his life. Meticulously, he cleaned and dried the razor. As he brushed his teeth, his mind replayed scenes he should have refused to take part in. Again, he closed his eyes; jaw clenched so tightly it hurt. Was it worth it? One moment of madness...

Except it wasn't one moment. And he'd been perfectly sane.

He straightened, spat into the sink, licked toothpaste from his top lip. Though his death would devastate Madeleine and their son Lucas, learning the truth would destroy them. Adam couldn't face that. In more rational moments, he knew the argument was specious. In reality, he knew he was a coward.

Not that he was scared of dying. He'd held patients' hands, whispered platitudes as they took their final breath. He stared unflinching into the mirror, dragged a comb through his hair. It wasn't death that scared Adam Graves; it was life.

Strong sunlight splashed through the casement window as Adam padded across the galleried landing. The deep ivory carpet warmed his soles. He lingered a while outside his son's room. Lucas rarely put in an appearance before mid-morning. Adam fought the urge to enter, bandy a few exchanges. It would be a bad move: this wasn't a day for firsts.

The grey linen suit he'd carefully selected was hanging on the outside of an ornately carved wardrobe. Adam dressed quickly and put a few items into a battered Gladstone bag. The bag had belonged to his father; Adam's continued use of it was an affectation that spoke of clinging to the past, of family loyalty and the comfort of familiarity. The irony didn't register with him this time as he slipped silently through the connecting double doors into his wife's bedroom. The peaches and cream décor was not to his taste. Unnaturally neat, it could have been used as a set for *Beautiful Interiors*. His lip twitched: very Madeleine. He inhaled the scent of her vanilla perfume as he headed for the bed. And as he slipped an envelope under her satin pillow, he told himself he was doing it for her.

But then Adam told himself a lot of things these days.

The handcrafted kitchen was a vast expanse of green tiles and dark woods. Madeleine Graves perched on a high stool at the breakfast bar, like a slightly overweight fairy in a forest. The diaphanous lilac negligee didn't do a lot for her. Neither did the pink chiffon scarf attempting to tame unruly chestnut locks. Despite her current sartorial shortcomings, she hadn't stinted cosmetically. Madeleine was probably more sensitive about the age gap than Adam.

She offered her husband a glowing peach cheek for the familiar peck. "What time will you be home, darling?" For the doctor's wife, it was just an ordinary day. She licked a finger, turned the page, apparently engrossed in a story about a thirteen-year-old who'd fathered triplets.

Maybe she sensed something in the pause, heard something in the silence. When no response came, she finally lifted her head, lines deepening between her amber eyes.

"About six?" Adam said.

No. He was fine. "Excellent." Madeleine blew another kiss through a peachy pout, frowned as she spotted a mark on his shirt collar. Her wagging finger and indulgent smile, beckoned him closer.

"I'm late already, Maddie. What is it?" He was backing towards the door.

She shrugged. The perfect doctor: patients always came first. He was obviously in a hurry. He wouldn't have time to change the shirt; and maybe no one else would notice. "No worries, darling."

Though she couldn't recall the last time her husband had cut himself shaving.

An elderly couple walking their teenaged Jack Russell through Hanbury Woods that evening spotted the battered Gladstone bag first. The scuffed leather case lay in a clearing to the right. It was an incongruous sight, but easier for the brain to process than the rest of the scene. The old woman wanted to believe that local youths had been throwing cans of red paint around again. Yobs had already targeted the church and parish hall. In reality neither she nor her retired police officer husband thought this was a mindless attack by vandals. But it was a more acceptable interpretation of what their eyes saw.

Scarlet grass? Leaves sprayed red? Their dog prancing round a man's body lying in a crimson pool?

The old man patted his wife's arm, told her not to move. He edged closer, gently coaxing the animal away. "Here, Nelson. Good boy, Nelson. Who's a good boy then?"

Not Nelson. The dog was tearing at a dark red gash that had once been a man's throat. And it was ruining a crime scene.

The old man turned to his wife hoping she wasn't in shock. "We need to call the police. Got your mobile, love?"

She lifted a hand to shush him. She was already on the phone issuing directions.

MONDAY
1

"Say again?" Tired and tetchy, the crime correspondent of the Birmingham *Evening News* regretted last night's Balti but not as much as the beer. And the brandy. It had seemed like a good idea at the time, but when the phone rang two hours down the line, Matt Snow was barely awake, let alone fully alert. The reporter tried sitting up but his head felt surgically attached to his sweaty pillow. A voice he couldn't place right now was banging on about a tip just phoned in to the news desk: man's body, major incident, Ladywood. Could be an exclusive. And there was a hole the size of Canada on the front page.

Ordinarily Snowie would have been well up for it. He loved his work: the kudos more than the cash. Which was lucky. And he was good at what he did. Strike that. He was ace. Just not right now...

"Look, mate. Give it The Bishop. He'll do you a good job." Matt didn't rate Toby Priest. The young reporter wasn't in the same league. If the story had legs it would soon come running back to papa Snow.

"Your call, dude. But I reckon it's got biggie written all over it."

Snow frowned, didn't care for the tone. Was it the new guy? Skippy? He raked fingers through a short straw-coloured fringe. Its normal tufted appearance was one of the reasons fellow hacks called him Tintin. Generally behind his back. The reporter swallowed a curry-laced burp. He was definitely torn between a warm duvet and a shit hot story. His weekly column and the occasional motormouth gig on local telly put Snowie in the big-fish-small-bowl class, but he lusted for Great White category. One lucky break and the pigmies he had to work with would be calling him Jaws. Even so, a guy had to get his zeds in. He drawled through a badly stifled yawn, "If you can't reach The Bishop, give us a call back."

"Forget it. I'm not your freaking secretary. I'll find someone who gives a shit."

Aussie dork was hanging up. "OK, OK. Hold on." He reached for the pad and pen he kept by the bed. "Sling us the address again." Details scrawled, he gave a muted, "Thanks, mate."

"Pleasure's mine." Pause. "Tintin."

He gunned the gleaming black Ferrari along slick city streets. Slick? Or mean? Matt Snow couldn't make up his mind. He was forever killing time by mentally drafting lines for his first block-buster. It was all in his head, not a word on paper yet, but Dan Brown, eat your heart. Snow reckoned his opus would make *The Da Vinci Code* look like kiddie Cluedo.

In the real world, the reporter was on the pavement outside his flat just off the Hagley Road in Edgbaston, freezing his balls off and failing to flag down a black cab. First week in October – whatever happened to an Indian summer? He stomped his feet to try and keep warm. Where were all the taxis? Jeez! It was only half one in the morning, and this was a main drag into town.

Snowie sighed, ruffled his fringe. The car keys in his pocket rubbed temptingly against his leg, but he suspected he was still over the limit; last thing he wanted was to lose his licence. A hack without a carriage was like tonic without gin. The locus (he liked that word; might use it) was only a stone's throw. The Churchill estate was well walkable. Then again…

The Fiesta started first time, which was good going. Recently he'd been calling it the Fiasco, and was trading it in next week. He wanted something with a bit more poke, bit more street cred.

He fancied a Midget but Bev Morriss would rip the piss something rotten if he went for a Morriss-mobile. Like he was bothered. He'd be more worried if she didn't give him a hard time. He and the spiky DS had crossed more swords than Lancelot. But Morriss was a good cop – even if she did have a gob on her.

Snow wasn't drunk or he'd never have got behind the wheel, but he drove like a snail on Mogadon to compensate. Even so it took less than five minutes to reach the less than salubrious location. The Churchill lay – lolled – cheek by jowl with the city's richest quarters. The five-star-first-class-top-banana-notch likes of the National Indoor Arena, the International Convention Centre, the Hyatt, the Rep were all in spitting distance. Which was most Churchill residents' speciality sport.

The reporter parked the car on a scrubby grass verge, killed the engine, re-acquainted himself with his surroundings. Every reporter in the city knew the housing estate; every police officer knew it better. Its grotty council semis and solitary tower block had been slung up in the sixties and slunk down inexorably since. Its streets were neither mean nor slick. They were dustbins and dog shit, gang culture and graffiti.

Most residents thought it was named after the dog that flogged insurance on the telly ads. Challenge Churchill? Yeah right. Given the crime tsunami round here, they'd be lucky to get third party on a pushbike.

And Matt was staring at the biggest wave: ASBO Tower. Nineteen floors pocked with pushers and pimps, felons and fuckwits. High-rise lowlifes who made it home-shit-home for the few decent folk who hadn't moved out: families clinging like hairs round a bath. Steel-railed balconies broke up the grim grey fascia, limp washing still hung on makeshift clotheslines, kids' toys and pot plants added the odd daub of colour, but even that was muted in the jaundiced glow of streetlights. Matt counted a dozen or so windows that showed signs of life: insomniacs. Or inmates up to no good.

He frowned. Something was missing. Cops cars were like lampposts on the Churchill: permanent fixtures. He reckoned residents could charge the Bill parking fees. But then they'd have to speak English. And talk to a pig. He doubted there'd be many who'd do both.

But there wasn't a copper in sight. And that made Matt uneasy. There should be shed-loads. The news desk had talked major incident. He glanced at the address he'd scribbled. Yep. One of the tatty little shops opposite ASBO, sorry, Asquith Tower. He checked out the row: launderette, butcher's, chippie, Spar, offie.

So where was the party? He tapped a seriously browned-off finger on the gear stick. Not so much as a solitary uniform. Should be a full crime scene: CID, SOCOs, meat wagon, the works. Unless? He scratched a nascent pimple on his cheek. What if the cops didn't even know about it? What if the informant hadn't called them? Or called the paper first? People round here had more faith in the tooth fairy than the law. They'd rather give a steer to Bin Laden than a boy in blue. Matt felt a tingle. Not an adrenalin rush, but a definite trickle. If he'd read it right, he wasn't just ahead of the pack, he was a nose in front of the police.

Best take a peep. His hand stilled en route to open the door. Anxious eyes scanned the street in front, took in the rear view via the mirror. The reporter wasn't a wimp, but he and Clark Kent had only one thing in common, and it wasn't being Superman. There'd been a shooting and six stabbings on the Churchill this year, two fatals.

When Snow's column wasn't taking a pop at paedos and perverts, it was full of rants against gang war and street violence. And it often carried Snowie's pic. He got more hate mail than Captain Hook. What if this was a wind-up? Or a set-up?

He sniffed. Best check with the desk; see if anything else had come in since he spoke to Skippy. He reached for his phone, cursed under his breath; knew he should've put the damn thing on charge.

Mind, if the battery was dead, so was this place. Ten minutes he'd been sitting here and the only sign of street life had been a feral tom picking at a road-kill pigeon. He sighed, knew he'd not sleep if he went home without at least taking a gander.

And these days he carried his own insurance.

His hand fumbled under the driver's seat, fingers sought out a Maglite, then closed round the handle of the knife.

2

Police officers hunt in pairs on the Churchill. PC Ken Gibson riding shotgun spotted it first: a flash of light, in a shop doorway. He nudged the driver, Constable Steve Hawkins, who glanced across. A youngish blond-ish bloke with a torch was hunkered down ferreting in what looked like a fit-to-burst bin-liner. The officers exchanged a weary glance. It spoke volumes: the amount of paperwork they'd be looking at if the bugger was about to take a pop at Booze Brothers. The off-licence attracted more visitors after hours than when it was open. None had calling cards. Torchie was staggering about now.

"Looks like he's had a skinful already," Hawkins drawled. The constable had twenty-odd years under a belt that strained against his girth. He'd been there, done that, didn't wear t-shirts. Bald and broken-nosed, when he was out of uniform he looked more baddie than sheriff.

"Could just drive on, Hawkeye?" Gibbo suggested hopefully. The younger officer could see the admin stretching over and above the call of duty, ie shift end at six.

Sorely tempted, it was with a resigned reluctance that Hawkins pulled the Vauxhall over a few doors down. On the upside, they'd faced far worse incidents on the patch. It would be two against one, and the bloke was no Incredible Hulk. "Nah. Let's sort it."

Softly-softly didn't work. The guy must have heard their approach. He spun round, eyes wild, hair all over the place. "Thank God you're here."

"Definitely pissed then," Gibbo muttered. Hawkins masked a smile, which wasn't difficult now he had a better idea what they were dealing with. The blond guy looked as if he was about to puke. Sweating, shaking, grey-skinned, he was probably a user, in need of a fix.

Gibson saw the knife first. Hawkins caught a stifled moan from his partner. Gibbo's wife had just given birth. The baby hadn't even been christened. And though officers wore protective clothing as a matter of course these days, anti-stab vests weren't proof against smackheads.

Furtively, Gibbons reached for his cosh, Hawkins took a tentative step forward. Calm. Casual. Play it by the book. "Best give that to me, sir. Don't want any troub…"

They had it. Hawkins froze. The druggie wasn't alone, and he had more than one knife. Behind the blond, in a doorway that stank of cat pee and human faeces, lay an old man's body curled in the foetal position: foetal and fatal. Hawkins mentally crossed himself. The vicious beating probably wasn't the cause of death. That would almost certainly be the blade embedded up to its glistening hilt in the victim's scrawny neck.

Shocked and scared, Matt Snow wasn't so far out of it that he couldn't decipher the look on the bigger officer's face. "You can't be serious? I didn't kill him!"

The cop looked as if he had difficulty swallowing. "Course not, sir."

"I don't even know him," Matt blurted. But did he? He needed time to think. The reporter had an inkling the victim was Wally Marsden, a paedophile who'd been on the sex offenders' register for years. He'd never seen the old lag in the flesh, only in a mug shot. But his hack's nose was twitching: the story could be a goer, big-time. And until Matt stood it up, he didn't want another reporter getting a sniff.

"Course not, sir." The officer reached out a hand. "So why not let me have the…"

"Get real," Snow snarled, jabbed the knife at the body. "I found him like this." He was sure of one thing: if it did turn out to be

Marsden, there'd be no shortage of suspects. Right now though, Snow reckoned he was top of the list.

"Course you did, sir," Hawkins said.

Snow flapped an impatient hand. Starsky and Hutch were getting up his nostrils. They clearly had no idea who the victim was, and even less who they were talking to. Shame that. The personal touch might have oiled the professional wheels. Snow came across a lot of cops on the job, but he'd not clocked either of these clowns.

"Look, Mr er…?"

The one who looked like a boxer gone to fat gave a thin smile. "I'm PC Hawkins. Steve Hawkins?"

"What's with the voice?" Snow snapped. "I'm not a retard." The reporter watched as they exchanged glances. Christ. They really did think he was a homicidal fruitcake. Sooner this was sorted, sooner he could chase the story, but it was a waste of time talking to plods. "I want to talk to a senior officer."

Gibson held up his radio. "I'll get on to it, sir."

Snow gave a satisfied nod. In the distance a dog barked, a car backfired. Hawkins's gaze never left the reporter's face. Maybe the guy was trying to place him? Could be he'd seen Matt's photo in the paper.

"Know me now?" Snow gave an encouraging smile.

"David Beckham?" Hawkins muttered.

Matt bristled. The body behind him was cooling, as was the killer's trail, and Clouseau was cracking one-liners. The reporter laid down the knife and the torch. "Matt Snow. Crime correspondent? Evening News?" He reached into a breast pocket. "The desk got a tip. I was checking it out." The cop didn't even glance at the proffered NUJ card. He was too busy snapping cuffs round Matt's skinny wrists.

"This is a crime scene," the reporter shrieked. "You should be calling it in, pal."

"I have." Gibson showed Matt the radio. "And you're in it. Up to your neck. Pal."

3

The zip wouldn't budge over Bev's bump. Red-faced, blue eyes brimming with tears, she breathed in so hard it was a miracle her rib cage didn't snap. Frankie tugged from behind. "Breathe in, my friend. It's stuck like a stuck thing from stuck land."

They were in Bev's bedroom at Baldwin Street. Frankie's face in the cheval glass was cool and unruffled as ever. But something wasn't right. And it wasn't just the wedding dress – that was an unmitigated disaster. Puffy mutton sleeves and myriad layers of ivory flounce, it resembled one of Bo Peep's cast-offs. Or a meringue on legs. And it didn't even fit.

"Shoulda got a bigger size, Bevy." Frankie smirked at Bev's V-sign. "OK. Two sizes."

Bev clenched teeth, then fists. Frankie had been her best mate since God was an embryo, but right now the girl was looking at a slap.

"Mum!" Bev wailed, wrung her hands. Emmy Morriss lolled on the bed, in a pastel blue two-piece and a hat the size and shape of a satellite dish. When she wasn't swigging Bristol Cream she was slurring, *Get Me to the Church on Time*.

"Mum!" The wail's volume increased. "You're not helping."

Emmy emitted a discreet belch. "No one's holding a gun to your head, sweetheart."

No. Just a Kalashnikov. The church was packed. A zillion prawn vol-au-vents were on standby at the reception. Not to mention the bun in the oven. Well, a chapatti.

"Bollocks." Slinky in a scarlet sheath, Frankie clapped a hand to ruby lips. "Got a safety pin, Mrs M?"

Bev peeked through fingers wet with tears. Her mascara was doing a runner, lippie bled all over the place. Her face looked like Jackson Pollock's palette. And now the freaking frock was history. Everyone was waiting. The Chief Constable would be there. Highgate CID was forming a guard of honour. This could not be happening. Bev groaned from the soles of her pink satin pumps, jumped a mile when the doorbell rang. Frankie sashayed to the window, peeped through the curtain. "Who booked the hearse?"

And that was it. Bev screamed, shot up. The dream panned out the same every time. And this was its fifth or sixth screening. Now wide awake, she hugged her knees, shivered as cold sweat trickled down her spine. She'd shared the nightmare with Frankie, tried making light of it, but impending motherhood obviously weighed heavily on her mind.

And elsewhere. Mouth turned down, she stroked her bump with trembling fingers. She was only three months gone, but her stomach had always been more pannini than pancake. No one had noticed, or at least commented. Yet. She sighed, shook her head. It was impossible to imagine Oz Khan's baby swimming around in there. Impossible to imagine anyone's. Christ almighty. Detective Sergeant Bev Morriss? Kick-ass cop? Maternal instincts of a sterilised cuckoo? Up the duff?

So why not terminate it? She lay back with her hands behind her head, stared at a lace doily cobweb on the cornice. Why had she kept it quiet? Why were her mum, Frankie and the guv the only people in the know? Was she in denial and talking about it would make it real? And what did that mean? That she didn't want it? Or did? And how many more stupid questions couldn't she answer? Ah, but she could. Trouble was the answers changed every time.

She took a deep breath, closed her eyes. Oz had a right to know. But did she want that complication? Would he? They'd been a good team while it lasted, partners on and off the job, carnal knowledge and criminal. But her erstwhile DC was now a sergeant in the Met. Oz had moved on. And she'd been happy to let him go. Hadn't she? So why dream about getting hitched? And what was with the hearse?

Eyes open, ears pricked, she breathed, "Yes! Thank you, God," Then banished every thorny thought for the thousandth time, as she reached for the landline. A ringing phone was one thing she could always answer.

A call-out to the Churchill estate was as welcome as bird flu on a turkey farm in advent. So how come DC Mac Tyler was chirpier than a sparrow? Slumped in the passenger seat, Bev cast a grumpy glance at her partner. Surely that level of perkiness was abnormal at this time in the morning? Not that it would last. Still a relative newbie, Mac was about to experience his first slice of life on the Churchill. That should bring him down to earth with a bump. Or maybe not. Bev cut him another glance. Mac's glass was never half-empty; he was a man with a perpetually full magnum. She reckoned it was down to his stand-up comedy. In the little spare time the job left, he was a regular on the amateur circuit. Not that he was joking as they exited the inner ring road.

"Caught some guy red-handed, apparently, boss. Uniform played a blinder. Gibbo kept him talking. Hawkeye disarmed him. Perp put up a hell of a fight, according to control." Mac's warm brown eyes checked the mirror as he indicated a right.

"Great." Distracted, Bev shifted her bum, subtly loosened the belt on her denim boot-cuts. Given her entire working wardrobe was blue, she could and often did dress in the dark. Shouldn't have grabbed this pair though, they were beginning to pinch.

"You OK?" Mac's bemused glance flicked back to the road.

"Hunky. This perp then? Got a name? Any form?" She scanned the nightlife, or lack of. The streets were dead, roads deserted. Not that they were in a hurry, or she'd be driving. But the body wasn't going anywhere, and the case looked cut and dried: the suspect was cooling his heels back at the nick, uniform had secured the scene, the SOCO guys were on the way, ditto the pathologist. She and Mac would be on site to ensure procedures were carried out, the gathering and handling of evidence, organising door-to-door, usual plod work. Yawn.

Mac shrugged a *dunno* to both Bev's queries, his speech now temporarily restricted by a mouthful of sausage roll. She sniffed. God, it smelt good. Having reluctantly downed a virtuous banana before Mac picked her up, she now flapped a half-share away and shot him a Morriss look. This one was from the mad-fool shop. Oblivious, Mac scarfed another bite. Bev puckered her lips. Guy was a fool to himself, really. With all the extra weight, he could body double for Danny de Vito. Not the legs – Mac's were too long. She watched a couple more inches of cholesterol disappear down her DC's neck. Couldn't be doing a bunch of good at his age. He'd not see fifty again; way he was going he'd be lucky to see sixty at all. And that'd be a shame, cause she had a soft spot for Tyler, even though he dressed like a lumberjack in a Lovejoy wig.

Her fingers tapped a beat on her knee. "Shouldn't eat when you're driving anyway. Cops should set an example."

"Yes, ma'am." Very Uriah Heep. Pity it didn't match the facial inflexion.

She sniffed. "Stick like that if the wind changes, mate."

Mac muttered something about rattled cages, but didn't finish the food. Bev saw him slip it back into a Gregg's bag. She felt a tad mean; shouldn't really take it out on him. It was Mike Powell's call they were here. The DI couldn't be arsed to get out of bed. He'd told her on the phone the experience would look good on her CV. Yeah right. If she cocked up again any time soon it'd be a P45 she'd be eyeing, not a naffing curriculum vitae.

The last big case she'd worked on had ended in a disciplinary:

insubordination, contaminating a crime scene, failure to communicate. Guilty as charged, m'lud. Mitigating circumstances and mega-grovelling were the only reason she'd clung on to her rank. But the brass had made it clear: one toe out of line from now on in and it'd be more than her footing she'd lose.

"That the doc's?" Matt nodded at an elderly Land Rover straddling the kerb opposite a row of rundown shops. The entire block was cordoned off, though the action was centred on Booze Brothers. A police lighting rig had turned the offie into a down-market gin palace, every illuminated inch being recorded on still and movie cameras by a police lens-man.

"Looks like it," Bev said. Confirmation came when a round-faced, middle-aged woman in a tweed cape clambered from the driver's door inadvertently flashing a thigh. Home Office pathologist Gillian Overdale could be dour and monosyllabic. Not flush with people skills, she was red-hot with stiffs.

"I'll grab a word with Overs," Bev said. "See what else you can get out of Steve and Ken." Hawkins and Gibson were standing round chatting to the SOCO team who were already geared up and waiting for a green from the pathologist. "Leave the keys, Mac." She was ferreting around in her bag. "I'll lock up in a min."

She watched as Tyler waddled off, hitching baggy denims over bum crack. Then reached for the remains of the sausage roll. It was tough but someone had to force it down. She checked the mirror for crumbs. Someone had to keep Mac on the straight and narrow.

As Bev headed for the off-licence, the sausage roll very nearly gave a repeat performance. The pathologist was turning the body, and though crime scenes often stink, this one reeked. Bev retched as waves of rancid body odour wafted from layers of filthy dishevelled clothing, and merged with human waste. Eyes watering, she mumbled, "Shee-ite."

Overdale was hunched over the victim, creased hazel eyes scrutinising every inch of visible flesh. She didn't need to look up. "Sergeant, if you're about to puke, back off. The last thing the crime scene needs is a contribution of vomit."

Bev curled a lip. The phrases sucking eggs and teaching granny were on the tip of her tongue. She had the nous not to let them fall. Fumbling in a shoulder bag the size of Surrey, she located her crime scene wet wipes, gave her nose a liberal dab of eau de lemon, then shoved the rest of the pack in her pocket.

Overdale's latex-gloved fingers were probing places Bev wouldn't venture with a tour guide. Not to mention a rectal thermometer. Even as an observer, she was keeping a greater distance than usual from this murder victim. Her initial glance had registered an old dosser, probably a wino. The stink of booze, matted unwashed hair, black nails gave away the guy's story. And the livid purple bruising and split lips didn't help a face already ravaged by rough living.

Bev had seen enough, turned her back, kicked a stone desultorily into the gutter where it joined yesterday's crumpled *Sun*. She couldn't see this making the headlines. An old alkie battered half to death then stuck like a pig? Prob'ly in a tiff over a can of Strong Brew? Yeah right. That'd double the print run. Not that the press had got wind of it: there were no neighbourhood ghouls around to tip the wink.

She tapped a Doc Marten and waited for the familiar emotions to dig in. And waited…

This indifference, this lack of empathy was a first for Bev, and it unnerved her. A good cop needs to feel for the victim. Every victim. Not cherry pick. She knew a small number of cops who didn't give a toss, many more who cared but hid it; she was one of the few who wore their heart on both sleeves. She hoped to God this was a one-off and not compassion fatigue. Because without that…

"You still look as if you're about to throw up." Overdale stood at Bev's side, running what appeared a professional gaze over Bev's face. "I thought you were inured to this sort of thing?"

Bev's unease grew as the unwelcome scrutiny continued. "Tickety, me, doc." She lifted a finger to a sallow moon. "Must be the lighting."

Overdale gave a brisk if-you-say-so sniff, then snapped off the gloves, dropped them in a steel case at her feet. Bev wasn't big on patience, but there was no point prompting. If the pathologist had anything useful to contribute she'd come out with it. Push and she could turn prickly. Pricklier. The hoot of an owl, the distant wail of a police car, a muted guffaw from Mac and the boys, then Overdale said, "He's been dead several hours."

Bev's heart hit the asphalt. The time of death meant there had to be another crime scene. Even Churchill residents wouldn't have ignored the lengthy presence of a stiff on their communal doorstep. So when and how was he dumped?

"I'd say he's been moved at least twice." Overdale blew her nose, stuffed the hankie in her pocket. She talked temperatures, gravity, pooling blood, primary and secondary lividity. Bev listened, groaned inwardly. Could it get any worse? An image of mottled purple flesh flashed before her eyes. Oh, yes. She shook her head to banish the vision. "Doc, when you say *several* hours…?"

"What do you want?" Overdale joshed. "Jam on it?" Perish the bleeding thought. Unlike Bev, the pathologist was smiling. "I may be able to narrow it down after the PM, sergeant. Let's say midday?"

As early as that? "Can't wait," Bev muttered.

Overdale looked set to leave, then turned back, thrust a hand in her pocket and looked down on the victim. "It was a vicious beating, sergeant. Sadistic, almost. And almost certainly inflicted before the fatal stab wound." She made eye contact with Bev. "And God forgive me, I can't get worked up about it. I've no

21

time for scum."

"Beg pardon?" Bev's mouth gaped. Even though she'd had a hard time feeling sympathy, she bristled at the woman's callous throwaway remarks. It was effing rich, a pathologist dissing a dosser. Who knew what circumstances had driven the poor old sod on to the streets? He didn't deserve to die like that. No one did.

Overdale flapped a dismissive hand. "I know what you're thinking... There but for the grace of God..." She pointed a scuffed brogue at the body. "But I don't like paedophiles." Bev's face said it all. "Don't you know who it is, sergeant?"

No. She moved nearer the corpse, took the closer look she'd baulked at earlier. "Jesus!"

"That's not what the media called him."

The tart observation went over Bev's head. Her brain was rapidly retrieving data from the memory bank. Walter Marsden, employed as caretaker, primary school. Wolverhampton? West Bromwich? Warley? As for taking care, the only thing Marsden had taken was three little girls' innocence. Seven years he got. Vile monster was how the tabloids described him.

"I was a consultant at Wolverhampton when the story broke," Overdale said.

Bev nodded. Thought it began with a W. "I didn't even know he was out."

"No." Overdale arched an eyebrow. "But somebody did."

Bev waved vaguely at the pathologist's departing back, acutely aware of her initial failure to identify Marsden. It wasn't that long since his predatory features had been plastered all over the front pages. She studied the raddled face, so engrossed this time she barely registered Mac's lumbering arrival.

"Hey, boss. I got a name from Hawkeye. The perp?" She couldn't read the glint in his eyes.

"Go on."

"You'll not like it."

She sighed. "Shoot, Mac. I'm not in the mood."

"Matt Snow."

"Tintin?" She lowered the volume and pitch. "As in the hack?"

"The very same."

"Yeah right." She folded her arms, tapped a foot. "And the punch line is…?"

4

Newsman Matt Snow looked anything but cool. Slumped on a metal chair in Interview Three at Highgate nick, even the reporter's fringe flopped. Four plastic cups with dregs of tepid tea equalled the number of hours he'd been cooped up. Dark marks ringed the armpits of his cheap brown suit, echoed the bruise-like circles under his eyes. A smell of sweat hung in the already stale air. Snow was acutely aware whose.

He heard a faint whistling and lifted his head. The out-of-tune dirge sounded like the theme to *Mash*, and it was getting louder. Snow was on his legs before the door opened.

"Thank God for small mercies," he muttered as a tall good-looking blond carrying a file sauntered in. "Inspector Powell. This is a joke, right?"

"Body with a blade in its neck? Hilarious." The DI sniffed loudly, pointed at a chair. Snow felt the heat of a blush rise on his cheeks. As an on-the-road reporter, he'd had several run-ins with Mike Powell; cocky bastard was enjoying this.

"The Churchill." Powell stroked his jaw. "Tell me about it."

Snow slumped into the seat. "I've already given one of your guys a statement."

"Yeah." Powell smirked, as he opened the file. "Reads like one of your little fairy stories."

The reporter's chair legs screeched across gunky floor tiles. "That's it. I've had enough." He was doing these dickheads a favour; he'd not be treated like scum.

"It's not even started. The Churchill. Talk."

"Or…?" Snow snarled.

"You'll be arrested on suspicion of…"

"What…?"

24

"Where shall I stop?" Powell ticked points with fingers. "Resisting arrest? Assaulting a police officer? Attempted burglary? Perverting the course of justice? Screwing up a crime scene?" Leaning back, he stretched his legs, crossed his hands behind his head. "Then there's the minor matter of a murder."

Snow sighed, resumed his seat. It was bollocks. He wasn't seriously in the frame. But he wasn't stupid. Fact was he had been at the scene, and though not prime suspect, he was key witness. Powell applying the heat meant he was on a fishing trip. The reporter knew full well what the DI was after: who'd tipped him off about the body. But he couldn't give him what he didn't have. Course, he could be reading it wrong. Birmingham Six. Guildford Four. Bridgewater Three. He'd no desire to be the Churchill One. "Do I need a lawyer?"

The DI picked a nail. "You tell me."

Snow calculated rapidly. Calling in a brief would take time he didn't have – not if he wanted to stay ahead of the game. It was a couple of hours since he'd been given the use of a phone. Natch, he'd rung in his story and had words with the news desk: disconcerting words. A bunch of stuff needed sorting, but until he got out of this dump his hands were tied. "Am I under arrest?"

Powell shook his head. "Police inquiries. You're helping." The inspector poised his PaperMate over an A4 pad. "So help."

Snow sighed. Sooner he talked, sooner he'd be released. He spoke uninterrupted for five minutes, giving a carefully edited version of the night's events. How he'd driven to the estate, found it deserted, saw what he thought was movement outside the off-licence, almost stumbled over the body, checked it for a pulse. And how relieved he was when the police arrived. He illustrated the last point with a winning smile.

The DI took a small mirror from his breast pocket, studied his reflection for at least a minute. He frowned, shook his head, stared again. "What do you think, Mr Snow?"

The reporter shifted uneasily in his chair. "How'd you mean?"

Powell rose, walked round the desk, leaned into Snow's face. "Yesterday, I was not born." The DI tipped the reporter's chair back with the toe of an Italian leather loafer. "Sunshine."

Snow slipped a couple of inches. "It's the truth."

"But not as we know it." Powell tipped the chair further. "I want the truth, the whole truth, and nothing…"

"I don't know any more," Snow shrieked.

The silence – like Snow's balance – was uneasy. Powell let both hang then lowered only his voice, pausing between each syllable. "Then how come you were there?"

"Told you." Truculent now. "A tip-off."

"From?"

"I don't know."

And that was the truth. He'd checked with the news desk. No one from the newspaper had called. The Aussie sub, Skippy, hadn't even been on shift. Until Snow knew what – or who – he was dealing with, he intended keeping his cards close to his chest.

Fresh from the Churchill estate crime scene, Bev stood framed in the window of Mike Powell's second floor office. Arms folded, deep in thought, she watched as Matt Snow's forlorn figure crossed the car park. She was digesting the DI's take on his run-in with the reporter. It was giving her wind.

"Why'd you hold him so long? Tintin's no killer. He's just a hack with attitude."

Not to mention an alibi for the most likely time frame.

"Yeah. I know," Powell said. "Fun watching him squirm though."

She shook her head. Not funny. Not clever. The press had enough anti-police axes to grind. She glanced round. Oblivious, the DI lounged in a padded leather chair, size twelves on the desk, hands in pockets, not one blond hair out of place. Nice work if you can get it. Not like rallying the troops on the ground. As if that straw wasn't tiny enough, it'd started tipping down. She ran a hand over her damp hair. The Guinness-coloured chin-length bob felt like a skullcap, and she'd swear the Doc Martens had shrunk. She gave an eloquent sniff.

"No harm in a spot of custody." The DI waved an airy hand. "Good for a newsman to get a new perspective."

"You'll be the one with a new perspective." She snorted. "From a sodding crucifix when he knocks his next piece out."

"A few hours in Highgate nick? It's hardly Guantanamo."

"Not the point." She circled Powell, took a pew opposite. "Snow was never a serious contender. No percentage rubbing him up the wrong way."

The DI sharpened his act, snatched his feet off the desk. "Look, mate, he was at the crime scene, had a knife in his hand, claims he got a tip but can't or won't say who from. And have you read his column lately?" Powell gestured at a pile of newspapers near his elbow. "I've skimmed a few," he said. "Way Snow sees it, castration's too good for kiddie fiddlers like Wally Marsden."

"Child molesters," Bev snapped. She hated the kiddie fiddler tag. It made the heinous sound innocuous, like some sort of game. She leafed through a couple of copies while Powell signed a few forms. The DI was spot on about the columns. Matt Snow made Richard Littlejohn read like Richmal Crompton. Bring back hanging for paedos? Yeah. By the scrotum. Over a vat of hot bleach. Wasn't just sex offenders Snow savaged: any form of low-life was fair game. But bark and bite. Snowie was a journo not a psycho: his keyboard was mightier than his sword.

"You all right, mate?" How long had he been peering like that? "You look dog rough?"

"Fuck's sake. I've been up since two o'clock." And sick three times.

He shrugged, muttered something with the words time and month in it.

Her eyes were slits. "What did you say?"

"Nothing. Keep your hair on." Why was he looking at her like that? "You putting on weight?" Powell didn't do PC.

"You looking for a slap?" Nor did she. Either way it was time to change tack. "Matt Snow," she said. "He's so far out the frame…"

"Look, Bev." Her name from his lips still came as a shock. Their working relationship was up and down like a busy lift. In recent months, they'd forged a sort of harmony, think hip-hop rather than Handel, but they were getting there, despite when he forgot and reverted to Morriss or Hey-you. "Just cause Matt Snow's a hack doesn't mean he's not capable of offing a toe-rag like Wally Marsden."

Her curled lip suggested grave doubt. "Assuming he's capable, he doesn't even know who the victim is." No one in the media did. The police would issue the identity at the mid-morning news conference.

"So?" Powell sat back, smoothed his tie, then his hair. "Snow's alibi had to be checked, or I'd've been failing in one of my duties as senior officer."

Senior officer's duties? Arse. Your. Own. Up. The checks made sense though, and given the reporter's alibi seemed sound, it meant Wally Marsden's killer was still on the loose.

"Best get off your bum and get on with the others then." She turned at the door, gave a mock salute. "Sir."

5

Cops are only human and though few would broadcast it, no one was moved by Wally Marsden's murder. The early brief in Highgate's smallest and shabbiest incident room lacked the frisson that comes when officers care passionately about a case. The only buzz emanated from a dopey bluebottle beating itself up against a window.

Bev leaned against a side wall, sipped ginger tea, observed the few squad members who weren't already working the Churchill. Uniforms and a couple of DCs were out knocking doors, canvassing passers-by, chasing CCTV. DI Powell had cobbled together a further six detectives, an exhibits officer and an admin clerk. Bev returned a few nods, but it was clear in the bored expressions and lacklustre body language that though they'd all do the needful to track the killer they'd not shed tears for the victim.

Contrasting images of the paedophile stared out from a couple of whiteboards at the front. Blown-up black-and-white mug shots and posthumous technicolor stills recorded a sharp decline in Wally Marsden's face and fortunes. From the sort of man you'd pass in the street to a lowlife who'd died there. Bev took another sip, wished she felt more.

DC Darren New – Highgate's answer to Tom Cruise, so Darren reckoned – caught her eye-line, patted an empty seat between him and Sumitra Gosh. Bev shook her head, raised the cup in a cheers anyway. A queasy stomach meant a quick exit could be in the offing. Darren shrugged a shoulder, shoved over next to Summi. Bev's sardonic eyebrow matched Mac's. Did Dazza have the hots for the delectable DC Gosh? Do dogs piss up lampposts? Mind, any bloke with a prostate fancied Sumitra:

waist-length curtains of blue-black hair, dark chocolate eyes and a figure to die for. Or diet.

Bev sucked in her gut, checked her watch. If the DI didn't get a move on, he'd be…

"Morning, all." Powell strode to the front, suit jacket flapping like dirty wings. Keeping his back to the squad, he made a show of studying the photographs. "Walter Marsden. Scumbag. Kiddie fid… Child molester." He paused a few seconds then turned to eyeball the team. "Bastard got what he deserved? Killer's done us all a favour?" Silence broken only by the kamikaze fly. "Anyone here feels like that? Do me a favour and get out." He pointed to the door. Another pause. "The room. The building. The police."

Bev turned her mouth down. The sentiment was pure guv-speak, but she'd not have ranked even the new improved Powell in Detective Superintendent Byford's professional league. Or personal. Maybe she'd misjudged the guy.

"Only joking." Powell winked, flashed a grin.

Yeah right. But joking about what? Marsden's shit fate? Or unfeeling cops? The vagueness could be deliberate to deflect potential flak: PC moles were everywhere. But Bev didn't rank Powell as that sharp a cookie – or he'd be acting detective super-intendent. Not that anyone could fill Byford's shoes. Eyes closed, she swallowed hard. It wasn't that she didn't still see the guv, but home visits weren't the same as having him round the nick. The superintendent was recovering – slowly – from life-threatening injuries sustained on the last case they'd worked. She missed him to bits.

"Keeping you up, sergeant?" Like Powell cared. Bev's blue eyes blazed. The DI lifted both palms, looked away. "'Kay. Problem one: Marsden was NFA. Slept rough most the time, occasionally crashed in one of the shelters."

No fixed address. So no pad, no neighbours, probably no paperwork, unless he carried it on him. Meant they'd be checking every doss house, every soup kitchen; talking to the Sally Army people, Big Issue sellers, the social, you name it…

"The Churchill Marsden's regular patch?" Bev asked.

Powell shrugged. "You tell me. No one's talking. That's problem number two. Feedback from our guys on the estate? Think blood out of brick wall. Punters either didn't know Marsden or don't give a stuff."

"Because he was a sex offender? Or because he was a dosser?" The questions were Carol Pemberton's. Tall and slim, with a dark glossy pageboy, the DC was classy and savvy. Bev had time for Pembers.

Powell rubbed the back of his neck. "Either? Both? What's it matter?"

"Shed-loads, if the killer targeted Marsden deliberately." Bev's casual delivery didn't disguise the serious point. One that opened several lines of inquiry, including revenge served several years cold. She made a mental note to get hold of Marsden's victims' files.

Powell tapped a finger against his lips. "Best run a check on the victims' families. Just in case. Far more likely Marsden was in the wrong place at the wrong time."

"Like Matt Snow." Dazza sniggered. Tintin jokes were already doing the rounds. Hack by name, hack by nature was the pick of the crap so far. But smart-arse remarks aside, the reporter's early presence at the crime scene raised a bunch of questions. The biggie being: who tipped him off?

Powell perched on the table, loosened his tie. "Any thoughts?"

Half the squad threw in its two penn'orth: most money landed on the informant being the killer, or pretty damn close.

"Close to the scene, sure," Bev said. "Don't follow he's the perp."

"Or knows who is." Dazza was on the same page. "Could be some joker passing by. Sees the body. Thinks: sod the plod. Tips off the press."

31

"'Xactly." She frowned. "Why Matt Snow, though?" It had bugged her since Mac first mentioned it.

"Matt Motormouth Snow?" Powell sneered. "Anyone who reads the *News* knows Tintin's name."

Yeah. But not his private number. Nor the right buttons to push to drag a journo out of his pit in the middle of the night. The mystery caller had editorial nous. And smart enough, probably, not to have left a telecom trail. They'd check Snow's phone records but Bev doubted they'd lead anywhere. Not that the tip had done the reporter any favours. He'd ended up in police custody, the so-called exclusive unexploited. It'd be a media free-for-all in a couple of hours, especially when the DI released Marsden's ID.

She added lines to her mental checklist as Powell assigned actions. Apart from the news conference that Mike Media-Tart Powell was keeping for himself, the straws were all short. Carol and a young officer whose name Bev could never remember would take the shelters. Dazza and Goshie would talk to rough sleepers on and around the estate. Thinking went that if Marsden had any mates, they'd be street people, fellow dossers who might be able to point the inquiry in the right direction. The priority was to try to establish Marsden's last known movements, but anything that shed light on the man's lowlife routines would help. Given they'd nada to go on…

Like any sex offender, Marsden had been on a register. In theory it meant tabs were kept. In practice, there were loopholes; Marsden had sleazed through the net. He'd not appeared on any official radar for weeks. That was the DI's third problem.

Powell jumped to his feet, clapped his hands. "Right. Someone out there knows something. Find them. Talk to them. I want this sewn up by the end of the week."

"Just like that," Mac muttered. The quip barely raised a smile, the squad's mood was still downbeat. Bev was musing on ways of extricating herself from Marsden's post mortem. Mac volunteering would be good, especially if she could persuade him it was his idea in the first place. Nah. He wasn't that stupid. She sighed, crushed the cup, lobbed it in a bin. Everyone was making leaving noises when the door hit the back wall.

The head of the police news bureau made a late entrance, and did not look ecstatic. Bernie Flowers was John Major's double: dapper grey suits, neat grey hair, glasses too big for his face. The bland image was misleading: Bernie had edited a national tabloid before a booze problem forced him out. Now sober and sharp as a scalpel, he had a better handle on the media than Max Clifford. Bernie didn't suffer fools at all, never mind gladly.

"Who the fuck leaked this?" 'This' was the lead on the front of the *Evening News*. Bernie brandished the paper like a red flag – and he was the raging bull. The headline ran: VILE MONSTER MARSDEN BUTCHERED IN BACK ALLEY. Alliteration v accuracy? No contest. Either way, Snow had his scoop. And the DI a fourth problem.

6

The Printers' Ink was a journos' pub in a narrow side street near the law courts. Bog standard red-brick-dusty-green-woodwork exterior, décor in the saloon was black, white and read: three walls lined with newspapers. Big stories like the death of Diana and 9/11 appeared alongside golden weddings and skateboarding ducks. Brian the landlord was a news junkie. If he fancied a change, he'd paste new pages over old. In places the papers were an inch thick. The latest addition was the lunch-time edition of Birmingham's *Evening News,* courtesy of its crime correspondent who was currently elbowing the bar.

Matt Snow's normal tipple was Banks's bitter; he was now on his third Grouse. But then his news editor was doing the honours.

"I'll say it again, Matt. Bloody good work." Rick Palmer was early fifties, but liquid lunches and late nights had left a legacy. His face wasn't lined, it had trenches. The unruly blond thatch looked like a wig, except for the roots.

"Cheers, Rick." Snow had been basking in bonhomie and backslaps for the better part of two hours. It almost compensated for the fact that some bastard had nicked his motor off the Churchill. He'd cabbed it to the estate soon as he'd been released from Highgate nick but the Fiasco had gone. Talk about insult to injury.

Still, the *News* had shat on the competition from a great height. And Snow was flavour of the lunch hour. The other hacks had drifted back to the newsroom, but Palmer had hung back. Snow had an idea why, and he didn't think it was small talk, or to discuss Toby Priest's feedback from the news conference. Snow hadn't covered it himself on the grounds he'd get a frosty reception.

"Toby reckons the police presser was a complete waste of time," Palmer said. "No new info. Just a witness appeal. Yawn. Yawn."

Not quite. Powell had issued Marsden's ID as well. The confirmation had come as a huge relief to Snow. When he'd rung his copy in from the nick he'd been ninety-nine per cent sure, but naming the victim as Wally Marsden had still been one per cent punt.

As well as the front-page splash, there'd been a stack of follow-up stuff inside. Virtually the whole coverage had gone under Snow's by-line including a backgrounder pulled together by one of the staffers. Natch, Snowie had bigged up his own role in the incident, and he'd taken a major pop at his police treatment. Not a bad night's work. The reporter savoured a sip of Grouse. Mind, if he'd cocked up, pear-shaped wouldn't be in it. His face would be an eggplant.

Palmer sidled a little closer. "Come on, lad. You can tell me."

"Tell you what?" As if he didn't know. He scratched an ear.

"Who tipped the wink?" The news editor rolled an unlit cigarette between his fingers.

Snow resisted the urge to tap the side of his nose. "Can't reveal my sources, Rick, you know that." Couldn't have been Skippy though. Snow had caught up with newsroom gossip: the Aussie intake editor had been fired a fortnight ago, buggered off back to Sydney. On sober reflection, Snow wasn't even sure the caller's accent had been antipodean.

As he suspected, trotting out the sources line on his news editor was a no-no. Palmer sidled closer, lowered his loud Brummie accent. "I won't breathe a word, lad. But I do need to know."

So did Snow. "Give me a day or two, Rick. I need to think about it."

"But you do have a name, lad?"

"Sure." It wasn't the first lie he'd told. But could turn out to be the one he'd most regret.

"Snowed under, Sergeant Morriss?" Detective Chief Superintendent Kenny Flint's bullet head appeared round Bev's door. She was flicking through *heat,* dipping languid fingers into a family pack of Maltesers. What's a girl to say?

"Rushed off 'em, sir."

"Yes." He stretched it to three syllables. "So I see."

She snatched Docs off the desk. "I was…"

"Save it, Bev. I'm aware of the hours you've clocked up today." He waved copies of her reports. Given it was now half-three, she was already into overtime. She was only hanging round to have a word with Mac.

"I've got a favour to ask," Flint said. "Nothing to do with the Marsden inquiry." They'd chewed the cud on the case earlier. The DCS was normally based in Wolverhampton; he'd been lead detective when the paedophile was last sent down. Flint had thrown a few suggestions into the inquiry ring, people it might be worth interviewing.

Bev watched as he took the swivel chair opposite, tugged his trousers to protect knife-sharp creases. If central casting was asked to supply a hard-nosed detective it'd deliver Kenny Flint: craggy features, cool blue eyes, greying buzz cut, think middle-aged Action Man. In a single-breasted suit. The guy sure looked the part, but that was about all Bev knew.

Flint had been brought in four months back to investigate an arson attack that killed three people including a young police constable. The brass had asked him to stay on as cover for the guv. DCS Flint held higher rank than Detective Superintendent Byford. Far as Bev was concerned Flint had yet to earn his stripes.

"What d'you make of this?" he asked. "Don't worry about prints." It was melted chocolate that worried Bev. She licked her fingers before taking the small sheet of paper from his hand. The words were typed – just four. Doctor Adam Graves. Suicide? "The envelope was addressed to Bill Byford," Flint told her.

She nodded. Guessed admin was passing everything on. "Name rings a bell." Where'd she seen it? She narrowed her eyes. Bingo. "Inquest report. Piece in the local rag." One of those she'd flicked through in Powell's office. Picture too. Good looking guy.

"Right," Flint said. "Family's local but the body was found in Hanbury Woods, so West Mercia have been dealing with it."

As she recalled, the inquest returned a suicide verdict. "Topped himself, didn't he?"

"Almost literally." Flint had liased with the investigating officer in Worcester. Graves had apparently downed a scotch and sedatives cocktail before slashing his throat with an open razor. "Nasty." Flint rubbed his chin. "No amount of pills and booze'd take the edge off that." Then saw her face. "Sorry. I wasn't trying to be funny."

Sorry? She knew clowns round here who'd consider the remark cutting edge comedy.

"What's your reading of it, boss?" She shoved the paper across the desk. The original and the envelope would be at the lab. Mind, anyone with a telly knew not to leave dabs and/or DNA. Even she picked up forensics snippets from *CSI*.

"I think the writer wants us to have another look," Flint said.

She shrugged. Why not say so? And give a name. She couldn't be doing with this cryptic anonymous crap. Cranky or what? The sleep deprivation was catching up. "Not our case, is it?"

"That's where the favour comes in. Bill has an interest too."

Byford? Unwittingly, she straightened, smoothed her hair. "Go on."

Flint explained how he rang the guv a couple of times a week. Didn't have to, just knew how he'd feel if it was him stuck at home twiddling his thumbs. Anyway, among a load of other stuff Flint had mentioned the note and it turned out Byford vaguely knew the family. "Or his wife did," Flint said. "Margaret Byford was a friend of the doctor's wife, Madeleine Graves."

Byford's wife had died of cancer eight or nine years back. Bev had never met the woman. "And?" she prompted.

"Look, Bev, the note's likely from a nutter. Prob'ly nothing in it… but I'd like you to have a word with the widow. Suss out her thoughts on it." She opened her mouth to protest; Flint hadn't finished. "It's on your way home."

She couldn't see the point, not that she had a choice. Favour? Yeah right.

"It's not just that." He rose, smiled. "It needs sensitive handling. And Bill reckons that's your baby." Oh, God. Not the B-word. "You all right, Bev?"

"Peachy, boss."

"I scribbled the address on the back."

She turned it over, recognised the street name, kept her glance down. "So the guv reckons I'm big on empathy?" She was fishing.

"Huge, he says. I wouldn't know, would I?" He popped a Malteser in his mouth. "Not been here long enough."

Touché. At least she had the grace to smile.

DC Mac Tyler looked like a bulldog chewing a lemon soaked in vinegar. "Tell me again, boss." He slunk into Bev's office, leaned both hands on the desk. "Why'd I get all the good jobs?"

"Jeez, mate." She grabbed the air freshener from her drawer. "Get outa my face."

"You any idea what the contents of a wino's insides smell like?"

She sniffed and sprayed. "Course I have." Floral Glade met rotting flesh and formaldehyde.

"Me? I could do a thesis on it." He lifted his arm, smelt the sleeve. "The stink'll never come out."

"Get over it; could be worse, you know." She pointed to a leaning tower of police files tottering in the in-tray. She'd told him it was a toss-up between Wally Marsden's PM or three hours marshalling crime stats for a Powerpoint presentation to the police complaints commission. She also said she'd take the post mortem any day, but it was Mac's call.

He snorted, slumped in the swivel chair. "How's the police complaints thing coming on?"

"Dandy." Her fingers were crossed under the desk. "So give." She listened as Mac delivered the post mortem's top lines. Overdale had confirmed conjecture at the scene that the stab wound killed Marsden. Close run thing though given the beating he'd taken, not to mention the state of his liver.

"Any tighter on the timings?" Bev asked.

"You know Overdale." He rolled his eyes. "'This isn't an episode of Morse, DC Tyler. And Ai'm not Mystic Meg.'" The impression was spot-on, even down to the cocked head and finger jabbing. Bev's grin softened her tired features.

"She wondered where you were, actually."

"Yeah?"

"Thought you might've gone off sick?" There was a question in his eyes as well.

"Fit as a Strad me, mate. Timings?" The eye contact was a tad longer than she liked but he didn't push. He consulted a dog-eared notebook. "She reckons he'd been dead at least ten hours. Body was like an aubergine terrine, boss. Huge great purple blotches…"

She lifted a hand. "Enough already."

"And she found marks round the wrists and ankles."

"Defence wounds?"

"Ligature. Thin cord, she reckoned. Like he'd been trussed up."

"Held in a confined space, then?"

"That'll narrow it down," Mac quipped.

"Yeah right." Bev wandered to the window, perched on the sill. It was a complication they could do without. A second crime scene widened the inquiry beyond the confines of the estate. Where did the murder take place? Where was the body held? Could they be looking at more than one perp? Marsden was no heavyweight, but it wasn't easy manoeuvring a dead weight.

"Told Powell?" she asked. The DI got snotty if he thought he was missing something.

"Yeah. Bumped into him in the corridor. Overjoyed, he was."

She stifled a yawn. It was only four, but they'd been on the go for fourteen hours. "Come on, mate." She grabbed phone, bag and jacket. "Early bath." There was a twinkle in her eye. "Though in your case…"

"Don't even go there."

They chatted through tomorrow's actions as they wandered down to the car park. Bev would continue tracing relatives of Marsden's young victims; she'd only spoken to two so far. Mac could maybe concentrate on the names Flint had suggested, mainly former associates of the paedophile. Doubtless there'd be follow-ups to the news coverage. Punters generally rang in after a witness appeal. In this case, she suspected, a trickle rather than a flood. And on past experience, loony tunes would muddy the inquiry water.

"Catch you later, mate." She was almost at the Midget when Mac shouted.

"Boss! Almost forgot." He lumbered towards her, hand in a back pocket of his jeans. "Overdale said to give you this." The envelope was crumpled, stained and a little too warm for comfort.

"Ta, mate." She frowned. Not at the misspelling of her name (the second 's' caught most people out) but the word Personal written top left and underlined. Twice.

7

Quentin Hawke's sharp eye was on the penthouse door as he stroked the smooth desert of Scarlett's silken thigh…

Silken or satin? Early evening, and Matt Snow, head down, hands in pockets, wandered along the Hagley Road, kicking aimlessly at an empty Coke can. Even he could tell the line didn't have blockbuster written all over it. Mind, the reporter was still half-cut from the lengthy liquid lunch, the creative juice wasn't flowing. And the fresh air and exercise wasn't clearing the mental mist. The sight that greeted him as he turned into Cavendish Close did.

"Stone me." Face in cartoon frown, the reporter stood stock-still for a second or two. What the hell was the Fiesta doing outside his flat? He approached slowly, hand spiking tousled fringe. He hadn't got round to reporting the motor stolen so the cops couldn't have dropped it off. He tried the door: unlocked. Had to have been hot-wired. Nah. That was kids' stuff. Joy-riders didn't have their wicked way then return the goods. Whoever stole it must've had a key.

A quick rifle through the glove compartment confirmed Snow's belief: nothing in it identified him as the owner. He straightened, scalp tingling as the significance dawned. The thief must have been at the crime scene. And known whose car it was.

Tiny hairs rose on the back of Snow's neck. For several minutes he sat racking his brain for scenarios that fitted. None did. Sober and seriously spooked now, he was halfway out of the door when he spotted a note on the driver's mat. The paper was creased and soiled from the sole of his shoe. Not that it mattered, the words were easy to read. It was the meaning Snow couldn't get his head round.

There's more where Marsden came from.
Don't talk to the police.
Hope you like the present.
The Disposer.
Present? What present? And who the hell was the Disposer?

Tudor Grange was a massive half-timbered pile on the edge of Handsworth Wood. It was the address Flint had given Bev, and from the outside it was all she expected. She'd done jigsaws of places like the Graves's pad. She locked the Midget, ran her gaze over lead windows, intricate chimneys, rambling roses. Hoisting her bag, she headed for the heavy oak door, Doc Martens crunching gravel.

Smells suggested a barbeque somewhere close. Her mouth watered at the thought of a hot dog. On the way here, she'd fitted in a quick dash round Sainsbury. The food she'd bought wasn't fast though, the boot was a junk free zone. Bev's housemate Frankie would scrutinise every purchase. No point cheating, the fall-out wasn't worth it.

The knocker weighed a ton. She rapped it twice. Either the house was empty or the occupants aurally-challenged. Once more with feeling. Nothing. Might as well have a butcher's round the back. The walled garden was more jigsaw fodder: massed ranks of flowers, emerald lawn, spouting fountain and a well-endowed Greek dude in bronze. The warm redbrick outbuildings had presumably been stabling for horses. As for the barbie action – it wasn't here. She turned to leave, glanced up, thought she caught movement at an upstairs window. She strode to the front, hammered the door again. Nothing. Maybe she'd imagined it. Should she slip a note through? Nah. The subject was difficult enough to broach face-to-face.

Okey-dokey. She'd have to make a return visit. She strolled to the Midget, deep in thought. Maybe she should do a bit of homework first. Talk to someone who knew the family. The thought perked her up. Good thinking, Beverley. She smiled. Not that she needed an excuse to pop round or anything. She already had a bunch…

The jiffy bag was propped outside Matt Snow's third floor flat. Brown A5, no name, nothing to indicate its origin. The reporter picked it up gingerly, darted wary glances round the lobby: four identical navy doors, a couple of terracotta pots sprouting plastic palm trees. No mystery Santa lurking in the greenery. If indeed this was the so-called Disposer's so-called gift. Snow lifted the package to his ear: at least it wasn't ticking.

The Disposer? What kinda…? Feeling like a character in a Bond movie, he slipped into the flat, checked out every room. It didn't take long. The selling point had been compact bachelor accommodation. Cramped was nearer the truth. He grabbed a cranberry smoothie from the fridge, drank it standing at the breakfast bar, tried processing a few thoughts. No sign of an intruder so the guy only had access to the communal areas. The low-rise block's security system wasn't exactly hi-tech. Maybe he'd blagged his way in, but could get no further without a key.

Please don't let him have a key! That the joker had access to the motor was bad enough; the thought he'd been in the flat…

Snow rattled the Jiffy bag again, clutched it in both hands, fingered the contents. Open it or call the cops? Should he bring the law in on this? Whatever this was. It was a mobile phone. Presumably pay-as you go. Everyone knows they're that much harder to trace. He upended the bag. No clue. No message. No directions. He found those later. In the bed.

Months of pain were etched on Byford's face as he opened the door. His six-four frame was leaner than it had been and his hollow cheeks just this side of gaunt. Never a denim and trainers man, he wore moleskin trousers and a pale blue shirt open at the neck. When he saw who'd come calling, the slate-grey eyes lit up and a warm smile diluted the detective's deliberately doom-laden delivery. "Beware of Greeks bearing gifts."

"I ain't Greek. And what makes you think they're for you?" Bev, eyes shining, peeked round a sheaf of sunflowers.

"Can't imagine," he drawled. Except his house was full of them. Every time she came she brought more. The place looked like an Impressionist painting. Byford stepped back, followed her through to the kitchen. "I might've run out of vases."

"Nah." She glanced round, grabbed a glass spaghetti jar. "Don't eat a lot a pasta, do you?"

"Not now." He raised an eyebrow as she jettisoned a few sad-looking strands bin-wards. Frowning and tilting her head, she positioned the flowers this way and that. Van Gogh couldn't have done a better job. As Byford watched, a smile tugged his lips. Something he couldn't or wouldn't name tugged other parts. The big man valued these visits more than he'd care to admit. In the early days he wasn't sure how he'd have coped without Bev. He could have stayed with Rich or Chris, but his sons lived miles away, had families of their own to look out for. Byford's physical scars were bad, but weeks in hospital on life support had left his confidence shot to bits. Bev had been there for him through the darkest days of deep depression. Was that why she gave him sunflowers?

"Where'd you want them?"

"Kitchen window?"

"Kushti."

Either way, they were a big improvement on her erstwhile floral offerings. His wayward sergeant used to present cacti by way of apology when she crossed the line; was a time his office had more succulents than the Sahara. In recent weeks he'd finally confessed he couldn't stand the sight of the things. It wasn't the only confession they'd shared since the attack that almost killed him. They expressed it differently. He found her attractive: she wanted to jump him. Either way, a spark was there that had yet to be ignited. As Bev would say: close but no cigar.

"Have you eaten?" Byford said.

"Thought you'd never ask." She winked. "Burgers? Chips? Pizza at a push."

He shoved her on to a stool, fixed omelettes and salad while she brought him up to speed on Highgate's inside track. If laughter was the best medicine, Bev was a pharmacy. Her face registered every emotion as she talked, and she had the bluest eyes he'd ever seen. Part of him wanted to take her to bed, wake up with her in the morning. Every morning. The senior-officer-in-his-mid-fifties-who-ought-to-know-better-bit couldn't get past the complications if he returned to work. Not *if*, he told himself, *when*.

And then there was the other little matter…

"Anyone said anything yet?" he asked.

"All them trained observers?" She forked half a tomato. "Not a dickie."

"Someone will. It's only a question of time." He forced eye contact. "Unless…"

She lifted a hand. "Don't. Please. Not now." A termination. They'd been there before. He thought she should have the baby. She was still undecided: to be or not to be. He ate in silence, cast the odd covert glance. She looked tired or tense, likely both. It was probably the toughest personal call she'd ever have to make. And one with an imminent deadline.

"Top nosh, boss." Plate pushed away, she sprawled back. "Gawd. I could murder a ciggie?"

"Again?" He'd never smoked, but knew the craving kicked in after a meal. Far as he was aware she wasn't even sneaking the odd drag at work.

"What's all this about Matt Snow?" He'd read the press coverage, but she needed a distraction. He washed, she dried as she told him about the reporter's heads-up on the Marsden inquiry, the one-liners going round the nick. Byford didn't see the joke.

"Keep an eye on him, Bev."

"Tintin?" Her voice couldn't get much higher.

He nodded. "I wouldn't trust him far as I could throw him." He knew what she was thinking, it was written on her face. "I'll just say this: don't underestimate the guy. He's no clown."

She shrugged, aimed the cloth at a hook on the wall. "Try telling that to Powell. He's spitting feathers."

"I'm not surprised." The cartoon in the *News* was the DI to a tee, save for the SS leathers and jackboots. Byford retrieved the cloth from the floor, chucked it in the Hotpoint. "But since when's Snow let the facts get in the way of a good story? He's ambitious. Wants to go places."

Another shrug. He sensed she was miffed, maybe she resented the input. No. She was usually happy to use him as a sounding board. Probably just knackered. "Fancy a nightcap?"

"Best hit the road." Were the yawn and stretch a tad forced?

"Before you go." He disappeared, returned seconds later with a photograph. "After Kenny Flint's call, I rooted this out. That's Madeleine Graves." He pointed to a stunning-looking woman, one of five adults shepherding a crocodile of little kids. Bev had never seen so many gappy smiles and half-mast socks. "It was taken a few years back now," Byford explained. "She was married to a man called York then. Adam Graves was her second husband."

Bev studied Madeleine's image: long chestnut hair, wide smile, open friendly features. "How well did Mrs B know her?"

Mrs B? Margaret would be turning in her urn. He masked a smile. "Not well. Mums at the school gate sort of thing, PTA evenings, sports day." He nodded at the picture. "End of term trips."

"Did you meet her?"

"Once or twice. Bit scatty; pleasant enough."

"Adam Graves wasn't on the scene back then?"

He shook his head. "As I say she was Madeleine York when we knew her. I can't remember her first husband's name. She was cut up when he died though. Heart attack, I think."

"And the note? Still want me to check it?" Not enthusiastic, she clearly had doubts.

"Humour me." He smiled. "I've just got a feeling about it."

"That'd be your feminine side coming out." Deadpan tongue embedded in cheek. She took a final glance at the picture before handing it back. "Fair enough. I'll give it another whirl. Can't do any harm, can it?"

TUESDAY

8

11.30!!! Miss it – you're dead!!!!! XXXX

The death threat was on the kitchen table when Bev moseyed downstairs in her Snoopy dressing gown. She read it, yawned, chucked it in the bin and popped two slices of Mother's Pride in the toaster for breakfast. The note was Frankie's – never a girl to mince her words. The appointment was for the antenatal clinic that morning. Pressure of work meant Bev had missed two already. At least that's what she'd told Frankie who'd turned up both times, and hung round the women's hospital fuming while her Manolo Blahniks cooled.

Bev pictured it now: a finger wagging Frankie in full-blown maternal hen mode. Christ, she was worse than Bev's mum. A half-smile twitched her lips as she poured boiling water on a ginger tea bag. Frankie had moved in months back to help Bev through a bad patch that had turned into a quilt. She sighed, couldn't see her best mate leaving any time soon. Which was a mixed blessing.

Frankie was bossy, self-opinionated, and gobby to boot. Lucky Bev was a self-effacing shrinking violet. She smiled, munched dry toast. OK, Frankie Perlagio could be a pain in the butt, but she was closer than a sister. Mind, Bev didn't have a sister. Lips puckered, she took another bite. Cardboard was caviar compared with this stuff. It was one of a long list of bland foods suggested on a medical website to curb nausea. Spooky really, cause if Bev hadn't already put in the net-checks, Overdale's missive would have been all Greek to her. She'd opened the pathologist's note late last night and it had put the wind up her a damn sight more than Frankie's early morning missive.

Overdale had written: *Tell me to mind my own business but I've been there... Nausea gravidarum is a bitch. Try Phenergan. Lots of ginger. And congratulations!*

Nausea gravidarum, medico-speak for morning sickness. The doc's words alone had been enough to make Bev gag and dash to the loo. Overs had rumbled the pregnancy – would she keep mum or mouth off? Still hunched over the porcelain, hot tears had pricked Bev's eyes as she realised that Gillian Overdale – a woman she barely knew – was the only person who'd used the word congratulations in relation to the pregnancy.

When Matt Snow threw back his duvet and discovered the note, he knew skin-crawling fear for the first time. His bowels quickened, heart raced, hands shook as he held the paper. Sleep had hardly come at all, let alone easily. The reporter had wrestled with theories, each less likely than the last. Facts were these: the Disposer had been in Matt's home, driven his car, knew his private number, tipped him off about a murder, observed him at a crime scene. It scared Snow witless. Had he been singled out by a nutter? A crazed fan of his column? Or a killer?

Twelve hours on, the reporter's overriding emotion was fury. He was back in the real world, a vast crowded newsroom, cocooned and comforted by the familiar paraphernalia of his professional life. No joker was going to jerk him around. Snow didn't do puppet. As for the message – who did the arrogant toe-rag think he was?

Keep the phone with you.
No cops.
Burn this.
The Disposer.

Yeah right. He'd chucked it in the bin. Not the phone. That was in his breast pocket. May as well hear the sad sack out before telling him to sling his hook. Anyway… Snow tugged his bottom lip: could be a story in it.

There was sod all in the one he was working on now. He glanced at his shorthand; the mugging details he'd gleaned off the police press office voice bank weren't doing it for him. Kids snatching an old biddy's handbag didn't have the same clout as the thoughts whirling round Snow's head. The Disposer crap had to be a wind-up, didn't it? But there was a niggle that wouldn't go away.

There's more where Marsden came from?

What was that all about? More paedophiles? More murders? More exclusives?

"How's it going, Scoop?"

Snow lifted his glanced, dropped the scowl. "Great. Great." Even managed a smile. Anyone but Anna Kendall would have got a mouthful; calling him Scoop was so old. But Snow had been trying to get into Anna's thong for weeks. He ogled as she sashayed towards the features desk, took her seat just past a column covered in prize-winning front pages. Snowie rubbed his chin, imagined the pert little bum under the shapeless orange frock. With her cheekbones and that hair, he reckoned she'd look a million dollars in a classy suit, stockings, suspenders, stilettos…

"Grow up!" Snow ducked. The paper missile could've been launched by anyone on the subs' desk; they all had their heads down, butter wouldn't melt. They were jealous; everyone fancied their chances with La Kendall. Snow had already had a couple of goes. He strolled over, casual hand in trouser pocket. "What you working on?"

"A woman in Selly Oak." She rolled her eyes. "Writes to guys on Death Row."

"Why?" Her irises were a blue-grey shade he'd not seen before.

"Cause she's barking?" Snow liked a woman who made him

laugh. He watched as she twirled a strand of shiny caramel-coloured hair. "I think she's hoping one of the sickos will propose so she can make a packet flogging the story. You know the kind of thing…" Anna adopted the urgent tones of a telly ad for the *Sun*. "…I married a serial killer…"

"…now I can't sleep at night." God, she had beautiful teeth. "Fancy a drink tonight?"

"Sure. Why not? As for Mrs Barking Mad – I suppose it's human interest, isn't it." She licked her top lip as she opened her notebook.

Personally, Snow had more interest in the bottom of a colostomy bag. But at that moment, he'd have agreed with every word Anna Kendall said.

Highgate. Mid-morning. The early brief had been exactly that. No developments, no leads, not even close. Powell was angling to do another telly appeal, but the media weren't biting. Darren New and Sumitra Gosh were still trawling doss houses and soup kitchens. Mac was on the Churchill with the rest of the squad mopping up outstanding door-to-doors. Bev had headed straight for her desk clutching a list of calls as long as a phone book, not many names had a tick. Eddie Scrivener on the other hand had rung back in response to a message she'd left yesterday. Scrivener's daughter had been one of Marsden's victims. Right now, the receiver was six inches from Bev's ear; given the man's volume, the phone was probably superfluous.

"I'd a taken 'im out soon as look at 'im. Shame someone got in first."

Fighting talk, but there was a catch in the man's voice. She studied Scrivener's face on her screen, the image grabbed from an on-line archive. It was a snatch shot, taken as Scrivener stormed out of Wolverhampton Crown Court on the last day of the Marsden hearing. It didn't do Eddie any favours. His distorted features gave Munch's *Scream* a run for its money.

The conversation had been painful. Until she'd broken the news, Eddie Scrivener was unaware the paedophile was dead. Her subsequent questioning resurrected memories. Not that the trauma had ever gone away. For three years Marsden had systematically abused little Tanya Scrivener. The damage had been a catalyst for the girl's later self-harm. According to Eddie, she'd fallen in with a bad crowd, started running wild, was eventually taken into care. Eddie hadn't set eyes on his daughter for months. Nor his wife. The marriage broke up a year after Marsden's conviction.

"So when you nail him, duck, let me know. I'll be first in line to buy him a pint."

Her heart went out to the man. It didn't stop her eliciting where Scrivener had been on the night of the killing. He'd be eliminated after the alibi had been confirmed. Or not. The same went for Tanya who was now eighteen. Everybody lied – even coppers.

Dispirited and a tad depressed, she hung up. Even if they caught the killer, it wouldn't end the suffering. As it stood, they had no witnesses, no CCTV, nothing back from forensics. Could be they'd never track down Marsden's murderer. Could be no one'd give a toss. She yawned, stretched, flexed fingers ready for another bout of phone bashing. After a few abortive calls, she nipped to the loo, came back, made a few more. Exciting, this detecting lark. Just for a minute she laid her arms on the desk, rested her head, closed her…

"Don't do that!" Eyes wide, she shot up. She hated being touched. Mac shoulda picked up on that by now. Giving her shoulder an ostentatious brush, she snapped: "What?"

Mac stepped back, palms held high. "Sorr-ee. Thought you'd like to know Powell's on the warpath. And that's before he catches you comatose."

Hiding the panic, she glanced at her watch. 11.35. Frankie.

Shit. She couldn't have slept that long. "Gotta dash." She grabbed bag, phone and keys. "Cover for me, Mac?"

"What with? A marquee?"

"Improvise." She flashed him a grin. "You're good at that."

"I'm a shit friend, Frankie. And I'm truly deeply sorry." Eyes down, Bev toed the dusty pavement, fingered the car keys in her pocket. Gridlock traffic on the Highgate Road had eked a ten-minute journey to thirty, the appointment was history and Perlagio was having a hissy fit. Pacing up and down like an expectant father, she turned, eyes flashing, hands on hips.

"Don't try that shit thing again," she snapped. "Forty minutes I've been hanging round. Smiling. Simpering. Making excuses."

"Like I did it on purpose, mate." Unlike the previous occasions when she'd watched the appointed hour arrive and turned her back on the clock. Why was that? She'd thought about it afterwards. Still wasn't sure, but fear was in there somewhere.

"What was it this time?" Frankie sneered. "Shergar sighting?"

Bev shrugged, stepped back to let a woman waddle past with a buggy. The toddler looked angelic. Until it stuck its tongue out.

"Bin Laden doing a spot of shopping in the Bullring?"

God, was she still banging on? Bev opened her mouth then buttoned it. Might say something she'd not regret. But if Frankie mentioned lucky…

"Lord Lucan in Mothercare?"

"That is so old." She sniffed, folded her arms "Fell asleep, didn't I?"

Wind. Sails. Then another gust. "Why'm I not surprised? Look at you. You're knackered." She curled a lip. "Christ, Bev, you can barely look after yourself…"

"Let alone a baby?" she hissed. "That what you think?"

Frankie was a head taller, but stepped back a couple of paces. "Bev… I'm …"

She lifted a palm. Heard it all before. Told herself the same thing enough times. How could she care for a newborn? Christ, in Year 9 she'd dropped an Encyclopaedia Britannica on the class hamster. A little knowledge might be dangerous, but not as lethal as a lot.

Frankie drew closer, stroked Bev's hair out of her eyes. "I'm not doing it for the good of my health, Bevy."

"I'm not asking you to do it at all." The soft delivery reinforced the body language: it seethed with unspoken resentment. It was Frankie, guilt trip gun in hand, who'd stood over Bev as she reluctantly made medical appointments. It was Frankie who insisted on the health food drive. It was Frankie who never missed an opportunity to extol the joys of motherhood. Maybe it was the Italian blood, but to Frankie bambinos were what life was all about. Bev scowled. Bloody woman should go and buy one. "Let it go, mate."

"Let what go?" Frankie snapped.

Bev shrugged. "It's no big deal. I'll get round to it." But would she? She suspected that once she'd seen a tiny blob on a monitor, there'd be no turning back. Which was exactly what her friend wanted. But unlike Frankie, Bev saw shades of grey, had no idea what the future would hold if she went ahead.

"Cool." Frankie perked up, checked her watch. "The 12.45 was cancelled. Florence Nightingale on the desk said if…"

Bev raised a finger, other hand scrabbling in shoulder bag searching for the ringing phone.

"My friend…" Frankie shook her head, reached a restraining hand. "Don't answer it."

Bev listened, nodded, asked for an address to be repeated, hit the end button, looked round for her mate. Frankie was about to turn the corner. Bev could have shouted, run after her, tried to justify it. But Bev had made her choice and Frankie had got the message.

Powell was sitting in an unmarked police Vauxhall a few doors down from the property in Sparkbrook. Bev cruised past, scanning both sides of the street. Bath Road and its environs were redbrick territory. Identical rows of terraces eyed each other up through tall sash windows, front doors opened straight on to narrow pavements. Tenants customised the look with colour schemes, the residential equivalent of go-faster stripes. She raised an eyebrow at some of the more lurid combinations, nosed the Midget between a Harley Davidson and a Reliant Robin.

Not that she could talk. A dodgy black-on-mustard re-spray meant the MG resembled a podgy bee when the doors or boot were open. Bev still loved it though. She stroked its battered leather soft top as she walked past.

The DI made a big show of checking the time. "Where you been?"

Uranus. "Sat in traffic. What we got?"

He nodded at a property with grimy windows, dull black front door. "Someone in there's called the murder room hotline nine, ten times. All hang-ups." *So?* "The number's listed to Wally Marsden's ex-wife."

Ah. Inquiries had revealed that Gladys Marsden did a moonlight flit from the marital home in Wolverhampton shortly after Wally's conviction. They'd had no joy tracking her down.

"Thought you could try your Mother Teresa bit – she might talk to you."

"With you here?" And where was Mac?

"Cheeky sod."

The door opened a hand's span. A woman's face appeared inches above the chain, and stayed there as she raked an uncertain gaze over her uninvited guests. Her papery skin had a yellow tinge; the eyes were the colour of dirty dishwater. If this was Gladys

55

Marsden, Bev reckoned smoking wasn't the only thing bad for your health: marriage to a paedophile came pretty damn close.

"Mrs Marsden? We're police officers." The warrant card could've been a library ticket for all the notice she took. "Can we have a word?" Fifteen, twenty seconds passed, again the only thing moving was the old woman's eye-line. "Inside, perhaps?" Bev prompted.

Realisation didn't dawn, nothing so rapid. But eventually the woman drew back the chain, turned on down-at-heel tartan slippers and traipsed listlessly down a narrow unlit hall, fumbling both hands along the walls as she went.

Bev and Powell exchanged bemused glances. The back sitting room – small, square, cluttered – was in semi-darkness. Heavy maroon damask curtains were drawn, half a dozen red candles flickered on a black marble grate, others cast gothic shadows across the ceiling. Bev glanced behind, half expecting Vincent Price to appear, all pointy canines and swirling cape.

Whoever said a woman could never be too thin had never come across Gladys Marsden. Skeletal limbs, sunken cheeks; the long horsey face was draped with lank, salt and pepper hair shot through with nicotine. Big yellow teeth reinforced the equine impression. The shiny black polyester dress didn't.

Bev clocked faint movement from a rocking chair in the corner. From Mrs Marsden or a more recent occupant? Had the not-so-merry widow noticed it too? Either way, she scuttled over, lowered herself gingerly on to a huge squashy cushion covering the hard seat.

"Mrs Marsden?" Bev prompted. Is there anybody there? "Mrs Marsden?"

The woman stared into the distance, frail fingers fluttered at her lips. Her other fist balled a scrappy piece of tissue. A cheap faded carpet muffled the rhythmic rock from the chair. When the voice came it was flat, matter-of-fact.

"He's not a bad man." Present tense. Common confusion among the recently bereaved. Relieved the woman was talking at all, Bev didn't pick her up on it. "He needs help, treatment…"

"Castration." Powell's snide aside wasn't helping. Bev glared, nodded at the furthest armchair. He rolled his eyes, mouthed *get a move on.*

"He knows it was wrong… knows he should…" She could've been talking to herself; Bev suspected Gladys did a lot of that. She moved in, knelt close, reached out. The woman recoiled, clamped her hands under her armpits.

"When did you last hear from your husband, Mrs Marsden?" The woman's glance – maybe involuntarily – darted to the left. A round table was covered with a scarlet tasselled cloth, a tumbler and white cards lay splayed in the centre, letters not suits. Strewth. If Bev's reading was right, they'd be having a word with Henry the Eighth in a minute, never mind Wally Marsden.

"Walter can't get through now. He's in limbo."

Aren't we all? Bev's heart sank. The woman was off her fucking rocker. Compassion vied with contempt. In a way, Gladys was another of Marsden's victims. But his only apologist.

"Why did you call, Mrs Marsden? Is there something you'd like to tell us?"

"Too late…"

"What's too late?"

The woman's lips moved constantly but no words emerged. Bev tried every tack in the tin. Nothing. Pins and needles finally forced her to her feet. She suspected the woman was on medication, must have a care assistant, home help, something of the sort. Maybe they could tackle it through a third party. "I'll leave this with you, love." Bev put a card with her phone numbers into the woman's hand. "Call me if you want to talk."

"Waste of time," Powell muttered in the hall. Bev sniffed. Most plod work was: leads that turned into dead ends, lines that went nowhere. Maybe the woman was a fruitloop, or maybe she'd had call to contact the hot line. Either way, Gladys wasn't sharing. Her wavering voice reached them as the DI opened the front door.

"He lied to me. He said he'd help Walter, or I'd never've…"

9

Bev slurped the dregs of a tepid Diet Coke, eyed Powell's Big Mac and mammoth fries. She'd already seen off a not so Happy Meal. Half two and ravenous by the time they'd finally wrapped up Gladys's interview, they'd stopped for a bite. They had more than food to chew over.

A man in a suit had apparently turned up on Gladys Marsden's doorstep flashing cash. For a hundred and fifty quid the old woman had parted with Wally's phone number. Thought she was doing her ex a favour. Fair exchange? No robbery. But had it led to murder? Full of remorse and self-reproach, Gladys clearly suspected it had. It was the reason she'd called the hotline so many times. She'd hung up because what could she tell them?

Through tears and gritted teeth, she'd given Bev what little she had. She couldn't remember the man's name, wasn't even sure he'd divulged it. She couldn't provide much of a description, and hadn't asked for identification. Given the cursory glance she'd cast at Bev's, he could have shown her a picture of the Prince of Wales and she'd have let him in. At first she thought he was from the social, then the probation. Maybe even the police. All Gladys knew was that the 'nice young man' had promised to get Wally off the streets, off the pop and into a job.

Bev sighed, fiddled with a straw, watched as Coke drops splattered the table. She couldn't get her head round the fact that Gladys still had feelings for a child molester. Marsden had rolled up out of the blue at Bath Road just after his release from Featherstone prison three months back. He'd not asked to stay, just told Gladys he'd like to phone from time to time to let her know he was still alive. Ironic or what? Bev's mouth twisted as she recalled the woman's words spluttered through racking sobs: Marsden had been a good father, never harmed a hair of their kids' heads. Yeah right. Wally junior was now in Wandsworth nick. Colin farmed sheep in New Zealand. Go figure. There was denial, and there was delusion.

The depressing train of thought was derailed when a couple of kids at the next table started chucking bits of lettuce. Bev glared at the ringleader who was probably all of ten. Years and stones.

"Hey, doughboy. Knock it on the head."

"Why? What you gonna do 'bout it, slag?"

"Find out, fatso." She leaned across the divide, gave a lazy smile. "Go on. Lob a bit at me. Make my day." Please don't. It'd mean five hours' paperwork, and he wouldn't even get his wrist slapped with an ABC. Acceptable Behaviour Contract? Arsie Bastards' Club. He needed a slap with something solid – and not on the wrist.

Buddha Boy dropped the stare first. "Sorry, miss."

She closed her mouth. "Better be."

"What you say to him?" Powell whispered.

"No big deal." She sniffed. "Treat kids with a bit of respect. S'all."

The DI had trouble swallowing a chip too. He managed to spit out something about Marsden's mobile. That the paedo had owned a phone hadn't occurred to anyone on the squad. Not that it would have led them anywhere. It was missing. Bev had even rung the path lab to get one of Overdale's underlings to go through Marsden's multitudinous layers of clothing again.

"Think it's worth sending Picasso round?" Powell gestured to his fries, slumped back, appetite spent, long legs spread.

"Ta." She grabbed the carton, considered the question. Al Copley was Highgate's best police artist. The verbal information he drew from eyewitnesses was as detailed as the likenesses he sketched. Word was, Al could get a self-portrait out of Stevie Wonder. In Gladys Marsden's case, he'd have to be that good.

"I reckon her sight's shite." Bev bit a chip in half.

"How'd you work that one out?"

"Wavy eye-line, trouble focussing, fumbling her way along the walls. And what was with the candles and sitting in the dark?" Light probably hurt her eyes.

"Nah," he scoffed. "Old bat's away with the fairies."

Bev shrugged. "Maybe." The confusion could've been genuine or was there method in the madness?

"Meaning?"

"It doesn't add up." Instinct? Intuition? Either way inexplicable. Eyes creased, mouth twisted, her thoughts had clearly moved on.

"Share." Powell said, pointing at her face. "That's an idea you're having – or a stroke."

She hunched forward, elbows on table. "Assume whoever visited Gladys was lying, right?"

"Goes without…"

"He's not from the social or the probation. And he's definitely not out to give Marsden a make-over."

"Life Swap?"

Incredulous frown. "Anyway, moving on… what sort of drongo goes round with a fistful of cash asking people questions?"

If he said Chris Tarrant, she'd bop him. There was a dip in the surrounding buzz. She could almost hear the DI's mental cogs clicking. Then it dawned.

Two minutes later they were in the car park at the back of McDonald's. Given that the DI's Matt-Snow-copybook was well blotted, they'd decided Bev should have a go this time. Gentle probing – nothing heavy. Tintin wasn't the only journalist with a fat chequebook. Just the only hack who'd arrived at the crime scene before the cops.

"Shame Mac's not around," Powell said. "I hear he's good at

tossing in the odd googly at an interview."

"No prob." She paused, key in the MG's door. "I'll pick him up on the way."

"From Matlock?" She frowned. The DI elaborated. "He took off like a bat out of hell before lunch. Got a bell from his ex. One of the kids was rushed to hospital this morning."

"Kids?" Mac Tyler? Talk about being decked by a feather. "Mac's got…?"

"How long you worked with him?" The criticism though tacit was cutting. Four months they'd been partners, he'd not breathed a word about having brats. Worse than that, caring sharing Mother Superior Morriss hadn't even asked.

The *Evening News* building is as central as it gets. Listen hard outside and Bev reckoned you'd hear the city's heart beat. Hemmed in by towering structures, the austere grey 1970s fascia was broken up by huge gleaming panes of glass. Catch the light right and it was like a wide-screen showing Cityscape the Movie. Right now, bits of blue sky acted as backdrop to the plush law courts opposite, the foreground was criss-crossed by streams of extras. Having left the Midget in a multi-storey, Bev had a walk-on part herself. A glimpse of her ruffled reflection – the look was hedge-backward not wind-tossed – meant a hasty digital comb-through as she lingered a few seconds taking stock.

She loved the buzz here; most of the second city's cultural, legal, financial and commercial gems were within walking distance of where she stood. She grimaced; bummer if you were a journo on expenses. Mind, Shanks's pony'd be a damn sight faster than horsepower given the traffic. Bars of music blared through gaping windows as cars crawled by: hip-hop, heavy rock, Hank Williams. Exhaust fumes vied with fried onions, hot fat, vinegar. Pavement traffic was chocker too: shoppers, office workers, a Big Issue seller with purple dreds, a pencil-skirted

Blackberry Woman clacking along barking orders saving at least one planet, a couple of briefs on the corner having a smoke, Rumpole wigs tucked under their arms. When a tourist with a branch of Jessop's slung round his neck asked in shattered English the way to the beach, Bev reckoned it was time to move on.

The news agenda had moved on too. Billboards sandwiching the paper's main entrance screamed Killer Winter. *Killer Winter?* How'd that work? Yeti axe murderers storming Broad Street? Christ, it was early October, barely autumn, and the rag was full of reports forecasting the Big Freeze and freak blizzards. And on that hot topic, she'd not called Snow before turning up. Forewarned was forearmed. Seemed to her, Tintin had enough people tipping him the wink.

"He's out. Sorry." A blowsy middle-aged receptionist lifted an indifferent glance though a long scarlet fingernail marked her spot in a Cosmo article on multiple orgasms. Bev had heard more sincere apologies from Bill Clinton. She cast a withering glance at the athletic poses illustrating the centre page spread: that'd be the G-spot the talon was covering. Bev's testiness could just as easily have been targeted at the Marge Simpson lookalike relishing every word. Bev stared in awe at the woman's wobbling lilac beehive. It defied every known law of gravity. Must be some serious underpinning going on in there. "Any idea when he'll be back?" Polite, friendly.

The woman licked a finger, turned a page, held an imaginary piece of string between outstretched hands. Bev wouldn't have been surprised to see her take off given how the bingo wings were flapping. Rocket up the rectum would do the trick too. She was half-tempted just to go find the newsroom, but even a cursory glance registered the high-level security: turnstile, swipe cards, CC cameras recording every blink. She tapped a foot on the tiles; Marge still didn't pick up the cue. Maybe she'd forgotten her line.

"P'raps you'd like to ask someone?" Bev's tone was dangerously sweet.

"Been there, done that. No one on the desk knows where he is. And he's not answering his phone."

Bev frowned, wondered who else had been sniffing round. Marge reached to flick another page found a hand in the way. "Who else has been asking?"

The woman stared at the hand; Bev slowly retracted it. "People are always after him. He's a reporter. Certainly not my job to keep track…"

"'Xactly what is your job lady?"

"Is there a problem, Rita? Perhaps I can help?"

Bev took her elbows off the desk, turned to find a young woman – early- to mid-twenties – hovering at her shoulder. The face was pleasant, the voice placatory but Bev's hackles had yet to fall. "And you are?"

"Anna Kendall." Wide smile. "I work here. I'm a writer. On features?"

Bev shrugged. "Good for you, love. How about getting Rita here to pull her finger out and…"

Anna quelled the flow with a raised hand. And was that a wink? "Let's find somewhere to talk."

Somewhere was round the corner of the L-shaped foyer where four chunky faux leather armchairs were arranged round a glass-topped coffee table. Anna Kendall hauled a seat out for Bev, before sinking into one herself. Rita was out of sight and earshot, if not mind.

"Don't mind her. It's not personal. She's a pain in the bum to everyone." The young woman arched a conspiratorial eyebrow. "I reckon she knows where the bodies are buried or she'd have got the boot years ago."

The laughter was infectious; Bev was immune. Didn't appreciate the rare feeling of being wrong-footed. She studied

Kendall closer. Gamine was the word that sprang to mind. The delicate features, almond-shaped eyes, small bones didn't amount to great beauty but the apparent warmth and openness was appealing enough. If you liked that kind of thing. The woman seemed vaguely familiar. Was it just the matey attitude or had they met before? "Do I know you?"

Slight twitch of the lips. "Aren't detectives supposed to remember faces, names, that sort of thing? Sergeant Morriss?" However gentle the tease, Bev didn't appreciate it. Kendall cottoned on to that fast. "Sorry. It was a couple of months ago. You were giving a talk at Hillside Comprehensive?"

Bev nodded. Balsall Heath. There'd been a string of complaints from people living near the school: rival girl gangs fighting in the streets, intimidating passers-by, swearing, spitting, flashing blades. Bev had gone along to give a bud-nipping motivational talk. Motivated one of the little buggers to slash a tyre on the police motor. She remembered it well but not the woman sitting opposite. "Still one up on me, love."

Kendall smiled, tucked a glossy strand of hair behind a tiny ear. "You probably didn't notice. I was right at the back of the hall. I wanted to grab an interview when you'd finished but the news desk called…"

"…with a better offer?" A thin smile diluted the irony.

"Sorry." She had the grace to lower a sheepish look. "I was impressed actually, thought you handled the kids well."

Yeah right. Bev shifted her sleeve, checked the time. 3.15.

"Sorry. You must be busy. How can I help?"

Stop apologising for one thing. "I'm after Matt Snow."

"I'll see what I can do." She was on her feet already. "You OK here for a minute?"

Bev watched as Kendall waited for the lift. There was something about her stance; the way she rubbed the small of her back. The loose fitting rust coloured smock hardly flattered the woman's figure. But maybe that wasn't the reason for wearing it?

A beep from her mobile cut short the speculation. The text was from Powell: Bath Road. Now. She frowned. Had Gladys Marsden finally seen the light? She was about to hit the DI's number when Kendall reappeared showing empty palms.

"Can't help. Sorry. Matt took off a couple of hours ago. There's no pointer in the diary. One of the subs thinks he took a call from a contact."

Bev rose with a can't-win-'em-all sigh, handed Kendall a card. "Ask him to give me a bell, would you, love?"

"It's Anna." The tone was icy. Oops. Didn't like the 'love'. Or was that Bev's imagination? All of a sudden, Kendall was Little Miss Sunshine again. "Tell you what… I'm meeting him for a drink later. If I don't see him before, I'll mention it then."

"Ta, love." The grin was a tad smug. She should've bowed out gracefully at that point but couldn't resist another. "By the way, when's the baby due?" In the one-upmanship stakes, Bev reckoned she was now on equal footing.

"January." Anna smiled, gestured to the door. "When's yours?"

Gladys Marsden would never see the light again. Powell, grim-faced, arms crossed, slowly shook his head as he stared at the wasted body slumped in the rocking chair.

"Coincidence or what?" His question was rhetorical.

Bev squatted close by, concerned gaze scouring the flesh for signs of injury. They were back in the now even stuffier sitting room at Bath Road where – an hour after they'd left – a carer had discovered Gladys Marsden's still warm corpse.

What sounded initially like a routine call had struck a chord with an on-the-ball operator in Highgate control. The report had been channelled straight through to the incident room. Lucky. Or it could've taken hours to filter down.

Bev had done a Lewis Hamilton getting here; shame it wouldn't be him on the speed camera. The sharp exit had also distanced her from Anna Kendall. But not the writer's parting remark. Once Bev had got over the shock, she knew the dithering had to stop. She'd called the clinic on the way over, arranged another appointment. Camera had probably clocked that too. At the moment there were more pressing issues to deal with.

Like most cops she didn't do coincidence but also acknowledged that from time to time they happen. On the other hand, Gladys had been a sick woman. The GP had been in the house when they arrived, and he'd given a rundown: cirrhosis, osteoporosis, dementia, glaucoma: mortality-pick-and-mix. Bev rose, pursed her lips. "Can't see nothing obvious. Could be natural…"

"I could win *The X-Factor* but it ain't gonna happen," Powell sneered.

"Too right. You have to be good at something." The response was automatic, her focus elsewhere. Something wasn't right here. Something missing? Something extra? Either way, she couldn't put her finger on it.

"I know this: we turn up asking questions and the old girl's dead before we've even shared it with the squad."

The thought had occurred. "The guy with the cash was watching the house? Realised we were on to him?"

"Could be." Powell shrugged. "Or maybe he'd decided to take her out anyway."

Damage limitation. Callous bastard. If it was murder. According to Gladys's doctor, the old woman already had one leg in the grave: she'd have been lucky to see in the New Year. Still no excuse for some scumbag pushing her over the edge. Bev unclenched her fists. No sense spoiling for a fight either. Not until they knew how she died. The DI was playing it by the book anyway. Crime scene guys were on the way, police tape cordoned off the house.

Bev prowled round, gazing at Gladys's prized possessions, trying to pin down her mental worry bead.

"Uniform are knocking doors," Powell said. "A neighbour might have seen something." He loosened his tie. The air was getting staler by the second. Bev felt it too. It was suffocating in here.

She scratched a cheek. "Maybe we were getting warm, if not close." It was an uneasy thought that their earlier visit might have inadvertently led to the woman's killing. Either way, it would be several hours before they knew the cause of death. The autopsy might not go ahead until tomorrow. Bev homed in on Gladys again. Death had even further diminished the poor old girl. Slumped and shrunken, her emaciated body seemed to take up even less space. Or was that because...?

Bev squatted again, gently moved Gladys so that more of the rocking chair was visible. She was right. No cushion. Even more gently, she took the hand that Gladys had refused to give her in life. It had been too easy, maybe, to dismiss all the marks as signs of old age. Sure, the scrawny skin was virtually covered in liver spots, but closer scrutiny revealed what Bev now thought were signs of death.

"What is it?" Powell asked.

She shook her head, glanced round the room, knew this time what she was looking for. She crawled across the grubby carpet, searched under chairs, behind the curtains, then scrambled towards the table, lifted the tasselled cloth.

"What are you looking for?" He was wiping sweat from his face with a linen handkerchief.

"Gladys's cushion." Still kneeling, she turned, met Powell's gaze. "The murder weapon."

And it wasn't here. For once, Bev didn't need Overdale's expert opinion. The death scene played in her mind's eye: the old woman gasping for breath as a shadowy figure shoved the cushion into her sunken features. The faint finger marks on the back of Gladys's hand suggested she'd put up a half-hearted struggle. Given her ailing health, it wouldn't have taken long for the killer to snuff out what little life she had left.

10

"Sorry I'm late, babe." A flustered Matt Snow leaned across the table, zoomed in for a close up. Deliberately or not, Anna Kendall slid along the dimpled leather bench and the reporter found himself kissing air. No more than he deserved given his entrance was forty minutes overdue. They were in the Manhattan, a new-ish cocktail bar in the Mailbox. Moody Woody Allen sepia skylines covered the walls; soundtrack segued from Gershwin to Sinatra. Play it again, Sam.

Anna smiled, patted the seat. "No worries. I've been keeping it warm for you."

He'd read her wrong. What a star. The kindness threw him momentarily; he hesitated, finger-combing his fringe. It made him realise how – tonight of all nights – he badly needed a friend. He took a deep breath, hoped to God he could play Mr Normal. "What can I get you?"

She raised a quarter-full glass. "Chardonnay, thanks."

Two snake-hipped waiters were dazzling a couple of chavs with their perfect teeth and dodgy American twang. Matt observed Anna in the mirror while he waited his turn. It was no hardship. Her Angelina Jolie lips curved in a private smile as she slipped a paperback into her bag, a crime novel going by the cover. Good way to kill time. Though it wasn't killing time that preyed on the reporter's mind.

A muscle twitched in his jaw. No worries, Anna had said. As if. The series of phone calls that afternoon had been deadly serious. If the man who called himself the Disposer was on the level, he planned to waste more perverts. Said his mission was to clean the streets of human dross. And he wanted Snow to write the story. The reporter would get exclusive access to every twist and turn of a seriously warped mind. It was a journalist's wet dream. But that was all it was: pure fantasy. Except the educated sober voice on the other end of the line had sounded as sane as Snow's. Which was why the reporter had told the guy to back off or he'd alert the cops. The response still chilled Snow's blood: speak to the police and I promise you'll beg to die. The Disposer had then described Snow's exact location, the brown suit he was wearing, even the woman in a burqa by the swings. Hardly surprising, given Snow had followed the Disposer's precise directions to sit on the bench near the kids' play area in Canon Hill Park. It was one of four places Snow had been ordered to hang round that afternoon. That was the stick. The carrot was a face-to-face with the Disposer. But it hadn't happened. Snow frowned, tried to recall the guy's final words. Something about trust being vital and that Snow had passed an initiation test. *An* not *the*.

The reporter scowled. Puppet? He had more strings than the Thunderbirds. But could he pull them to his advantage? Food for thought? A mental feast, but Snow wasn't sure he had the stomach for it. Make that guts. This was land-mine territory. Every journo joked they'd kill for a good story. Could he really stand by while the Disposer did it for him? OK, that was well over the top. The reporter was a bit-part player, a bystander, an observer, but didn't it boil down to the same thing? If he knew what the Disposer planned – and did nothing to prevent it? He sighed. Snow wasn't just out of his depth; he was drowning.

Anna caught his glance in the mirror, winked and smiled. God, she was gorgeous. Anyone else and Snow would have cancelled tonight like a shot. Given the distractions, he wasn't exactly in the mood for small talk.

Anna spoke before he sat down. "Before I forget, Bev Morriss is after you."

Both wine glasses clattered as he placed them on the table,

a few drops of Snow's Rioja spilled on the glass. If Anna noticed, she chose not to comment. "She was sniffing round reception at the paper. I saved her from a fate worse than death." She wiggled her eyebrows. "Well, Lethal Rita anyway."

Matt tried to match Anna's smile. "What did Morriss want?"

She gave a one-shoulder shrug. "Didn't say." Anna clinked her glass against Matt's. "We didn't exactly hit it off to tell you the truth."

He was desperate to blunt the edges with alcohol, couldn't trust himself to lift the glass without trembling. The Disposer's threat still echoed in his head: *talk to the police and you'll beg to die...* "Morriss is a lippy bint."

Anna turned her mouth down. "Seemed OK to me. I'm sorry we got off on the wrong foot actually. Anyway. I said I'd get you to call." She handed him a card from her pocket. "Number's there."

"Great." Like he was going to.

"Could've been something to do with Gladys Marsden..." Anna picked a loose thread from her dress, oblivious of Snow's slack jaw.

"What could?"

"Why the police wanted a word. Mind, I don't think they'd discovered the body then." She drained her glass. "Matt...?" Snow couldn't hear over the blood pounding in his ears. He was about to disappear into the Gents anyway.

"I'm forever blowing bubbles..." The teetering soprano could shatter double-glazing. "Pretty bubbles in the air." A scalded cat with a frog in its throat would sound more mellifluous. "Dum-de-dum-dum-dum..."

Bev stretched full length in the bath, twizzled the hot tap with a big toe, snuggled under a soufflé of soapy vanilla froth. Scented candles filled the air with cranberry and cloves, a glass of chilled

Chablis was at hand. Apart from Johnny Depp in a towel, what more could a girl want? Johnny Depp in a flannel? The singing detective wiped a leer off her face.

"Dum-de-dum-dum-dum."

"Put a sock in it." Frankie's ears hurt and she was in the kitchen.

"Dum-de-dum-de-dum-dum-dum."

"I'll give your dinner to the dog."

"We haven't got a dog."

"I could fix that."

Bev grinned. Glad they'd got over the spat, hated being at odds with her best mate. Only mate? The mental barb had niggled before. Cops tended not to fraternise outside the force. Well, Bev didn't. Was that a failing? Who cared? Not tonight any way. Let it go...

Frankie was determined to celebrate. She was chuffed to bits Bev had rescheduled the antenatal appointment, and Frankie had landed a couple of gigs at venues she'd not played before. Considering she was a seriously good session singer, Bev was surprised she'd not stomped up to pull the plug by now.

Mind, Frankie was wearing her Domestic Goddess hat too. Going by the occasional whiff of garlic and basil, Pasta Perlagio was on the menu. Frankie's signature dish differed a dash and drizzle every time. Not that the Domestic Dingbat was carping. Bev's culinary prowess knew no beginning. Then again her deductive powers hadn't been so hot recently. She blew flushed cheeks out on a sigh, ducked ensuing clouds of bubbles.

Actually, she took issue with herself, that's not true. She'd been bang on at Gladys Marsden's place. Overdale had phoned the DI with the post mortem's preliminary results. As well as the bruising on Gladys's hand, the pathologist had found petechial haemorrhaging in the soft tissue of the old woman's eyes, mouth and larynx. Asphyxiation would go on the death certificate: posh for a cushion in the face. Despite the heat, Bev shivered.

According to Overdale, Gladys was so weak she wouldn't have been able to put up much of a fight.

Unlike Matt Snow. The slimy little bastard had given Bev the slip. Before knocking off for the day, she'd tried all the obvious places, plus a few dives where she knew the reporter drank occasionally. She'd left messages with everyone who knew him, even had a word with her old mate Jack Pope. She gave an unwitting smile. Ridiculously good-looking, Pope was a resistible blend of boyish charm and macho bullshit. A former cop, he was now Snow's equivalent on the *Sunday Chronicle*. There was no love lost between the rival crime correspondents whereas Pope was one of Bev's old flames. She reckoned he still held a torch for her. She tilted her head, turned her mouth down. Make that a flickering match. Whatever. He said he'd keep an eye open for Tintin.

"You decent?" Frankie's hand appeared proffering Bev's mobile. "It's Oz."

Water and bubbles sloshed over the sides as Bev shot up. No way could she talk to Oz, she'd not returned his calls or texts for weeks. "I'm out."

Frankie came in, glared at Bev. "She says she's out."

Bev glared back, shooed the phone from her face, mouthed a panicky, "No!"

She was scared witless. Scared he'd find out about the pregnancy when she still wasn't convinced she wanted the baby. She closed her eyes, pictured her former lover's beautiful sculpted features. The phone was still inches from her face. The pain in Oz's voice brought tears to her eyes. "Bev? If you don't want to talk at least have the bottle to tell me..."

Bev hid her face in her hands, counted ten, fifteen seconds. He must've thought she'd hung up. He'd not have said it if he knew she could hear. The volume was lower this time, but the words rang in her ears.

74

"'Kay. Fine by me… fuck you, lady."

DC Mac Tyler made it a rule never to drink alone. Nearly midnight by the time he arrived back, he closed the door on his soulless Balsall Heath bedsit and headed straight for the bottle. The last few hours had been a nightmare. He'd driven like a maniac to reach Matlock. God knew how he'd arrived in one piece. Not that he had. He'd been in bits after the call. En route he'd replayed his ex-wife's hysterical voice on the phone telling him that George, their eight-year-old, had been knocked over by a van on a pedestrian crossing. The under-age uninsured driver was in police custody. George was in intensive care, a head injury causing concern.

Concern? Unspeakable churning terror. Mac had never endured anything worse. The thought of losing…

His hand shook as he poured two inches of Bell's into a chipped mug, leaned back against the sink. His stomach was empty, the spirit burned his insides. He downed it in two gulps. Whenever he closed his eyes all he could see was George's cheeky little face on the pillow, white skin mottled damson and mauve.

Alone and lonely, the detective sank his face in his hands. George had regained consciousness – thank God – by the time Mac arrived at the hospital. The skull fracture was hairline, doctors said recovery should be quick and complete.

But the relief was tempered by the absolute agony of countless what-ifs… Pacing the corridor outside the IC unit, a memory had flashed unbidden into Mac's brain: his mum, years ago, saying she'd died a thousand deaths when he was growing up. Now he knew what she meant.

Mac poured more alcohol. Was it worse for mothers? When he told Jess he'd be going back to Birmingham that evening, she'd flipped, screamed at him to bugger off; the job had always come first. Had it? He took a sip, sucked the liquid through his teeth. Like a lot of blokes, he compartmentalised. But he loved the boys more than anything on this earth. Blanking them out at work was a coping strategy. Being a cop was a dangerous game, without distractions. Could women do that? Would Bev be able to?

He sloshed the dregs round the mug. It wasn't just that though. With the marriage breakdown, he only had limited access now. Not seeing the boys every day hurt like hell. Just thinking about it brought tears to his eyes. It was why he rarely talked about them. The transfer to Birmingham had made it easier to keep emotional baggage to himself. Early on, he'd sussed out who ran the Highgate rumour mill, chucked in a seed or two about going through a messy divorce. Generally speaking, people had left it at that.

Maybe it was why he'd extended the same courtesy to his spiky sergeant. For a couple of weeks now, he'd suspected she was pregnant. But it was down to her if and when she told people, assuming she was going ahead with it. Would he think less of her if she had an abortion? Yes. No. Maybe. He shook his head. Poor bloody woman. What a decision to have to make.

He pushed himself up, wandered wearily all of eight paces to an unmade single bed. Self-disgust washed over him. He'd promised himself it would only be a few weeks, but four months now he'd lived in this dump. The beige anaglypta walls were like vomit, grotty carpet tiles stuck to the soles of his shoes. He perched on the edge of the mattress, took a photograph from a wonky bedside table. It was the only thing in the place he valued. George, like his older brother Luke, had inherited Mac's dimples. He ran a stubby finger over their faces, mirrored their broad grins. Despite the fear, the pressure, the pain of having kids – Mac knew his boys were the best thing in his life. Not for a second did he regret being a dad. Maybe it was time to risk getting his head bitten off. And mention the joys of parenthood to Bev.

WEDNESDAY

11

Early morning. A whiff of autumn in the air. Mellow fruits and mistiness? Petrol fumes and dog poo. But then, Cavendish Close was a popular spot for pooch-walking. The MG was parked outside Matt Snow's flat. Bev perched on the bonnet scarfing breakfast. Her long navy coat was new, felt a tad big on her. She scowled. Not like her feelings last night. Fuck you, lady, Oz had said. Small didn't begin to cover it. Minuscule. Mortified. Murderous. How could Frankie...?

Oz has a right to know, my friend.

Mayo oozed from the end of a six-inch BMT sub and she licked it quick. Course Oz had a right to know. She was aware of that. Didn't mean she was ready to tell him. She'd told Frankie to shove her pasta up her bum. It was the last cordial exchange they'd shared. A mound of viscous black-peppered penne had stared accusingly at Bev from the kitchen bin this morning. Talk about having your bubble burst...

Starving, she'd stopped off at Subway and was now making up the dietary deficiency. Frankie would find a scribbled note when she got up. If she didn't like it she could lump it.

A flash of light on glass alerted her to action at the door of Snow's apartment block. Bev hastily wrapped the sub in a napkin, shoved it in her bag. This was one bloke she did want to talk to. She jumped up, wiped greasy hands on a tissue. All a touch premature. A middle-aged woman walked out of the building in a corporate suit that said she worked in a bank or a building society. So where was Snow? Bev'd put a call through when she pulled up twenty minutes ago. He'd just stepped out of the shower, said he'd see her in five. Unless she wanted to come up and rub his back. Cheeky sod.

She strolled down the road. Traffic rumble would soon be a roar, not far off rush hour now. Would she make the early brief? Quick glance at her watch: 7.15. Not if Tintin didn't get a move on. She frowned, couldn't afford to lose Brownie points, not when she needed a favour from the DI.

A russet-red carpet of leaves rustled underfoot. She had a quick look round, kicked a bunch in the air. Then another. And another. She grinned, recalling the days she and Frankie waded through leaves walking to school, always arm-in-arm, always having a giggle. Enough already, button it, Beverley.

Maybe she'd give Powell a quick bell, early warning she might be late. She scrabbled in her bag, picked a few shreds of iceberg off the touchpad. Sodding leaky sub. The phone rang as she was hit about to hit the DI's number.

"You're not gonna believe this." Matt Snow.

"Try me."

There was a pause; it sounded like he was sitting in traffic. "I forgot you were outside. The desk called. I'm in…"

"Shit so deep – you're gonna sink, matey."

He said he was in the motor on the way to some job on the other side of town. Bev took a calming breath. "There's a stack of questions need answers, Snow. I'll give you an hour to get to Highgate nick."

"What if I can't?"

"Fifty-nine minutes, forty-five seconds." She slung the phone in her bag, stalked back to the motor. "Catch you then, you little turd."

Bev checked her watch as she crossed the car park at the nick. If she raced, she'd just make it. She clattered up the back stairs, burst into the squad room. A fat guy in a loud shirt was staring at a computer screen. It took a second to realise who. "Looking rough, mate." She rifled through printouts, sneaking the odd covert glance at her DC.

Mac Tyler gave a one-shoulder shrug. "Don't hold back, sarge."

"Dog rough then." A wink softened the edge, but it was true. Desperate Dan stubble on both chins, pink flaky patches on his cheeks, and the eyeliner was an unflattering red. Shit! She'd forgotten. "Sorry Mac. How's…?" Christ, she didn't even know the kid's name.

"George. He's OK." He told her briefly what had happened: the accident, the hospital, the doctors' verdict.

"Great." Shifty eyes, shuffling feet. She didn't really do kid talk, and it looked as if Mac's eyes were tearing.

"How 'bout you, sarge? Stomach still giving you gip?" He sat back, rested beefy hands on porky paunch. Loaded question? Meaningful look?

"Tickety. Comin'?" She dashed out, clutching a sheaf of overnight incident reports to skim on the way: shots fired in Handsworth, non-fatal stabbing on the Lozells Road, four houses turned over in Moseley, fatal RTA in Digbeth, bingers' brawl on Broad Street. Yawn yawn. Same old.

Their joint appearance at the brief interrupted Powell's flow. "Good of you to drop by." He waved an arm in extravagant welcome. Sarky sod. Bev bit her tongue; she'd still not asked the favour. She flashed him a smile, sat at the front, pen poised, all ears. Three or few new faces had joined the squad. Gladys Marsden's murder had clearly upped the ante.

Powell perched on the corner of a table, swinging a leg encased in fine grey wool. "As I was saying, instinct tells me we're looking for one killer. Nail Gladys's and we've collared her old man's. And given the complete lack of progress tracking Wally's – that's kinda lucky."

"Dead lucky for Gladys," Bev mumbled. Mind, in a cack-handed way, the DI had hit the nail smack on. Establishing Wally Marsden's movements was like pinning down fog. A homeless dosser, Marsden had gone wherever the fancy took him. Gladys had neighbours, a carer, a mate or two, presumably. As for her gentleman caller, a team of detectives was in Bath Road now trying to flush out information from the locals.

Powell looked at Bev, eyebrows raised. "And then there's the Matt Snow connection."

She waggled a hand. "Loose connection." Her account of the farce outside the reporter's flat raised a few titters. "Said he for-got I was there." Outrage incarnate. "Can you believe that?"

Even the DI had a ghost of a smile. "Bloke must have a death wish."

Quick time check. "He's got five minutes, then the wand comes out."

Caught between a rock and a hard place? That'd be a breeze. Matt Snow's quandary was off the register. Hack off the Disposer or risk Morriss getting one on her? Make that another one. Bloody woman was nosing round like a pig in a truffle market. If the Disposer got wind of her inquiries, odds were he'd think Snow had blown the police whistle. And the reporter had no wish to die.

Right now he was tapping the wheel, stuck at a red on the Stratford Road, heading for Lidl's at Small Heath. He'd taken the Disposer's directions over the phone, just minutes before Morriss's early morning call. Snow glanced round nervously, half expecting a Highgate posse on his tail. The reporter knew he'd have to talk to her sooner or later; the current jaunt was only putting off the inevitable. But he had to square it with the Disposer first. Make it clear the police were after Snow, not the other way round. The reporter had no intention of blabbing to the Bill.

A horn blared. Snow glanced in the mirror, curled his lip at a wally in a white van. The reporter was hacked off being shoved round, had half a mind to get out and deck the guy. He didn't have time, hit the gas instead. Apart from doing his Thunderbirds impression he had a column to write, for Christ's sake. Hadn't given it a thought so far, nor the nascent bestseller. What price make-believe when he was in the middle of the real deal? Scared and out of his depth he may be, but he was a reporter... Play it right, and it could be the biggest coup of his career. Or cock-up.

He flicked the radio, nudged the volume, just missed the top of the news.

"... found dead in her Sparkbrook home yesterday has been named as Gladys Marsden. West Midlands police say the woman died from asphyxiation. They're treating the death as murder and are appealing for witnesses..."

Snow loosened his cheap brown tie, ran a finger round his collar. Morriss's third degree would have to wait. He'd text her saying he'd get to Highgate soon as. He had questions of his own first for the Disposer. The reporter lowered the window, inhaled cool air, wished he could turn down the heat.

"Sergeant Morriss?" The voice on the landline was warm, friendly. It took Bev a couple of seconds to place it. She was at her desk, writing the tenth or eleventh report of the morning. Bliss on a Bic. Not. Months ago, she'd read an article: Sir Ronnie Flanagan, chief inspector of constabulary no less, had worked out that fifty-six million police hours a year went on paperwork. Bev reckoned fifty-five million of them were down to her. Any distraction was welcome. Usually.

"Ms Kendall." Clipped, cool.

"Anna, please." Bev heard the smile, ignored a pause for her to respond in kind. "Sorry, sergeant. If you're busy...?"

"Get to the point, love." Churlish. Childish. Why was she such a cow to the woman?

"I could call back…"

Exaggerated sigh. "What you want?" Bev doodled on a piece of card: a witch with warty chin, hairy hooked nose.

"I work on features, right?"

Bollock-alert. She blackened a witchy tooth. "And?"

"You're a female detective fighting crime on the front line."

"Hold it right there, love." She was seeing a wall with a fly on it. And herself writhing under a media microscope.

"Come on, Bev, you're a great role model. I watched the way you handled those kids at Hillside. I'd love to shadow you for a few days. See how a modern day cop copes with the pressures policing the mean streets. Tell it like it really is. You'd be ace, Bev."

Lick my bum, why don't you? As for first name terms – in your dreams. "Paperwork and plod, Ms Kendall."

"Not all the time. And when it is… I'll say so." Another pause. Letting the sincerity sink in? "Honest, Bev, I'm not in the habit of making it up as I go along. I'm sick of seeing the police get a bad press. Why not show it from a cop's point of view for a change?"

Bev knew Kendall was bullshitting, but… "Yeah, OK. I'll think about it." It might be worth keeping her sweet. The writer worked alongside Snow, could pick up the odd titbit, pass it on to Bev. It might open newsroom doors without getting a warrant first.

"Fantastic! I've already run the idea past the police press office." Had she indeed? Sharper than she looked then. "I reckon we could get a series out of this. Crime's so sexy at the moment… when I say sexy… I mean…"

"Don't worry. I get the drift." Her lip twitched in a wry smile, picturing Kendall's unease. Not to mention Powell strutting round in Rocky Horror gear. "Give us your number. I'll get back

82

soon as."

She provided three. "Did Matt Snow call by the way? I gave him your card last night."

"Spoke to him first thing." No detail. None to give. Not that she would.

"Was he OK?"

"Yeah. Why?"

"Just that he called in sick this morning. Stomach bug, I think."

"Did he now?" Keeping Kendall sweet was a no-brainer. She'd just revealed a big fat Snow porkie. Git said the news desk had called him out. She'd keep that up her interview sleeve when the lying rat came in later. The reporter hadn't shown at Highgate this morning, but had sent her a text with a new ETA.

She glanced at her watch. It was late o'clock. "Gotta dash, Anna."

"OK. Thanks for your time. Oh and Bev? That comment about the baby? I was completely out of order. You're only just starting to show, aren't you? If you're anything like me, you're not making a big thing of it yet. I don't know how you feel, but I was dead scared early on… losing it… you know?"

"Yeah." She cut the connection, laid a hand on her belly. "Something like that."

"Talking to yourself, boss." Mac stood in the doorway.

She scowled. "You *ever* knock?"

"The DI says you're nipping out?"

"Couple hours tops." Powell had OK'd the favour. P'raps she ought to bite her tongue more often. She threw a few bits into her bag. Damn mayo everywhere. "Personal stuff."

"Fine by me." He sauntered to the desk, carrying a file. "The DI wanted you to have a look at this." She cut it a glance. Shit. The label read: PCC/crime stats/DI Mike Powell. "He's keen you're familiar with the format." Mac raised an eyebrow. "Should you ever be asked to do one."

Palms held in mock surrender, she flashed a guilt-riddled grin. "It's a fair cop, guv."

Mac nodded at the doodle. "Self portrait, boss?" Deadpan nonchalance.

"Touché." She blew him a kiss. "Deputy Dawg."

The figure wore a black hoodie emblazoned with **The Who Live At Leeds.** A mobile phone concealed much of the face, one eye was flush with the camera's viewfinder. Matt Snow was in its sights, looking as if he was having a hot flush. Finger on the shutter: click.

What was visible of the mouth curved in a sly grin. Lidl's stinky bottle bank wasn't the coolest place to hang. Then again neither was Bath Road, or Canon Hill Park. The reporter hadn't looked over the moon on any of his recent assignments. The photographer had quite a portfolio to choose from now. One more shot. No rush. Wait until the reporter was in frame. Click.

12

Bev was so far out of her comfort zone it felt like she'd entered Room 101. Least there were no rats, just women in varying stages of pregnancy sitting round, banging on about babies and water births, big boobs and breath control. Christ, she'd be swapping knitting patterns and recipes for pureed kumquat soon. And thinking 'bout rats, where was Frankie? Her faithful forgiving friend. Bev gnawed her thumbnail. Scary being here at all, let alone without a mate. Guess the note she'd left that morning hadn't mended any fences. She sniffed; sod Frankie.

The orange moulded plastic chairs wouldn't win any comfort awards. Bev sprawled anyway, folded her arms, closed her eyes. Wasn't just blanking the clinic, she hated hospitals full stop. They evoked memories of her dad's cancer, sobbing her heart out in an empty corridor. Death and disinfectant. Past shadows. Future fears.

She tried tuning in to the present. A couple of women in trackie bottoms were talking soaps, a woman in a scarlet and gold sari was doing the *Guardian* crossword, a surly kid with an eyebrow piercing was picking a scab on a bony knee. All human life…

Bev sighed, reached for a dog-eared *Reader's Digest*. And another. Christ, she'd pod the kid here if they didn't call her in soon.

"Beverley Morriss." Least she was a name not a number. "This way, sweetheart."

Sweetheart? OK, Hot Lips. Actually the young blue-eyed blonde did have an attractive mouth; it was currently set in a warm smile. Bev's faltered. It was novel being patronised by a woman, specially one who didn't look old enough to have A-levels.

"Relax. We don't bite." The nurse sat behind a desk. Bev's glance took in a leaping dolphin screensaver, cup full of pens and a page-a-day calendar of George Bush-isms. "My name's Clare. I just need to take a few notes."

The room was light, airy; the walls pale lemon. Bev shucked off her coat, hung it on a hook, spotted a stain on the back. Dried mayo looked like bird shit. Could life get any better?

"Is this your first visit?" Clare reached for a file.

"Yeah, I missed a couple appointments." Bev looked down at her hands.

"No problem. Just a few questions."

For few questions read full medical history. Bev replied mono-syllabically to Clare's attempts at small talk. She was edgy because she knew what was coming.

"Now for the good bit." Clare smiled. "You get to see your baby for the first time."

And maybe the last? Either way an ultrasound was unavoidable. No scan, no termination. It was hospital policy. Bev could come up with a zillion reasons why it would be madness to have a kid, but what if she fell in love with a faceless grey blob? What if she already had feelings for it? Her head was on fast spin. She was a cop, she made occasional life or death calls. Why was she a quivering wreck?

"Take a seat outside," Clare said. "Someone will call you. And cheer up, sweetheart, it might never happen."

What if it already has? Eyes brimming with tears, Bev grabbed her coat, hoisted her bag, stomped through the waiting room, headed for the exit.

"Hey, my friend." Frankie's voice stopped her at the doors. "You're not running out on me again are you?"

"Where's Morriss?" Mike Powell burst into the squad room, silk tie over his shoulder.

86

An admin clerk held out empty palms. Mac Tyler looked up. "I think…"

Powell flapped a hand. "Save it. She said two hours max. It's four o'clock now."

Mac could've kicked himself for not thinking on his feet, covering Bev's back. She was only an hour late, but given the recent disciplinary… More to the point, she'd not called in. "Something must've come up."

"Got that right. A triple-nine. Five minutes ago." Powell shoved the paper across Mac's desk. "Man's body. Small Heath park. Stratford Road. Uniform are on site. A crime team's on the way. Get over there now."

Mac grabbed his jacket. "Boss, Bev wouldn't…" What? By the time he'd fashioned a comeback, Powell was out the door.

"Where were you?" Bev slumped in the same plastic orange moulding as before, bottom lip jutting.

Frankie swivelled in her seat, arms folded. "Hello Frankie! Great to see you. Thanks for coming. How are you, my…?"

"No friend a mine." Bev cut the snipe-fest.

"Leave you to it, shall I?"

"Fucking dare."

The banter was hushed because a couple of toddlers were close by, giggling as they raced Dinky cars across the floor. They were all nappy bums and dimpled thighs. Bev found a smile on her face, not sure where it came from.

"See." Frankie tilted her head at the kids. "Better than the telly any day."

Bev shook her head. "Even for you, that's barking."

Frankie shrugged, pulled a pack of Revels from her pocket. They chomped in companionable silence for a spell.

"I'm scared, Frankie."

"Come on, it'll be cool. Whatever happens I'm here for you…"

Must be true given the missive she'd left Frankie. Get your ass to the Women's at one. Big love, Bev. "Like the note?"

Frankie sniffed. "Diplomatic service is crying out for people like you."

"Ms Morriss?" It was a man in a white coat this time.

Frankie whispered, "They're coming to take you away." It didn't help.

White coat held the door open. Bev caught a whiff of coffee breath as she swept past. Guy was quite fit in a spiky blond kind of way: David Bowie cheekbones, big teeth, tiny diamond ear stud. Badge on his chest said: Marc Kingsley, Radiographer.

"Excited?" he asked Bev.

Frankie flashed a smile. "She's speechless."

Bev half-listened to Kingsley's spiel as she glanced uneasily round the suite: pastel pinks and blues, metal filing cabinets, blank monitors. Business end was obviously the big leather couch. Kingsley dragged a chair next to his. She was about to perch when he pointed at Frankie. "It's for your friend."

The paper sheet rustled under Bev's bum as she lay back. She watched Kingsley peel on latex gloves then reach for a tube. She winced as he rubbed gel on her belly.

"Cold?" Smiley face.

Polar. "Tad nippy." She simpered.

Sleeves rolled, he wielded what looked like a TV remote. "I'm just going to run this over your tummy. You won't feel a thing."

Wanna bet? Watery smile.

Kingsley moved his toy this way and that, his eyes creased in concentration. Frankie's shone with excitement "Look, Bevy." She was on the edge of her seat like it was a Big Brother double eviction or something.

Reluctantly, Bev turned her head to the monitor. Palms damp, pulse hiked, she tried to make it out. Shadows and shady bits. Then she saw something. She narrowed her eyes.

"Yep," Kingsley said. "There you go." His finger pointed to a tiny black blob. "That's your baby's heart. Beating like a drum."

Vaguely aware of Frankie's hand in hers, Bev's focus was on the moving image. She squinted. Glance flicked across the screen. She held her breath. Blood whooshed in her ears, drowning a similar noise coming off the speaker. She stretched an arm to the monitor, finger hovering over the pulsating blob. "If that's the heart…" She moved the finger a few inches to the right. "What's that?" An identical shape. Beating. Like a drum.

Kingsley peered closer. "Hey! Congratulations. You're having twins."

Stunned silence. Frankie squeezed Bev's hand. "One each."

The quip wasn't funny and the bonhomie was forced. Frankie was as shell-shocked as Bev. It was clear in the voice. Bev couldn't see Frankie. Bev couldn't see anything. Not with eyes tight and hot tears streaming down her face.

13

The scrubby parkland with spindly trees backed on to Lidl's car park. Rusty iron railings separated the litter-strewn sites; a Tesco carrier bag snagged on a spike, flapping desultorily in a light breeze. Through the gaps a straggly row of motley shoppers gawked at the crime scene. A podgy bleached blonde in a pink shell suit shovelled popcorn like she was watching *Casualty*. Her moon face beamed when a local radio hack thrust a mic towards it. Put new meaning into sound bite. Mac scowled as he ran past. Further along the line, he spotted a couple of school kids videoing the action on their mobiles. Others were yacking into theirs, probably inviting mates round for a viewing.

Panting and wheezing, Mac pulled up at a police cordon protecting the ongoing drama. He tried to catch his breath as he took in the scene. Whoever made the 999-call hadn't got all the facts straight. There was a body. But it was breathing. Just. It lay on a slatted wooden bench; the way the hands were crossed it looked as if it had been laid out. Except for the battered bloodied face, spattered with white chips of bone and teeth. Two paramedics in green scrubs knelt at the victim's side attempting to insert a drip. To the right, a couple of white-suited crime scene guys were waiting to move in. Two more were already fingertipping patchy yellow grass round the edge of the tape.

Tyler left them to it, scanned the surroundings for someone less occupied who might be able to fill in the blanks. Darren New and Sumitra Gosh were questioning a group of youths over by a Mr Whippy van. Carol Pemberton and another DC were stopping and questioning people leaving the park via the main gates. Half a dozen uniforms with clipboards were dotted across the grounds also talking to potential witnesses. It didn't look as if Powell had arrived. Or Bev, despite increasingly urgent messages Mac had left on her mobile. He parted a path through more rubberneckers and press people, and headed for the nearest uniformed officer.

"What've we got, Paul?" Still puffing slightly, Mac now regretted the hundred-yard sprint from the Vauxhall he'd left straddling the Stratford Road. More than that, he resented the sneer on Paul Doyle's patrician face. The young constable was a runner; Highgate wags called him Paula as in Radcliffe.

"White male. Late thirties? Early forties? Taken a right hammering." Doyle swigged noisily from a bottle of Buxton water. Behind his back, stroppy Canada geese strutted and scrapped over breadcrumbs.

"Name?"

"Not yet." The tall blond wiped his mouth with the back of a hand. "Two old dears over there?" Mac's gaze followed Doyle's finger. Silver-haired biddies perched on the opposite bench, heads bobbing like a brace of pigeons. One clung on to a tartan shopping trolley, the other a walking frame. "They saw three yobs go through the victim's pockets then leg it over the fence."

Mac's eyes widened. "They witnessed the attack?"

"No. The guy was already lying there. The old girls didn't realise he'd been beaten up, couldn't see the injuries."

How long had the victim been on public view? How many people had passed by, looked the other way? Mac scratched his head. "What is this place? Al fresco funeral parlour?"

Doyle shrugged. "Guy's not dead yet."

Powell was tearing across the park, black trench coat flapping, a stray dog yapping and snapping at his heels. Mac waved his whereabouts, carried on talking to Doyle. "What else did you get?" The old women had told Doyle the park was a haven for what they termed dossers and druggies.

"Alkies and smack heads to you and me." Doyle raised the

bottle in ironic toast. "They come here to sleep it off. If you're homeless, I guess that bench is as good as a room at the Ritz."

"The guy's face is raw mince, Doyle," he hissed.

"Couldn't see the face when I got here." He swallowed a burp. "His head was under a newspaper." SOCOs had already bagged and tagged a three-day-old copy of the local rag, he told Mac.

Doyle's attitude left everything to be desired. Mac turned, scowl deepening when he spotted a regional BBC crew that had set up as close as it could inch to the police tape. A pencil-thin blonde who'd overdone the blusher was spouting into the lens what Mac assumed would be a load of tosh. The hushed delivery and loud hand signals were superfluous given the drama unfolding behind her, though as she was centre frame, viewers would be lucky to catch a glimpse of the real story: paramedics working to save a life.

Mac rolled his eyes. Who watched this garbage anyway?

"All right, Ruby?" Powell did. First name terms no less – and he'd inadvertently ruined the shot in passing. As for his four-legged friend, it was now trying to copulate with the boom mic. The DI didn't see the reporter run an imaginary razor across her throat.

"Known as a wrap in the trade," Mac muttered to Doyle who struggled to keep a straight face.

"OK, guys. Shoot." The DI smoothed his hair, cast occasional glances over his shoulder as he listened to Doyle's account. He nodded, asked Mac for his take. "What you reckon? Is the victim another dosser?"

Mac shrugged. "Didn't look it to me, boss." The jeans and jacket looked respectable enough. Not Armani but…

Powell turned to Doyle. "The old girls? They seen him in here before?"

"They didn't say."

Powell curled a lip. "Go and ask then."

"Paul?" Mac hitched his jeans. "Miss Marple and her mate?

Did they get a good look at the sickos who rifled his pockets?"

"Usual gear. Hoodies. Ski scarves. Combats."

"Pass it to the press office anyway," Powell said. "They can issue a release."

"Already called it in." Doyle nodded over the DI's shoulder where he could see the victim being stretchered to the ambulance. Powell turned, then pointed Mac towards the action. Mac waited until one of the paramedics was closing the doors.

"Anything you can give us, mate?"

"Still unconscious but he's stable now." Latex gloved fingers ran through a mousy crew cut. "Most of the damage is to the head. What it's done to the brain… Your guess's good as mine. Give IC a call in a couple of hours."

Intensive Care. Mac shuddered, and censored an emerging flashback.

"Hey, guv?" Darren New shouting, arm-waving. He was still over by the ice cream van, talking to a lad in Lennon glasses. Mac trailed over with the DI, filled him in on the victim's condition as they walked.

Dazza was in what Bev called Andrex puppy mode. He jabbed an excited thumb at the kid whose ginger curls poked out of a Dodgers' baseball cap. Poor lad couldn't do much to hide a face pebble-dashed in spots. "Listen to this, guv. OJ here's got something."

Chicken pox? Powell smiled, applied his young-people-skills. "OJ? Drink a lot of juice do you, son?"

Blank stare. "My name's Oliver Jenks." He held out a hand – not in greeting. "I didn't nick anything. It was like this when I found it."

There was no money in the wallet, and the tan leather had dark stains. Sticky. The blood not dry yet. It had been lying near a bin in the park. Likely the thief had taken any cash before ditching it.

Too late, but Powell slipped on gloves. There were receipts, a cinema ticket, AA membership. The DI showed the driving licence to Mac. It was a decent picture. Even with the victim's appalling injuries, Mac could tell it was the same guy: Philip Goodie, thirty-nine, Sutton Coldfield address.

What Mac couldn't work out was why Matt Snow's business card was tucked in there as well. And given the park was crawling with press – where was the big-shot crime correspondent himself?

Matt Snow was in New Street, nursing a medicinal brandy in the Bacchus bar at the Midland hotel. If the reporter had thrown a sickie earlier, his gut sure churned now. Excitement? Fear? Blend of both? He sipped the liquid, making it last; he was here to talk business, needed a clear head. He sat in a secluded alcove far away from the loud suits jostling at the bar. The Disposer had arranged the meeting – up close and personal, he'd said. Snow scanned the low-lit cavernous interior again. Timekeeping clearly wasn't high on the guy's agenda.

He sighed, tapped a beer mat against the table. By rights, he should be in Small Heath park covering some attack. Rick Palmer had phoned when the story broke, and hadn't been over-impressed when Snow said he couldn't turn out, that he was already working a potential lead – massive compared with a glorified mugging. Then Snow mumbled something about a bad line and cut the connection.

He checked his Timex again, watched the bar gradually fill. Closest he had to company was a marble bust nestling in a wall niche. Every time he turned his head right, he was eyeball-to-eyeball with Bacchus and it looked as if the god of wine had been on a bender. Snow scowled. He wasn't pissed, just pissed off. Fury rising, he wasted another hour before realising the Disposer wasn't going to show, probably never had any intention.

More mind games? The latest absurd test? The guy was a control freak. Snow had plenty of questions, zero answers. By the time the cab dropped him home, he was in a foul mood, and it worsened when he entered his flat.

Senses alert, he stood motionless in the narrow hallway. Someone had been in. Had to be the Disposer. The bedroom door was open, a light burned in the study. Snow tensed, ears strained. A noise? From the study? Was he still in there? More rustling. Adrenalin fizzing, Snow inched forward. "Hello? Anyone there?" His hand shook as he opened the door wider. The room was empty, curtains wafted in the draught from a window. The reporter let out a noisy breath. Not afraid now, fired up.

A piece of A4 was propped against his computer. Snow entered cautiously, glanced round half-expecting the guy to materialise out of the ether. Up close, it was clear there were two sheets. The first was a message for Matt.

I want the attached in tomorrow's paper.

"Yeah right." Lip curled, the reporter perched on the edge of the desk, undid the top button of his shirt as he read the second sheet.

I am our children's protector. Paedophiles steal our children's innocence, tarnish their lives, shatter their dreams. Paedophiles are scum. Paedophiles are vermin. Like rats they need to be exterminated. I will destroy them. I will wipe them off the streets. This is my mission. My solemn promise. The Disposer.

Snow snorted. This was all he needed. The guy was a joke; a homicidal pied sodding piper. No way would the paper print the ramblings of a sad sack. And anyway, Snow reckoned he'd danced enough to this loony-tune.

The pay-as-you-go was in his pocket. Startled, he reached it on the fourth ring.

"Took your time, Matthew."

Snow narrowed his eyes. Was the guy watching the flat? "Look, mate…"

"I'm not your mate. This is business. Got a pen?" There was a superior smile in the classy voice. "Of course you have. There's a penholder on the desk next to the photograph of your mother." The pause was deliberate, provocative. "Attractive for her age… isn't she, Matthew?"

Snow reached for the recorder in his top drawer. He wanted this psycho on tape. "Is that supposed to be a threat?" he hissed.

"I never make threats, Matthew." The implication didn't need spelling out.

"What do you want?" He pressed record, held the machine close to the phone.

"That's better. Sitting comfortably, Matthew? I have a story for you." Snow listened both appalled and fascinated as the Disposer talked, furnishing details about Wally Marsden's death only the killer could know. Further, he had chapter and verse on the attack in Small Heath park. The Disposer might be mad as a box of frogs but he was no fantasist. He told Snow he wanted the story and his statement on tomorrow's front page.

"Another exclusive for you, Matthew."

"The cops'd be on my back before the ink was dry."

"Don't worry about the police. I've decided it's time you had a little chat." Inevitable, he said, now he was showing his hand, raising the stakes. "It'll be fine as long as you stick to the script." Another pause. "My script."

"It's not some game of poker," Snow sneered. Or maybe it was. Maybe Snow could play too. String the Disposer along – and keep the cops happy. At least until he saw how the deal panned out? Why fold, if he was on to a winner?

The guy talked for ten, fifteen minutes. Snow smiled as he watched the tape record every word. The game had risks – but he had an ace or two up his sleeve.

"What the hell were you playing at?" DI Powell hands jammed in trouser pockets, circled the desk, loose papers wafted in the downdraught. Bev sat straight-backed; metaphorically under the carpet, feeling crushed. "Skiving off and…"

"Not…" Bev's protest petered out.

"If you'd been doing a proper job," he snarled, "you could've asked Snow yourself."

She looked down at her hands. Powell had summoned her into his office after the late brief of which she'd caught only the tail end. Her tardy arrival had gone unremarked, though he was making up for it now. Not that she'd missed much. She'd heard the bottom lines: the Marsden inquiry was still stalled, initial fears that the Philip Goodie attack was linked had been more or less ruled out. Goodie was neither wino nor dosser. A librarian, living alone, they were still trying to trace next of kin. Big unknown was why he'd been carrying Matt Snow's card?

Which was what had provoked Powell to throw his toys out the pram. Even worse, Bev knew he was right. If she'd been doing what she got paid for, maybe she could've found out.

"I'm sorry." She picked dirt from a thumbnail.

"Great. Bev Morriss is sorry. All's well with the world."

Except it wasn't. The ultrasound bombshell was doing her head in.

"Felt crook. Must've been something I ate." Food poisoning wasn't far off the truth. She still felt gutted. There'd been no way she could've just headed straight back to Highgate. She'd abandoned an uncharacteristically floundering Frankie, and driven the MG around aimlessly before finding herself outside the guv's house. Even if the big man had been in, would she really have opened up? Or was that more madness? Christ, next thing she'd be blaming everything on her hormones.

"Got a phone, haven't you?" Loose change jangled in his pocket.

Duff battery? Lent it to ET? Dropped it down the bog? "Should've called, sir. There's absolutely no excuse."

That shut him up. Head bowed, she knew he was staring, trying to work out if she was winding him up. The contrite apologies, lack of lip, and unsolicited 'sir' were so not Bev. Head still bowed, her rueful smile had a touch of bitterness: guy probably thought there'd been a death in the family. As opposed to...

Grey tasselled loafers came into view as Powell took his favourite pew on the edge of the desk. "It's not clever, Bev."

Course it wasn't clever. The missing hours weren't a hangable offence, but the disciplinary meant she was on a tighter lead than a rabid rottweiler. She knew a bunch of hawks was monitoring her professional behaviour. Which was why that solicitous 'Bev' was worse than a bollocking. She swallowed the lump in her throat.

"Want to talk?" Powell asked.

"Nope."

"Anything I can...?"

"Nope."

It was dark now, rain skittered across the window. Through lowered glance, she saw their reflection in the glass. The DI's hand was inches from touching her. Christ. She'd had enough shocks for one day.

She sat up smartish, grabbed her bag. "I'll get in early, make up time." Two hours if the fluttering fingers were anything to go by. "See you then."

Early night? Or go for an Indian? An image of Oz Khan flashed unbidden into Bev's brain. Been there, done that. She sniffed, slipped the key in at Baldwin Street, craved a drink. Blunt the edges of a shit day. Litre of pinot would do it. Yeah, cause getting hammered would be so sensible. Shutting out the world, she leaned against the wood, closed her eyes, took a few calming breaths.

"Never could do things by halves, could you?" The mock-censure held a smile.

Even open wide she couldn't believe her eyes. "What you doing here?" The guv. Walking into the hall from the kitchen. He'd never been in Bev's house before. How'd he get in? What'd he want? Why'd he...

"Great to see you too." He tapped his brow.

"Sorry." She loved his smile. Bet her hair was a mess. "Just... it's a ... "

Hold on. Never do things by halves? That must mean he knew about the scan.

"We going to stand here all night?" Byford asked.

The Moët was on ice on the draining board. First thing she saw. Second was a sink full of sunflowers. She turned, mouth gaping. He looked as uncertain as she felt. She scratched her head. "Dunno know what to say."

"That'll be a first." He smiled. "Come here, Bev." He brushed a single tear from her cheek with his thumb, held her in his arms, stroked her hair. Frankie had called, told him she was concerned, he said. She'd let him in then made herself scarce.

"Scared in case you deck her for spilling the beans," Byford teased.

"Me who's scared, guv." She searched his eyes, looked for what? Answers? Reassurance? Magic wand? "What'm I gonna do?"

"Drop the guv for a start." He led her through to the living room, sat close to her on the settee. Subdued lighting reflected the mood. The big man listened as she talked him through her fear: the mother of all double-whammies. Crippled with doubts about whether she could cope with one baby, the prospect of caring for twins was inconceivable. But going ahead with a termination would mean taking not one but two lives.

Desperate eyes searched his face. "How the hell can I do that?"

"Bev." He tucked a strand of hair behind her ear. "You can't." He told her she was more than capable. Made her sound like a cross between Madonna and Sherlock Holmes in a skirt. Total bollocks but it was what she needed to hear. It was past midnight when Byford rose, gathered the champagne glasses.

"Don't go, guv." She laid her hand on his. "Not tonight."

Gently he pulled her to her feet, kissed her eyelids, her nose, her lips. They walked upstairs, arms wrapped round each other. Thoughts spinning, drained emotionally, her eyelids drooped as she waited for Byford to finish in the bathroom. If she hadn't been so knackered, maybe she'd have stayed awake.

THURSDAY

14

After a working breakfast – early worms on toast – Bev was first to show her face at the brief. She slipped into pole position, sat back, sipped ordinary tea. Bliss. She'd felt forced to drink enough ginger gunge to last a lifetime or two. Yeah. Well, that was all going to change. Pregnant or not, she'd make the decisions how she ran her life. She blew the fringe out of her eyes. Knew it wasn't as simple as that, but at least Byford had helped put it in perspective.

Bev-new-woman-Morriss had opted for her one and only tailored suit. The cut and Oxford blue hue was a tad business-woman of the year. Must be rubbing off. Her desk was almost an admin-free zone, she'd already put in priority phone calls and read – as opposed to skimmed – the overnight reports. Little Miss Smugface crossed her legs, smoothed an imaginary crease from a sharp-pencil skirt.

Might have imagined spending the night with Byford were it not for the note he'd left on his pillow: *You need your beauty sleep. Catch you later!* That last phrase was a Bev-ism. Maybe she was rubbing off too? She gave a lazy smile: need your beauty sleep indeed. With the zeds she'd caught last night, she should be Keira Knightley's double by now. The smile broadened: would they really have got it together if she hadn't sparked out?

"Glad something's tickled your fancy." Mac flopped on the next chair, pulled a notebook from a pocket of his lumberjack shirt. He flashed a page full of names, people who still needed interviewing, mostly Gladys Marsden's neighbours in Bath Road, a smattering of Churchill residents who'd not been in

101

during door-to-doors. "Could do with a hand, boss."

"Sure." Once they'd spoken to Matt Snow. The reporter had topped her list of early morning calls. She'd certainly wrecked Tintin's beauty sleep. Threatened to speak to his editor if he didn't show his ugly mush at the nick any time soon.

She glanced round, counted heads: full squad more or less. The DI got the door with his bum. He entered ferrying a steaming cup in one hand and a load of files in the other. The customary spring in his loafers was currently more autumnal amble. Not surprising given the inquiry was going nowhere fast.

He ran through the state of play, reassigned actions that needed another look in case anything had been missed first time round, then: "Any bright ideas?" Blank faces all round. "OK. They don't have to be bright."

"Maybe look at the motive again," Dazza suggested.

"Doh." Powell groaned.

"Yeah, but listen, boss," he argued. "We're all assuming Marsden was bumped off cause he was a paedophile. What if – like I said before – he just happened to be in the wrong place at the wrong time?"

"Random attack?"

"Wino squabble?"

"Big boy's mugging?"

Bev's phone trilled. She took the call while the squad tossed thoughts round. Maybe it was her body language or the fact the colour had drained from her face. Powell was first to notice. "And?"

"That was the General." The hospital had also been high on her call list. "They spoke to Philip Goodie's ex-wife about an hour ago. She didn't want to know. Said the marriage broke up yonks back cause he'd been abusing their little girl. He got sent down for two years."

The atmosphere changed in an instant. The DI voiced what

was probably on most detectives' minds. Was Wally Marsden first in a line that now numbered two? "So it's more than likely we're looking at a nutter who's targeting paedos?" Powell chewed his lip, thought it through. "We need a police guard down there now." Bev shook her head. "Christ's sake, woman. The perp's only got to read the papers to know he didn't kill Goodie. What if he goes back – finishes the job?"

"He'd be a bit late," Bev said. "Goodie died ten minutes ago."

No one had yet used the phrase serial killer. The fact that Detective Chief Superintendent Kenny Flint was suddenly senior investigating officer said it all. Mid-morning now and a recently ousted-from-the-top-spot Powell scowled from the sidelines. The brief had been hastily reconvened with a bigger cast. Bev felt a tad sorry for the DI; a high profile case could've given him a chance to shine in the guv's absence. Pitying Powell? Christ. Pregnancy really did mush the brain.

She glanced round, did another head count. The squad now stood at a dozen detectives. Human hard disk Johnny Blake was information officer, exhibits and logistics roles had been dished out to the two Ronnies: Sergeants Cater and Fox. Bev sat next to Mac, keeping her head down, swinging a leg, praying the poisoned chalice would pass to some other sucker this time.

Flint's steely gaze swept the incident room. She sensed it homing in. "Look after media liaison, would you, Bev?"

I'd rather eat shit, sir. "Sure thing, boss." She dropped her pen, almost banged heads with Bernie Flowers who bent to retrieve it at the same time. The news bureau boss handed it over with a smirk. "Safe pair of hands needed on this one, Bev."

Sickly smile. "I'm an octopus me, mate." Thanks, God. Weak sunlight glinted behind thin grey cloud. She doubted it was a sign from above.

"I don't want the press getting wind the murders could be

down to one man." Flint warned. "Last thing we need is a feeding frenzy." Bev pictured a tank of piranhas with her as *plat du jour*. "We don't know for sure that's what we've got yet," the DCS stressed. "Only link so far is the fact both victims were paedophiles. As we all know, serial killers almost always stick to the same MO. That's certainly not the case here."

Marsden's throat had been slashed. A blood clot on the brain had seen off Goodie, following the savage beating.

"Unless the killer was disturbed," Bev said.

"Deranged," the DI muttered.

Flint raised a hand. "Hear her out."

Bev shrugged. "Marsden died from the knife wound, but he was beaten to a pulp first."

"Then the killer dumped the body some hours later." Flint's stubble rasped as he rubbed his chin. "Maybe this time he didn't have that luxury. The murder wasn't so well planned. Or executed?"

"Maybe lost his nerve." Beating seven shades out of someone in a public park was high risk. Not everyone looked the other way.

"Or lost control," Mac threw in.

"Or they could still be unrelated," Powell said.

Bev's pensive gaze moved along the whiteboards. But what about poor old Gladys? Why had she been snuffed out too? She frowned. Was that a hint of reproof in the old girl's glassy eyes? Whatever. It was up to the squad to establish connections.

Shiny black lace-ups squeaked as Flint stalked the room, hands clasped behind his back. "We need to find out what – if anything – these men had in common."

Background checks then, liaising with prison and probation services. Had Marsden and Goodie served time together? Had either been threatened or assaulted when they were inside? Computer checks too, other forces, similar inquiries. Even cold cases going back a while. Sighs of relief almost all round when Flint assigned Dazza and Carol Pemberton the bulk of the plod work.

"What about other men at risk?" Mac asked. "Should we be warning them?"

"How long've you got?" Bev'd done a bit of homework. Latest national figures showed almost thirty thousand names on the sex offenders' register, well over two thousand in the West Midlands alone. And officers needed to know where to look. Offenders routinely got lost in the system. Only high risk level threes were closely monitored. Add that to a severe shortage of approved accommodation, long waiting lists for nowhere near enough treatment programmes and… The squad got her drift.

"Academic anyway," Flint said. "Unless we establish it's the same killer." He drained a glass of water, gathered his files. "And we'll not do that sitting on our backsides."

Heads snapped round when the door took the topcoat off the back wall. Vince Hanlon's bulk more than filled the frame. It took a ten on the Richter scale to get Highgate's veteran sergeant off the front desk. Normally. His huge face was flushed puce. Not, Bev reckoned, down to the flight of stairs. "You lot need to see this," he said. "It's just come in."

The *Evening News*. Vince held the paper aloft. The lead headline was just two words, no quotes, not even a journo's judicious question mark: SERIAL KILLER.

Vince read the small print aloud. "*Convicted paedophiles in Birmingham are being targeted by an anonymous killer. In a letter to this newspaper, a man calling himself the Disposer claims his mission is to wipe out human waste. He's already claimed two…*"

Bev's fists were balled. The exclusive had Snow's by-line. Where was the little shit?

"Oh, and Bev?" Vince called. "Matt Snow's downstairs. Wants a word."

15

Matt Snow, head down in his own newspaper, was propped next to a wanted poster on the wall in Highgate reception. The front page was a winner. The reporter's late night and early morning had paid off. Coverage looked good, decent size by-line too. It had been the devil's job persuading his boss to print the material. He'd told Ricky Palmer it had arrived in a package – addressed to Snow – at the *Evening News* front desk. Ricky saw the potential straight off, but the editor wanted to run it past the police. Snow winged it. Sure, later, he said, but the accompanying note made it clear the cops had a copy. If the paper held back, he argued, the exclusive would be lost, along with possible future communication from the serial killer. Maybe it was the prospect of losing out to the competition more than Snow's clout that swung it. Either way, the strategy had worked.

What was one more shed-load of lies?

Snow was still lounging casually when Bev took the stairs three at a time giving him a quick once-over on the way down. His sludge suit looked as if he'd slept in it; the Hush Puppies were scuffed. She reckoned the laid-back pose didn't match the tremor in his hands. Could be he'd need the brown trousers.

"That an asbestos suit you're wearing, Mr Snow?"

"Come again?"

She nodded at the newspaper. "Play with fire – you get burnt."

"If you're gonna mess about..." He pushed himself off the wall, made as if to leave.

"Don't even think about it, sunshine. Follow me."

DCS Flint was already installed in Interview Two, a copy of the *Evening News* face-up on the metal desk in front of him. Bev did the introductions, told Snow to sit. The reporter took a brown envelope from his jacket pocket, looked pretty smug until Bev reached for a tape, tore the cellophane with her teeth.

"What is this?" Snow spluttered. "I came here voluntarily."

"Big of you," Bev murmured.

Flint was impassive. "You're not under arrest, Mr Snow. You're under caution. You can leave any time." He gave a tight smile. "I strongly advise you to answer my questions first. Sergeant?"

Bev started the recording, ran through the spiel: who, where, when. They were going by the book in the hope of putting the wind up Snow. Neither seriously suspected him guilty of more than gross stupidity. They wanted answers that a bit of police pressure might elicit.

"This information?" Flint waved a dismissive hand at the newspaper. "Where did you get it?"

Snow handed Flint the envelope. "This arrived at the paper, addressed to me. The killer's statement, details about the attacks." He held Flint's glare. "It's why I'm here. In good faith – to help…"

"After rushing it into print?" Flint snarled. "Why didn't you bring us in on it?"

"Didn't you get one too?" Ingenuous. Insolent. Bev reckoned Snow was trying to be clever. Trying too hard. It was a polished act. But that's all it was.

"Sorry, chief," the reporter said. "I assumed he sent it to everyone, police, media…"

"So you thought you might as well use it anyway…"

He leaned back, ankles crossed. "Just doing my job, Mr Flint."

"Giving self-proclaimed serial killers a channel of communication?"

"The public has a right to…"

"Puh-leese," Bev groaned. Not that again…

"What about your responsibility?" Flint said. "It was your

duty to report it to the police."

"It's my duty to keep readers informed. I write stories in the public interest, not yours. If there's a serial killer out there, they need to know."

"They need the truth."

"Are you saying there is no serial killer?" Defiant? Daring? There was a challenge in the reporter's eyes. This was the Matt Snow Bev knew, writ large. Was he standing on someone's shoulders? Were he and the so-called Disposer more than just pen pals?

"This letter?" she dropped in casually. "Is it the first contact you've had with the killer?"

"Course it is." No eye contact. Lying through his teeth? She made a note. Tapping the pen against her own, she recalled the tip-off that put Snow ahead of the game at the Wally Marsden murder scene. Had the so-called Disposer pointed the reporter in the right direction then as well? Had the killer chosen Snow as a tame conduit to get his sick message across? And was Snow arrogant enough to imagine he could deal with that?

"How'd it get to the *News* building?" Again, her tone was indifferent. "This letter?"

Snow frowned. "Post, I suppose."

"Personal delivery?"

Needled now. "How should I know?"

Pensive, she pursed her lips. "Be on camera anyway." It was bullshit, but Snow appeared shaken. The paper's reception area did have saturation CC coverage, but the chances of the Disposer handing over the letter in person were slim. Make that skeletal. On the other hand if there was nothing on tape, could that in itself be significant? Fingers crossed the techie boys would come up with a pointer or two.

Flint leaned forward. "Whether the letter's genuine or not, you're playing into the man's hands." Oxygen of publicity. Fifteen minutes of fame.

Snow shook his head. "That's where you're wrong. We're showing him he can trust us. Trust me. If he believes that, he'll contact us again. Contact me again. Maybe he'll get careless, let something slip." The reporter straightened, then leaned forward, mirroring Flint's posture. "Look, superintendent, there's nothing in that letter to indicate who he is, where he's from, or who his next victim will be. Surely if I develop some sort of relationship with him, win his confidence…?"

"What?" Flint snapped. "That you'll expose him? Bring him to justice? Save lives? Let me work this out, Mr Snow." He raised a finger as if he was seeing the light. "You're not a sanctimonious self-serving little prat. You're actually doing us all a favour."

"Exactly." He sat back, arms folded.

"Interview suspended." Going by the look on Flint's face, Bev suspected it wasn't the only thing he wanted to suspend.

DCS Flint dipped a chocolate digestive in a mug of tea. "What do you make of Snow?"

Bev turned her mouth down. They were taking a short break in the canteen. Mac would be on board when the interview resumed. Flint needed to prepare for an imminent news conference – undoubtedly a rougher ride.

"Truth's not his big suit." She brushed KitKat crumbs off her jacket. "I reckon he knows more than he's letting on. And he's enjoying this."

She'd been mulling over Byford's warning about Snow being nobody's fool, a journo who wanted to go places. Maybe he saw this story as his ticket out. She narrowed her eyes, struck by a sudden thought. What if he was doing more than writing it? What if the Disposer didn't exist? What if Snow was making the news, not just breaking it? Impossible. Off the wall. They needed forensic evidence, not flights of fancy.

Maybe they'd get something back from the lab. The package was now where it should've been in the first place. Not that they were holding their breath.

Bev gazed down on to the car park. Snow's stories had certainly sparked the feeding frenzy feared by Flint. The media circus was already setting up camp. She spotted radio cars, TV wagons, a couple of OB units. From this height it looked like media toy town. And boy were they gonna have fun. "Sooner you than me, boss."

Flint followed her gaze. "I'd best get going." He slurped the rest of his tea, and headed for the exit.

Seconds later he was back. "Bev? I meant to ask. What happened with the Graves woman?"

Bollocks. She'd let it go. The doctor who topped himself. She was supposed to have chased the widow. Flint must've seen it on her face.

"Soon as you like, Bev." The senior detective's patent disappointment was worse than a drubbing. "Another note arrived this morning."

"How's the gut, Mr Snow?" Bev swept in to Interview Two, file under an arm, Mac on her heels.

The reporter straightened from an almost horizontal sprawl and fingered his fringe. "Is this gonna take long, cos I've got better things to do. I came here…"

"Of your own free will. Yeah. I know." She perched on the edge of the desk, cast him a curious gaze. "Stomach bug, was it? Why you didn't show for work yesterday?"

He stretched both arms over his head, yawning wide. Playing for time? Winding her up? The reporter couldn't claim he'd been ill. He'd told Bev the news desk had called him out.

"Where'd you hear that, sergeant? I was on a story."

Anna Kendall had let it slip. And in the truth stakes, Bev knew where her money lay. "What story?" she asked.

"It's not relevant." He tapped his foot.

"Where'd you go to cover this story?"

"Leave it," he snapped. "It's not important."

Push it? Press on? She narrowed her eyes. They'd nothing to hold him on. If she got up his nose, he could walk. Anyway there was probably more fertile ground. She moved to the business side of the desk, switched to police-speak. "The tape please, DC Tyler."

The reporter pursed his lips, sat back arms folded.

"Where were you yesterday afternoon, Mr Snow?" Bev asked. "From midday onwards?"

"At home. Working on my column." Quick. Too quick?

"Can anyone verify that?"

"I cleared it with the desk. Why?"

"What's the column about?"

Slight pause. "Police corruption." The smirk didn't last long.

"So you weren't taking a stroll in the park?" She opened the file, casually shuffled through police photographs from yesterday's crime scene. "Small Heath park?"

"No! I finished the piece then went for a drink."

"Where?"

"The Bacchus bar."

"What time?"

"I dunno. Five, six-ish? Are you treating me as a suspect?"

"Philip Goodie. How'd you know him?"

"I don't. Only what details the killer supplied."

"That you claim he supplied." She waited until Snow made eye contact. "Philip Goodie had your business card in his wallet." The comment provoked what she suspected was the reporter's first genuine reaction. Confusion? Shock? Uncertainty? Shame she couldn't read it.

He shrugged. "Punters call all the time. Maybe he had a story for me."

She raised an eyebrow. "He did that, Mr Snow."

"And Gladys Marsden?" Mac threw in, as arranged, from off field. "Did she have a story?"

"Who?" Snow shifted in the seat.

"Wally Marsden's wife," Bev said. "How much did you pay her?"

"I've never met the woman." But he knew something. There'd been a flash of fear in his eye – Bev was almost sure.

"The poor old girl was dying anyway," Bev said. "Did you know that?"

"Are you charging me with anything?" They couldn't. They'd not a shred of evidence against him. Gut feeling told her he knew more about Gladys Marsden's murder than he was letting on, probably more about the paedophiles' deaths. Sin of omission? Last time she looked that wasn't a crime. As for her off-the-wall theory that the Disposer was a figment of the reporter's imagination – she wasn't even convinced Snow was capable of killing let alone culpable. They couldn't detain him. Reluctantly she shook her head. Chair legs screeched against floor tiles.

"Where you going?" she asked.

He cast a glance of contempt. "Some of us have got work to do."

16

A serial killer with an agenda and a penchant for publicity was a story with legs to die for. The press had dubbed Birmingham Murder City. National TV were planning live inserts into main bulletins. *Newsnight* wanted to record a down-the-line interview with Flint. Radio phone-ins had scrapped schedules to go with the paedophile flow. Upside far as Bev was concerned – her media liaison role had been passed up a rank.

Far as the press went, it was all chase-tail-and-catch-up. Matt Snow's head start had put journalistic noses out of joint. A regional hack perceived as a joke had shat on national reporters from a great height. More than that. Snow, as the Disposer's perceived personal contact, was part of the story. And the crime correspondent wasn't sharing. A seriously miffed media couldn't shoot the messenger so at the police news conference and in much of the ensuing coverage Flint had taken most of the flak.

Why hadn't police linked the killings sooner? Why hadn't they issued a warning? What steps were being taken to protect potential victims? What leads were being followed? How imminent was an arrest? Would the Disposer strike again?

By the 18:00 brief for what was now Operation Wolf, the squad felt it was in the firing line as well. Head down, DCS Flint paced in front of the murder boards. "It ends here." Deliberate or not he'd stopped in front of Philip Goodie's photograph. "There'll be no more killings."

Bev sniffed. Brave words. Easy to say. Patrols had been stepped up in areas known to be frequented by low-lifes, warnings had been disseminated by officers calling at shelters, halfway houses, approved accommodation. Forewarned – forearmed? Piss in a gale force. Released paedos didn't exactly advertise their whereabouts in the community. And not all paedos fitted the sleaze bill. Look at Philip Goodie. The guy appeared to have turned his life round: decent suit, respectable job, low profile.

Bev reckoned the media was doing a better job warning the public than the police. Not many punters – let alone paedophiles – could be unaware by now that a killer was on the streets of Birmingham taking out child sex offenders. Downside was this: some people didn't give a toss; a fair number were with the Disposer all the way. How did the cops know? Because Outraged of Edgbaston et al had e-mailed their views to newspaper letters pages, some had been allowed local radio airtime. They'd all get a police visit. Those who'd supplied names would get one quicker. Way Bev saw it, issuing warnings was a sideline. The main event was staring them in the face.

"Something on your mind?" Flint asked.

"That." She nodded at one of the whiteboards where a blown-up copy of the Disposer's missive to the *Evening News* was displayed. "What sort of person writes a letter like that?"

There were mutters of nutter, psycho, sad sack. Bev shook her head. "Try victim." She watched as squad members took a fresh look. Facial expressions differed, some were sceptical, others clearly on the same page.

"Someone who's been there?" Daz asked.

"Or whose kid has." Bev's focus was still on the words. "No one has time for paedos. But whoever wrote that loathes them. Look at it: 'Paedophiles are scum. Paedophiles are evil. Paedophiles are vermin.' Has to go deeper than bog standard skin crawl."

"'I am our children's saviour.'" Flint quoted this time. "Like he's on a mission to protect rather than destroy."

She nodded. "Sounds to me like a personal crusade."

"Being waged in public," Flint snarled. Everyone knew his Paxman grilling was due that evening.

Everyone also knew a large part of the inquiry would now be devoted to tracking down more people like Eddie Scrivener: fathers, families, even close friends of children who'd suffered abuse from convicted paedophiles. Shit. The Scrivener alibis. She'd not got round to checking. Mental note: pass it to Mac.

Mind, Scrivener was the tip of a vast iceberg. She tapped a pen against her teeth. How far back would they look? And over how wide a field? Goodie's case had been tried at Nottingham Crown Court fifteen years ago, and they had no way of knowing if it was the oldest on the killer's hit list.

Flint split the graft as best he could between the team. Like they didn't have enough to play with: potential witnesses to be re-interviewed, God knew how many hours of CC footage still to be viewed. And calls to the incident room in response to the saturation news coverage were increasing every hour. The incoming flow needed serious monitoring and follow up.

It was a subdued squad that filed out ten minutes later. Bev reckoned compared to what they were looking for, a needle in a hay barn would be a piece of gateau.

Just after seven and feeling a touch brighter, Bev pulled up outside Madeleine Graves's pad in Handsworth Wood. Locking the MG, she gazed across its dusty leather roof. Tickety. Tudor Grange showed signs of life. Grey smoke drifted into a pewter sky from a bonfire round the back; amber light glowed through leaded windows at the front. Bev's upbeat mood was down to more than the fact someone was home this time, she'd also recouped Brownie points with the boss, wiped the earlier disappointment from his face. Though DCS Flint would never be 'guv' to her, she didn't want his disapproval either. She'd fallen into step with him as they'd left the nick – poor bloke was en route to a BBC telly studio in the Mailbox. She'd relayed Anna Kendall's request to shadow her for a news feature. Flint was quick on the uptake, recognised the potential straight off; agreed that getting inside track on Snow would be even more useful now. He gave Bev free rein, happy for her to use her own judgement dealing with the hack, looked even happier when she casually let slip where she was off to.

Crunching gravel underfoot for a second time, Bev caught a whiff of the smoke and smiled. The pungent odour, evoked bonfire nights from years back: her and Frankie pushing a raffish Guy Fawkes round in a wonky dolls' pram, getting soaked bobbing for apples, air writing with sparklers. Lost in reverie, it took a second to work out where the lah-di-dah voice was coming from and who it was addressing.

"Door's on the latch, dear. Let yourself in. I'll be down in a jiffy." Bev glanced up, spotted a woman with a warm smile calling her through an open window on the first floor. She'd clearly mistaken Bev for someone else. Be rude not to oblige though. The woman brushed strands of thick wavy hair out of her eyes, glanced towards the road. "Are you sure your car will be big enough?"

For what? Bev waved a reassuring hand, stepped in smartish, didn't need asking twice. She wiped her Docs on a rush mat as she took in the hall. It was twice the size of her mum's sitting room. Tad gloomy though. The subtle lighting wasn't enough to offset the effects of all the oak panelling and heavy drapes. What with that and a tiled chessboard floor, she half expected to see a knight in armour lurking in the background. Flared nostrils detected beeswax and pot pourri. Predictable pongs in a place like this. Eyes narrowed, she sniffed again. If her nasal radar was on the money, something a lot less predictable lingered. She raised a curious eyebrow. Ganja was so not Tudor Grange.

Nor were the bulging black bin bags lined against the wall, or the muffled blasts of heavy rock from above. She cocked her head. Guns N' Roses? Yep. She put the sudden hike in volume down to someone not having Sympathy For The Devil. The music faded and was replaced by a low murmur of voices. Couldn't catch more than the odd word. Not for want of trying.

Quick shrug, then she ventured in a few paces, wondered idly who Mrs Graves – if that was the woman she'd spotted – had been expecting. Given Bev's predilection for wearing blue, she'd been taken for a social worker in her time, even the odd meter reader. The life-size painting on the far wall stopped her in her tracks. Her low whistle was maybe involuntary. She stepped closer, eyes creased. No mistaking who that was. The newspaper pic hadn't done Adam Graves justice, and he'd looked tasty in that. Unwittingly she licked her lips. The man was drop dead gorgeous. Sharp dark suit, soft dark hair, sultry dark eyes. Forget Milk Tray, this was Green and Black man.

"You're admiring the portrait?" Deep stair carpet, soft tread. Bev jumped. The woman from upstairs stood at her side, fiddling with a fussy chiffon scarf round her neck, the warm smile was a little cooler now. "My late husband. A friend of ours is a well-known artist." Mrs Graves gazed at the canvas, could've been talking to herself. "It's hard losing someone you love. I miss him very much."

Bev couldn't take her eyes off the widow. How the heck did Mrs Beast bag Mr Beauty? Nobody likes a bitch, Beverley. Even so...

Dumpy was maybe a bit strong, but the spread was definitely middle-aged and the two-inch heels only just brought Madeleine Graves up to Bev's five-six height. The matronly figure was unrecognisable from the guv's photo. Shame really: underneath the slap, the face probably retained a trace of prettiness. Juliette Binoche's mum – on a bad day? Trouble was La Graves had tried too hard. The heavy hand with the cosmetics hadn't worked. Only made her look older. Last thing she needed given her old man could've passed for her toy boy

"It must be very difficult," Bev murmured. She sensed the widow's focus shift; they made eye contact for the first time.

"You can have no idea." Not bitter. Factual, telling it like it is. She straightened, seemed to pull herself together. Moved on mentally too. Bev watched her walk away. "The stuff's here. I'll give you a hand. It was awful going through Adam's clothes, but I know it's what he would have wanted. It's for a good cause." Oxfam? Cancer Research? Age Concern? Bev didn't say a word. When she turned back, Mrs Graves held a bin bag in each hand. "They're not heavy but they'll take a lot of room. You may even have to make two journeys."

"Mrs Graves, I'm…" Struggling here.

Toffee coloured eyes clouded with uncertainty, confusion. The woman dumped the bags at her feet, put a hand to fleshy lips. "Oh Lord. You're not one of Claudia's people, are you? The jumble sale? She said she'd send someone along around seven. I assumed…"

"Easy mistake to make, Mrs Graves."

The mouth tightened; there was steel in the soufflé. "Then you are…?"

"I'm a police officer, Mrs Graves. Bev Morriss. Detective Sergeant. I'd like a word about your husband." People look guilty when the law's around, even when they haven't broken it. Madeleine Graves almost seemed to relax.

"There's coffee in the kitchen. Come through. We'll talk there."

People grieve differently. Some clam up, can't even mention the dead person's name, let alone wax lyrical. Not Mrs Graves. It was Adam this… Adam that… Adam everything. Bev quickly realised her police status was immaterial; the woman just needed someone to listen. Which she was happy to do. For a while. She waited and watched as Madeleine drifted round her domain pouring coffee, arranging cakes on a plate, talking incessantly about the man she described as her soulmate. Bev shifted in her seat, felt what? Uncomfortable, sure, the woman was pouring her heart out to a stranger. But humbled too. Bev didn't think she'd ever felt such passion for anyone. Just chatting about Graves had taken years off the widow's face. The lines were softer, the eyes shone, the smile was infectious. Displacement activity of course. Mrs Graves wasn't stupid: Bev wasn't there as a grief counsellor. But Bev was warming to the widow. Maybe it was the latte and home baked chocolate brownies.

"So." Madeleine struggled on to the stool next to Bev. "Tell me why you're here."

"I'll show you." She licked crumbs from her fingers, took a copy of the anonymous note from her pocket. "It was sent to a senior officer at Highgate police station."

Madeleine nodded. "Wording's exactly the same as mine. More cake, dear?"

"Yours…?" Gob. Smack.

"I received two in the post." She took a genteel sip of coffee. Don't tell me you binned them. "Could I take a look?"

"I burned them." She shuddered. "Poisonous cowards. If someone has something to say – they should come out with it. Not hide behind a cloak of anonymity." The voice. It was like the plummy one in the Archers. Jill? Sod the voice, Bev. Listen to what it was saying. That was an odd phrase she'd used.

"'If someone has something to say…'" Bev quoted. "You think someone has?"

Coffee sloshed as Mrs Graves banged the mug on the breakfast bar. "Whatever gives you that impression? Of course not. There's not a sliver of doubt my husband killed himself… and I… have to live with that." She paused, eyes brimming. "Can you imagine the pain? The guilt?" There was a catch in the throat, the head dropped. Bev waited patiently. A measure of calm restored, Mrs Graves looked up, held Bev's gaze. "A thought that tears me apart? Adam was so desperate he took his own life.

119

And I had no idea what he was going through."

Some soulmate. Bev swallowed, still had to ask. "Did he leave a note?"

"No." Her glance flicked to the left. It was as good as a lie detector. Bev pursed her lips. The porkie didn't mean a lot; it wasn't uncommon for a wife, husband, close family member to destroy a suicide note. But not before they'd read it. Bev's voice was soft and low. "What did it say, Mrs Graves?"

The probe was gentle, but enough to send her off on one. She cradled her head in her hands, rocked slightly as her shoulders shook.

"Leave her alone." Vocal knives.

The whiplash was almost audible as Bev spun round. There was a young guy in the doorway. With attitude. The sort that must've cost his parents an arm and leg. No need to ask who he was. He was a shorter thinner paler version of his father. Still fit though. And knew it.

"It's all right, Lucas." Madeleine sat up quickly, wiped tears with the sleeve of her kaftan. "Sergeant Morriss is just doing her job."

"Her job's to upset you?" The drawl didn't quite go with the Russell Brand look. Still, he'd got the black drainpipes, natty waistcoat, round-necked shirt off to a tee. He just needed to borrow one of his ma's scarves.

Madeleine began, "This is…"

"Your son." Bev wondered how long Lord Snooty had been listening at the door, and if his timing mattered. She flashed her brightest smile, hopped off the stool, approached with hand outstretched. "I'm Bev Morriss." It was a little test she often used. Lucas Graves passed, but only just. His none-too-clean fingers barely touched in the fleeting shake. This close she could see what he'd done to his hair. The black tips looked as if they'd been dipped in a can of scarlet paint. She repeated why she was there, asked for any input he might have. He didn't. You don't say?

"If that's it…?" he asked. "I was just on the way out." She watched as he shucked into a black leather jacket, kissed Madeleine's cheek. He turned at the door. "I didn't mean to be rude, officer. It's just… my mother's going through a hard time." He'd dropped the drawl; was the charm just another act? "Nice to meet you." He gave a mock salute.

Doubt. Benefit. Bev nodded. "Snap." Ten minutes later, Bev was making tracks herself. She'd pushed Mrs Graves again on the anonymous letters. Apart from extracting a promise from the woman that she'd contact the police if more arrived, that was it. As to the existence of a suicide note, the widow was adamant there'd not been one. On balance, Bev couldn't see it mattered. Cause of death wasn't suspicious. She'd seen or heard nothing to set antennae twitching.

She paused in the hall. "Want me to drop those for you?" The bin bags.

"I wonder why Claudia's girl didn't come? The sale's on Saturday."

"For…?"

"The Conservative Party."

Christ on a bike. Frozen rictus. Two went in the boot; two on the passenger seat. Madeleine waved from the door. Bev's weak smile died as she unlocked the driver's door. Talk about insult to injury. Some toe rag had scrawled FILTHY in the dust on the soft top. She peered closer. Or was it FILTH?

"As excuses go… that's on a par with cutting your granny's toe nails." There was a smile in Byford's voice. Bev was on the phone explaining why she couldn't go round to his place that night.

"Straight up, guv. I've gotta drop them first thing."

He pictured her surrounded by bin bags, sorting through the

Graves's cast-offs. "Must say, I never had you down as a closet Tory."

"That is so not funny."

He laughed. "What are you hoping to find? Cameron's policies?"

"Ever considered stand-up?"

"With you and Mac around?"

"Later."

Byford smiled, shook his head, ended the call. He retrieved his tumbler from the kitchen, headed for the best seat in the house. His body-shape indent in the leather recliner was proof of that. From here through the picture window, the big man liked to look out on the cityscape in the distance: jagged shades-of-grey skyline during the day, now a mosaic of twinkling lights. Better than the box any time.

He sipped Laphroaig, replayed Bev's call. Had it just been an excuse not to see him? Had she feigned sleep last night? And was a tiny bit of him relieved? He gave a wry smile. Whatever the future held, Bev'd be a handful and a half. With or without babies.

He rolled the malt round his tongue. Either way he knew he wasn't into one-night stands. Never had been. For him it would be long-term or nothing. Was he ready for that? And what about Bev? Commitment was an alien concept to her. He sighed. Whether she liked it or not, motherhood would force a change. Clipped wings and cramped style could lead to compromises she'd never otherwise consider. Including him? He downed the whisky; the angst was going nowhere.

"As Bev would say, 'Get over it'," he chided himself, and reached for his book: Ian Rankin's *Exit Music*.

It's not as if you're asking her to get hitched.

FRIDAY

17

Mouldy five pence piece and a bunch of fluff. What more had Bev expected? A handwritten note: *I, Adam Graves, being of decidedly dodgy mind, topped myself cos...* She smiled to herself: yeah, like that'd happen outside an Agatha Christie. Most of the gear she'd gone through hadn't even belonged to the doc. Flipping heck: Frankie had fancied one or two of the skimpy tops herself. God knew what the widow looked like in them. Mutton and unborn lamb sprang to Bev's mind.

Traffic was rush-hour-heavy; she took a rat run to avoid Moseley Road's worst bottleneck. Anyway, she'd got shot of the bin bags. Come to think of it, the old woman she'd handed them to looked a bit like Christie. Not that on the button though, given she'd tried persuading Bev to join the Conservatives. Bev had eschewed the party invitation and legged it. Maybe she should've stuck round, picked up some detecting tips.

Operation Wolf certainly needed a few steers, according to the expert currently reading the eight o'clock news. Bev tapped a finger on the wheel. *West Midlands police admit they're no nearer an arrest in the so-called...*

Yada yada. She curled a lip, opted for a blast from Snow Patrol instead. Revelled in the freedom, the simple pleasure in flicking the switch. After her attack a couple years back, she'd had the CD player ripped out of the Midget. Couldn't listen to in-car music without getting flashbacks of the rapist. Yeah. Well that was history now. And the panic attacks. She hiked the volume, sang along at the top her voice. *Give me a chance to hold on, give me a chance...* It didn't quite drown current fears. Or future concerns. She reached higher, pulled out another vocal stop.

Then pulled down the visor; bright sunlight was making her squint. Windscreen could do with a clean. She leaned forward peering through grease streaks and bird shit. Washers weren't doing it. Christ, it was filthy. Like the roof. She'd wiped that particular F-word off the soft top this morning. On reflection she reckoned Lucas Graves's dabs could've been all over it. Could be wrong but his fingers had been decidedly grubby in last night's reluctant handshake. Payback for upsetting mummy? Maybe. On the other hand loads of kids had problems with cops.

No doubt Anna Kendall would soon be finding that out. It'd only take five minutes tailing a cop round some parts of the city to feel the love. Bev had caught up with the hack on the phone yesterday evening. She'd made provisional arrangements to hook up with the writer after lunch depending what had come in overnight. And assuming nothing vital came up at the brief.

Real bummer 'bout the bin bags though. If she'd not been otherwise engaged, maybe she would've spent the evening with the guv.

"You didn't catch Flint and Paxo? You missed a blinder, sarge." Mac offered Bev half shares in a bacon butty as they scuttled along the corridor trying to avoid a late arrival at an early brief already put back an hour. Before leaving home, Bev had wolfed two boiled eggs and a platoon of Marmite soldiers. Mind, that was ages ago, least an hour.

"What's on it?" Nose screwed suspiciously. "And no I didn't."

"Thought Flint was gonna land him one. Daddies' sauce."

Rude to say no. "Ta, mate." Must be the eating-for-three kicking in. "Edited highlights. Shoot."

"It was national pop-a-cop-day. Paxman was like a terrier in a bone yard. Made the boss look a right clown." Mac was a wicked mimic. "'No cause for alarm? Are you entirely serious, Detective Chief Superintendent?' Then he gives Flint the eyebrow."

"Give him a starter for ten as well?" she snorted.

"Finished, have we?" The DCS. Behind them. The question was rhetorical. He certainly didn't hang about for an answer. Bev and Mac stepped aside sharpish and sheepish. Flint swept through, spine ramrod straight, and marched in to the briefing room. Suitably chastened, they fell in line behind.

Going by the massed ranks' sudden hush and badly concealed smirks, Mac wasn't the only one who'd watched the media savaging. Flint clearly had a problem with it. Building up a head of steam? Full body. He stood centre front, hand in pocket, ran his gaze over the fifteen or so squad members assembled. "Let's get this straight before we start," he barked. "I'm sick of taking stick from ignorant gits. It's bad enough when the press has a go. I'll not tolerate it from my officers."

Tough. At the back, Bev bridled. Then actually gave it some thought. The man had a point. Heading up a major incident inquiry wasn't easy even without gratuitous pops. Not that she'd personal experience of the top job. Nor likely to. But she'd seen the heavy toll a high profile case could take, knew senior detectives who used chemical crutches to get through: baccy and booze being the legal ones. People like Flint, the guv, even Powell, were the guys with a neck on the block. They called the shots and it was there the buck stopped.

As for the press, it was easy to take swings from the safety of a desk. Shame a few more hacks didn't have Jack Pope's insight Her old mate Popie had thrown in the badge for a press card couple years ago now. Over a boozy Balti, not that long back, he'd made what for him was an intelligent observation that had stuck with Bev. He reckoned the two jobs had a lot in common. In police work and journalism, no two days were the same, each shift brought something new – often volatile situations that had to be defused using people skills. Instant communication and connection with complete strangers went with both career territories. Big difference though. "At the end of the day, babe…" She recalled Jack's winning combination of cliché and condescension. "Reporters don't make life and death calls. They just write about it. The only deadline bothering me is my editor's."

Three deaths in as many days were bugging Flint. Any more critics on his back and he might buckle. Bev jotted a reminder on her to-do list, half listened as the DCS ran through the stats: hundred and twenty statements, tapes from seventy street cameras, ninety-eight calls to the hot line. Number crunching really. Nothing to go on.

"Short of catching the killer red-handed," Flint said opening a shaving nick as he rubbed his chin, "we need quality information." Without forensic evidence and video footage, a breaking case often boiled down to that: the one phone call that pointed police in the wrongdoer's direction, the one tip that led to an arrest. Or the crim gets careless. Or cocky. Cops aren't clairvoyant; they don't have visions, blinding flashes of inspiration. That sort of bollocks was for the box.

"What about *Crimewatch*?" Powell had starred with the lovely Fiona Bruce once, probably fantasised about repeating the performance with Kirsty. "I'm pretty thick with one of the producers."

Pretty thick? Bev masked a smile, made another note.

"Christ, Mike," Flint groaned. "I hope we nail the killer before that." The monthly programme had gone out last night. Double-edged sword as well. Prime time telly could really open the fruit-cakes' floodgates.

"Reconstruction?" Daz mooted.

"Maybe, lad." Flint didn't sound convinced. Re-creating the last known movements of a pair of paedos didn't have a lot going for it in the simpatico stakes. Flint threw the brief open, and officers ran through results of tasks assigned. It didn't take long. No news in this case not being good news. There were still masses of boxes to tick, phones to bash, doors to knock. Routine, methodical plod work. Pulses were not racing.

Bev tucked her pen behind her ear. "I reckon the killer'll be in touch before long."

"How'd you work that one out, Morriss?" Powell sneered.

"Enjoying it, isn't he?" She mimed writing. "Corresponding with a tame hack. Getting his story splashed all over the front page. Bet he's got a taste for it."

"Keen for more." Flint nodded, sighed. Maybe he was thinking the same as Bev. Fact was the Disposer wasn't the first psycho to enjoy seeing his name – and words – in print. Look at the Zodiac killer in the States. Forty years since his homicidal spree in California, but films and books chronicling the story were still being churned out. The Zodiac wrote to three newspapers claiming more than thirty lives. Crammed with taunts and cryptic clues, the correspondence added to his notoriety and the public's fascination. Course, the first – and still most infamous – serial killer to get his rocks off writing to the press was considerably closer to home. And just as elusive.

Neither Zodiac nor Jack the Ripper had even been identified – let alone caught.

"Bev." Flint tapped her on the shoulder on his way out. "More pressure on Matt Snow, I think."

18

"More fan mail, Matt?"

Snow scowled as he flicked his head round. Anna Kendall was peeking over his narrow hunched shoulders. He might fancy the pants off her, didn't mean he appreciated the prying. Mind, in the pink shift dress she was a sight for runny eyes. Maybe he was just getting paranoid?

The reporter had come in early, thought he'd have the news-room to himself for a while. Wanted first dibs at the early post he'd brought up from front desk. Amazing how time flies when you're not enjoying yourself; the whole team had drifted in by now. And Anna's question couldn't be further from the truth.

"Some nutter reckons he's the Disposer." Snow waved a sheet of lined paper that had clearly been torn from a spiral notebook. "Says he's gonna wipe out redheads next."

"Couldn't start with Chris Evans, could he?" Anna perched on the edge of his desk, crossed her legs, probably oblivious to what her hemline was up to. He returned the tongue-in-cheek grin, aware of a slight relaxation in his taut nerve cells. He'd felt wired to the national grid since his last contact with the killer. And the cops.

"Evans is OK." Snow lounged back, hands crossed behind his head. "How 'bout Anne Robinson?"

"What do you reckon the Disposer would say to her?" There was a gleam in her eye. "You are the…

"…weakest link. Goodbye." He completed the limp line. Their laughter was forced. The unsolicited mail had a serious aspect. Every Tom, Dick and hoaxer was jumping on the bandwagon.

"How many letters now, Matt?" Leg casually swinging.

"Stopped counting after thirty." He tried meeting her eye-line but given the distraction it was difficult. "Look at that." He pointed a Hush Puppy at screwed up balls of paper on the floor. No room in the bin.

She slipped elegantly off the desk, squatted, skimmed some of the offerings. "Shouldn't you let the police take a look at this stuff?"

He snorted. "It's complete bilge, Anna."

"Even so…" She licked her lips as she read. "Are they all anonymous?"

"Pretty much. 'Cept for the note from George Bush. Oh yeah, and the one from Tony Blair." Snow rolled his eyes. "Fuckwits."

"With fingers clearly on the political pulse," she quipped, then sat cross-legged, lowered her voice. "Do you think he'll write again?"

"Tone? Any time." Snow aimed for a casual crack, missed by a wide margin. He knew damn well who she meant. Fact was the Disposer had already made contact; his words were imprinted on the reporter's brain. Snow shivered, suddenly cold. "Have to wait and see, won't we?" It was almost a relief when the news editor called Snow to his office. Anna waited until Rick Palmer's door was closed before gathering the letters and slipping them into her attaché case.

Bev didn't want to piss on Anna Kendall's paper parade, but a quick butcher's at the scrawled contents of the first few creased sheets wasn't hopeful. "This is great, Anna," she fibbed. "Thanks a bunch." She told God it was a barely white lie. Like He'd care. Unlike Anna, who might take offence and not come to the wicket again with potential goodies. Mind, Bev might've overdone the effusion.

It looked as if Kendall was blushing; the Twix-coloured eyes were lowered. "Hope they won't waste too much of your valuable time. But they were being thrown away, and you never know, do you?"

Know what? That every loony on the planet had picked up a pen? A near matching stack had been sent to the nick. Bev shoved the letters in a file, promised to get them fine-tooth combed later. Mac could have a look-see when he got back from Wolverhampton.

Bev had been looking forward to a nose round the newsroom but Anna had called to change the location. The writer had been on assignment over Highgate way. Made sense to drop by after. She'd just come from interviewing a woman who was marrying for the eighth time. "Get all the good jobs, I do." Anna had laughed, broken the ice before handing over the letters.

Bev popped the file atop a wobbly in-tray. She'd opted for her office rather than an interview room. More user-friendly. She sat back, flexing her manipulation muscles, asked Anna to talk in more detail about her request. Bev observed more closely than she listened. The young woman was like a breath of fresh air. Mind, she waved her hands a lot when she spoke. Had to admire the passion, GSOH too, maybe a touch naïve. Anna made a good case, but Bev had already drawn mental lines. She was only interested in access to Snow. Like she'd tell Anna that. Magnanimously she agreed in principle to Anna shadowing, but only when it didn't impede Operation Wolf. "Priorities and all that." She smiled, hands spread.

"I absolutely understand." Anna leaned forward. Close and cosy. "We can still do the general interview stuff, though?" Puppy dog eyes. She put Bev in mind of Daz when he was doing his Andrex bit.

Bev sighed. "Journos aren't too popular round here at the mo, Anna. Might be best to hang fire till we get a handle on the case."

She nodded, clearly disappointed. "Unless…" Pen tapped perfect teeth. Bev's fingers were crossed under the desk: Go on, gal, she urged silently. "Maybe some time when you're in town you can pop in? I can record a chat in the newsroom easily enough."

Result! She waggled a hand. "See what I can do."

Anna opened her mouth, maybe thought better of it, lowered her eyes again.

"What?" Bev's lip twitched. Girl was certainly no hard-nosed hack.

"Tell me to get lost. I won't mind, but any chance of me looking round an incident room? Just to pick up the buzz. It could add veracity to the front line cop features."

Yeah right. Girl was a cop tart: one step up from a crime scene gawper. She just wanted a gander. Bev thought it through. Two minutes wasn't going to hurt. And it could pay-off big time. But. "No can do. Sorry."

Anna shrugged, reached for an expensive looking case. "No prob. You know what they say... If you don't ask..."

Too true. Same 'they' talk about hot irons and striking. "How's Matt Snow coping in the spotlight?"

She turned her mouth down. "Struggling, I'd say. He likes people to think he's Mr Cool, but I think the pressure's getting to him."

"Pressure?" Bev scoffed. "Screwing the opposition? Guy gets more scoops than Mr Whippy."

Wasn't one of Bev's best, but it made Anna laugh. "I suppose... but Matt didn't ask to be singled out. Right now he's got every nutter in the city on his back, the management breathing down his neck, the police on his case. Oops. Sorry. I..."

Dismissive wave. "No worries." Anna reached for her jacket. Now or never. Worse thing she could do was tell Bev to fuck off. "Wanna help him?"

She paused, one arm in a sleeve. "Matt?"

Bev nodded, adopted a serious expression to counter Anna's uncertainty. Sounds of silence. The tick of Bev's wristwatch was audible. For a few seconds she thought she'd made a bad call, then...

"Sure." Anna sat back, crossed her legs. "Truth be told I feel a bit sorry for him. Some of the other hacks are giving him a hard time. Jealous, I suppose. What can I do?"

Bev held her gaze. "Keep an eye on him for me."

Incredulity? Contempt? The writer straightened. Miss You-Can-Not-Be-Serious. "Are you asking me to be your snout?" Bev shrugged. Win some, lose some. "Yeah, go on then. I'm up for that." Anna's giggle was infectious. "Tell me more."

Phew. Not lost her touch then. Bev asked Anna to keep her eyes, ears, mind, open. "Can't tell you what for exactly." She puffed out her cheeks. "Anything out the ordinary piques your interest, twitches the antennae. Try and find out who he talks to, where he goes, what he's up to. If you can get him to open up, maybe he'll drop his guard, let something slip. Problem?"

The frown deepened. "Why do I get the impression he's being treated as a suspect?"

Bev's turn to lean forward. "Not that, Anna. I think a killer's playing him like a fiddle. I reckon Matt's out of his depth. He assumes he's in control. He's not. And it's a dangerous game."

She nodded. "He's aware of that." Guessing?

"Is he?"

"He's scared. I sensed it this morning." Anna looked down at her hands.

"Go on."

"I asked if he thought the Disposer would write again." Eye contact now. "Way Matt reacted – I think he already has."

Bev probed but could extract no more. Anna's gut feeling wasn't proof. Made sense though. Could explain why Snow hadn't returned any of Bev's calls. Again. He'd certainly not been at his desk since first thing. "You heading back to work now?" Anna shook her head. "Next time you see him? Get him to give me a bell?" She pushed her chair back. "I'll walk you out."

They had to pass the incident room. Bev popped her head round the door. Busy? More buzz in a defunct beehive. She beckoned Anna. "Two minutes, OK?"

Bev was no clock-watcher, but by 18.43 she'd had enough. A stack of papers at her left elbow represented eliminations: calls put in, checks made, follow-ups done and dusted. At the right lay further actions. It was a much smaller pile but the tasks in it needed deeper digging: phone interviews where she'd picked up vocal nuances, felt she'd elicit more face-to-face. Meant she'd gabbed a lot too. Hoarse wasn't in it. Three bottles of Malvern water she'd necked, throat still felt like barbed wire. Please God, don't let me be coming down with anything. The weekend beckoned, as did Byford. The plan was to spend it together. Starting tonight.

She ran a finger test on her hair. Yep. Needed washing. No problem. The big man wasn't due to come courting till nine. She couldn't remember the last time she'd had two days off running. Not that she'd be doing much running. She gave a lazy smile.

Arms high, she stretched kinks from her spine, revelled in the prospect of a long lie-in followed by a bit of duvet action. Unlike uniform. Poor sods would be posting fliers first thing round the crime scenes on the Churchill and in the park. She'd mooted it at the late brief. Got the green light from Flint. Designs were at the printers now. Bit like wanted posters only in this case it was information they were after. Were you in blah-blah on such a date? The leaflets would be tucked under windscreens, tied to lampposts, pushed through letterboxes. Might get a result…

After the brief, she'd finally got round to filling in Flint on her abortive visit to Madeleine Graves. The DCS seemed happy enough, agreed the ball was now in the cryptic correspondent's court. Without more to go on, they'd done all they could.

Assuming there was more.

As for the Disposer and the possibility he'd contacted Snow again, Powell had the dubious pleasure of chasing that particular ball. No peace for the wicked: the DI was on duty all weekend. Course, if hell broke loose, leave would be cancelled and she'd be back in like an Exocet. Perish the thought.

She rifled her emergency rations drawer, came up with half a Mars bar. Mouth was chocker when the phone rang. She made a stab at giving her name.

"Boss?" Mac. She could hear his puzzled frown.

A chunk of caramel was stuck in her teeth, jammed to the roof of her mouth. She garbled her name again.

"That you, boss?"

Swallow. "Nah. Amy Winehouse."

"Touch-ee. You sounded like Daffy Duck. Thought I'd got a wrong number."

"I was masticating." Came out all hoity-toity. Stifled guffaw noises down the line.

"You'll choke in a minute, mate." A smile curved her lips.

"S'OK. Just had this vision of you mast…"

"Enough already. This a social call or what?" As if. Mac had been chasing alibi leads in Wolverhampton.

"Scrivener lied, boss."

Wolf whistle in the corridor. Door slamming in car park. Bulb flickering in Bev's head. Eddie Scrivener. Father of Tanya: a victim of Wally Marsden. "Give."

"Told you he was playing darts? Tournament at The Bull? Drop too much jolly juice? Home to beddy-byes?"

"Check."

"Bollocks."

Mac Tyler didn't do broad-brush strokes. Mostly he paid more attention to detail than Bev. He told her that though the pub landlord had corroborated Eddie's story, something smelt iffy. So he asked for the names of other darts' players, other regulars. Mac had paid several house calls. Three men backed up the alibi. Two swore they'd not set eyes on Scrivener for a month.

The mental bulb was still only a flicker. It was a long way from mendacity or even a simple mistake to murder. She licked a finger, mopped chocolate flakes from the desktop. "What's Scrivener saying?" Mac would've visited the house, didn't need telling.

"Not there, boss. Not been seen since Tuesday."

Not since her phone call. "Neighbours?"

"No idea where he is."

"Shit." She saw Scrivener's face again, screwed in hate when he'd been photographed storming from Marsden's trial at the crown court.

"There's more."

"Go on."

"Smell of gas coming from Scrivener's place." Eau de fishy bullshit.

"Never." Shock, horror.

"Thought it best checked."

"Deff." Breaking and entering – without the breaking. Saved time, cut red tape.

"And?"

"Place is a shrine to his kid. Pictures all over the walls, cabinet full of baby clothes, lock of hair tied with pink ribbon."

"She ain't dead, Mac, and she ain't a kid." Eighteen if Bev remembered right.

"Had her childhood wrecked, boss."

Stolen innocence, tarnished lives, shattered dreams. Phrases from the Disposer's letter. Bev pursed her lips. Eddie Scrivener had never let go, never moved on. He adored the child Tanya had once been; how much did he hate the man who – in effect – had taken her?

The bulb burned brighter. Very least they needed urgent words with Scrivener. She'd get the news bureau to issue a release, ask Wolverhampton to keep an eye on the house. "Nice work, Mac."

"Not finished, boss. Scrivener kept a scrapbook. Crammed with paedophile court cases, trial reports, mug shots."

"Wally Marsden?"

"Page one."

Flash bulb went off in her head.

It was gone eight by the time Bev pulled up kerbside at Baldwin Street. No lights burning inside. Frankie must be off crooning somewhere. As she locked the motor, foodie fumes floated in the night air. World cuisine in walking distance, one of the things she loved about her Moseley pad. Spanish, Greek, Thai, Indian, Italian, Chinese, French, you name it... Mind, she'd kill for a chip butty right now.

The thought brought her up sharp. Had Eddie Scrivener killed for a damn sight more than a fish supper? Jury was a long way out. But at least Mac's dogged persistence had thrown up a lead. Before leaving Highgate, she'd briefed key players like Flint and Powell, liaised with a bod in the news bureau, swapped a bit of banter with Mac who was last seen pawing over a hot keyboard. She smiled, shook her head. Mac had finally – and tentatively – invited her to a comedy night. He was on the stand-up bill at The Dog in Digbeth on Sunday. Shame. She'd sure as hell go along for a heckle, but Byford had a prior booking. She shivered, spine tingled, hadn't felt so girly in yonks.

She chucked her keys on the hall table, curled a lip at the local rag Frankie must've left there. Hopefully, Eddie Scrivener's mug would make tomorrow's front pages. Not that the cops were pointing fingers yet. But Scrivener had questions to answer. 'Needed to help with inquiries' was the wording on the news release.

Sitting room was neat as a pin. Had her mum been in? No. Friday was one of the days her ma worked. Bev slung her coat over a chair, kicked off a Doc, watched in horror as it almost decapitated a piece of Frankie's Capo di Monte. Guilty sniff. Prob'ly a rip-off anyway. Even so, she eased her foot gently from the other shoe before giving the knick-knack a once-over. Teeny-weeny chip. Who'd notice that?

Right. Bit of mood music. Stones? Nah. Reminded her of Oz. Moby? Cold Play? Travis? Nah. Annie Lennox? Heather Small? Sade? Nah. Her nail flicked through more CD cases. Yeah. Dylan'd do it tonight. *Just Like a Woman*, featuring Bev Morriss on backing vocals.

Thank God for the latest media report on alcohol in pregnancy. This week, a glass didn't do any harm. Next week? Dicing with death probably. The first sip was pinot nectar.

She sighed. Couldn't ignore it any more. The answerphone had been flashing since she came in the door. It'd be her mum; Emmy Morriss ran on clockwork. Bev's heart sank. It wasn't that she'd avoided her ma since the scan… Yeah right. Only like the bubonic. Just that Emmy had wet her knickers knowing one baby was on the way; her maternal ministrations now would make a mother hen look negligent. Come on, Bev. Share. Don't be a heel.

Best hear what ma had to say first. She hit Play. It wasn't Emmy. It was Byford. Couldn't make the weekend. Sorry.

Stunned silence then furious shout. "Fuck you, big man." Bastard hadn't even got the bottle to call her mobile. Wine glass drained, she poured another, slid down the wall, sat on the tiles, hugged her knees. Tears streamed down her face. *She breaks just like a little girl*, Dylan sang. Damn right, Bob.

SATURDAY

19

Matt Snow lit a Marlboro, red-rimmed eyes creased against the smoke. Tonight was the first time he'd touched tobacco in five years. There were four left in the pack. Hacked off, he shoved it in his trouser pocket. Along with half a dozen other addicts, he was huddled in the cold on the pavement outside The Prince. The road surface glistened after a heavy shower; a canvas for fuzzy lights, wet leaves, street art. Urban Impressionism.

Giggles and guffaws as a fellow smoker cracked a joke. Snow didn't crack a smile. He was close to, but not part of, the group. A position he happily occupied, normally. Outsider was pushing it a bit, but the reporter had no close friends. Maybe even cultivated the loner image, reckoned the aloofness added a touch of authority. Superiority? Mystery? He sniffed. Yeah right. No point kidding himself. It was other people kept their distance. He was no Mr Popular. Peers respected his ability, viewed him as a ruthless bastard: a bullyboy who'd flog his grannies for a down page filler.

The reporter took a long hard drag, flicked the glowing stub in the gutter. What the hell had he sold to the Disposer? And what was in it for him, exactly? He sighed. It was a bit late for second thoughts.

Snow fought his way back to the bar. Terracotta tiles were tacky with beer slops, cream walls were coated with nicotine. The Prince wouldn't have been his pub of choice: the cop shop was only a two-minute walk. Last thing he needed was to bump into the Bill. Or Bev. Mind, they probably had better things to do on a Saturday night.

Snow ordered another Stella, lingered near the bar. Brash big mouths with loud accents and braying laughs meant he could barely hear himself think. Probably no bad thing. He checked his Blackberry. No texts. Bunch of voice messages from Morriss and Powell. The pay-as-you-go was on vibrate in his breast pocket. He was waiting for the Disposer's next contact. When it came, perhaps he'd ask the bastard why he'd told Snow to hang out at the Prince. Least of his worries really. The Disposer was ballistic after that morning's Eddie Scrivener coverage. Reading between the lines, it was clear the cops had Scrivener in the frame for the Wally Marsden murder. The Disposer wasn't into glory sharing. He was threatening action that'd get the national media creaming its collective jeans. Have to get their arses back to Birmingham first. Terror alerts in the capital meant most of them had returned to base.

"Tintin. How you doing, mate?" Jack Pope, crime correspondent on the *Chronicle*. Great.

"Watch it!" Snow snapped. Pope's heavy-handed backslap had jettisoned Stella all over Snow's shirtfront. Ineffectual dabs with a tissue only spread the stain.

"'Nother drink?" Pope winked. "Or have you just spilled one?"

Snow itched to whack the smirk off his face. Pope was a walking cliché: the tall dark handsome smooth talker. Jack the lad, and one of the lads. Everything the short, pallid, bland Snow wasn't. On the other hand Pope couldn't write his way out of a split paper bag. Ex-cop, for Christ's sake. Didn't have a clue about crafting a story.

"What brings you here?" Snow asked. Like he could care less.

Pope tapped the side of his nose. "Little bird." That figured. Guy had an aviary at his disposal. Not that Snow was bitter or anything.

"When's the next one, Snowie?" Jack wiped the back of his

139

hand across his mouth.

"Next what?"

"Bin collection. Come on, Tintin. Don't be a wanker." His beer-laced burp hit Snow in the face. "Your new best buddy. When's he sending another paedo packing?"

"Like I'd tell you." Snow snorted. "If you were on fire, I'd piss the other way."

"Cruel." Jack pouted, all hurt. "Might drown one of your Hush Puppies."

"Snigger away, dickhead. I'll have the last laugh." Snow's fist was balled.

"Oh?" Jack cocked his head. "Gonna piss on the opposition again, Snowie?"

"Buy yourself an umbrella, Pope."

"Tell me more."

Snow had already said enough. "Fuck off, pretty boy." He turned his back.

"Tut tut, Tintin. Swearing's sign of a shit vocabulary. Still, anyone reads your crappy column knows that."

Snow had never seen red mist before. Never attacked anyone either. He smashed the Stella bottle against the wall, took an almighty swing. Jack instinctively protected his face but jagged glass ripped the skin open on the back of his hands. Shocked gasps and women's screams. Rough hands dragged Snow away; others restrained Pope from retaliating.

Two blokes frogmarched Snow through the crowd. At the door, the reporter shook them off and turned. Spittle flecked his lips. "Next time you're dead."

"Ballistic wasn't in it, babe." Jack Pope looked pale and sounded shaky. "I'd never've thought the slimy runt had it in him."

Arms folded, Bev tapped a toe, watched a young casualty nurse at the General bandage Jack's ragged wounds. Beyond the cubicle curtains, a depressingly familiar Saturday night drama played: binge drinkers and street brawlers, fuckwits in fisticuffs, blacked eyes, bleeding faces, broken bones. Soundtrack was slurred snatches of *Danny Boy*, and *Angels*. Bev sighed, felt like punching out a few lights herself.

Jack had got off lightly. No stitches, no permanent damage. She thanked the big man in the sky Jack hadn't lost an eye. Right now both were ogling the earthly angel wielding the lint.

"Hey, Jack, tell me: what part of 'give me a bell if you find him' didn't you understand?" Bev's anger was directed at herself more than Pope. Her call had unwittingly endangered the guy. She'd enlisted him in her pathetic little hunt for Snow. They'd divvied out the reporter's haunts and watering holes. Jack had struck lucky. Or not. With hindsight it had been madness. She'd never have asked if he hadn't been an old flame. And she hadn't had something to prove. Or better things to do on a Saturday night. Screw Byford.

"Come on, babe," Jack cajoled. "You weren't exactly expecting this?" He lifted a bandaged hand. She shook her head. Never in a month of Sundays. "Exactly," Jack said. "I was just having a friendly little chat with the guy before bringing you in."

"You pressing charges?" Bev asked.

"Pressing a knee in his nuts next time I see him." The nurse giggled. Bev gave a token smile. Typical Jack. Should've known he'd cock up. Being a team player was an alien concept to the guy. She snorted. Hark who's talking. Bev had been out on a forest of limbs in her time. But Jack wasn't a cop any more, didn't share her priorities. She wanted a word with Snow; Jack would've wanted a story.

"What sparked him, Jack?"

"Search me." Reckoned she'd find something too. Jack had a guilty glint in his eye. Pound to a penny, he'd wound Snow up. But to blow like that? Big questions: was Snow on a knife-edge?

Or had the capacity for violence always been there?

"Wait till we get home, shall we?" Jack asked.

Bev was miles away. "What?"

"Before you search me." Suggestive eyebrow. Kiss-kiss lips.

"Hey, love," Bev addressed the nurse. "Sure his brain's not damaged?"

Snow lay on the leather settee, throbbing head clutched in bloodstained hands. Felt as if a chainsaw was hacking his brain. Painkillers hadn't kicked in yet. Couldn't counter the booze, perhaps. A bottle of Grouse stood on the carpet, half its contents swirling round the reporter's gut.

How had he got home? He frowned, dredged vague memories of stumbling out of a cab into the gutter. He chuckled. No idea why. Get a grip, man. Couldn't afford to lose it again. Why had he let Pope needle him? If the guy pressed charges, Snow would be out of a job. Christ, was he already out of his mind?

Snow felt like a schizo, but wasn't cut out for the double life. Pretending everything was normal when he shat himself every time the phone rang. Price was high considering he'd never even met the man at the end of the line. Course the pay back was appealing. But the pressure was patently getting to him.

Why else had he shot his mouth off to Pope? Snigger away, dickhead. I'll have the last laugh. Hilarious. Snow groaned. Talk about showing your hand. Hopefully Pope wasn't quick enough to pick up the drift. Or was the booze adding to Snow's paranoia?

He staggered to stockinged feet, stumbled to the window, pressed feverish forehead against cool glass. "It'd be Pope's word against mine."

A piss-head weaved across the pavement. Snow's thin lip curled in contempt. He didn't see the dark figure against the oak tree. The nearest streetlight was out, the slight form was barely distinguishable from the bark. The watcher was aware of Snow's every move, had been most of the night, and was sober as a stone cold judge.

Byford tugged the cashmere scarf more snugly round his neck, dug gloved hands deep into fleece pockets. Silver light danced across the surface of the dark ocean, the moon a perfect milky circle against midnight blue velvet. Silhouettes of three, no, four small fishing boats were just visible from the shore, tiny red lights twinkling from the masts.

The big man gazed out from the shoreline. He loved the sea, loved the ever-present sound of the waves; always there, constantly changing, soothing, reassuring, hypnotic. Never jarring, like the cacophony of city noise. He loved the water too, a moving palette with a million shades. Dark now, dark dramatic landscape too, except for the moon's stage lighting.

His son's phone call had come out of the proverbial blue. Richard's marriage was falling apart, Stephie needed space, she'd taken the kids. Byford couldn't remember the last time he'd heard Rich cry. It was a tough call: Bev or the boy? The big man had packed a weekend bag, headed to his youngest son's home in Cumbria, a village on the coast, Silecroft.

Well-oiled and emotionally drained, Rich had drifted off to sleep around midnight, the big man had slipped out for air, exercise, a little solitude. He wanted to wave a wand, take away his son's pain. That wasn't going to happen. From what he gathered, it looked as if Rich and Stephanie needed a miracle, not magic, to avoid divorce.

He sighed, pondered his own little domestic difficulty. The silence from Bev was pretty predictable, he supposed. Stroppy was her default mode. Even so, it wouldn't have hurt her to give him the benefit of the doubt. As it was, she wasn't picking up the phone, hadn't returned his calls. Was she hurt? Fed up? Furious?

All three probably. And down had crashed the emotional shutters – up had clanged the personal drawbridge.

Maybe he should've been more explicit when he left the message. But whatever he said boiled down to the same thing: my kids are more important. She'd love that.

Did she love him? He didn't know. Maybe his sudden dash was the excuse she needed. He sighed, rubbed a hand over his face. Maybe it was the excuse he needed. He cared for Bev, of course he did, but boy could she be prickly. She made Naomi Campbell look a model of reason. He took a nip of malt from a hip flask. God, he was too old for all this soul-searching. Anyway, he was a bloke, he was from Mars.

SUNDAY

20

As venues go, the back room of the Dog wasn't big, more comedy stall than store. Produce-wise, a few of the gags were past their sell-by. Who cared? Bev had sunk a few bevies, spirits were high. Good job there was no comedy equivalent of karaoke or she'd be up there. Wouldn't even need a friendly shove from the girls. Bev, Frankie, Sumi Gosh and Carol Pemberton had bagged the table nearest the front, prime spot to catch Mac's act.

Caz, looking tasty in red, strolled back from the bar, dished out roasted peanuts and pork scratchings.

"Ta, mate," Bev smiled. There was only so long you could wallow in self-pity. By Sunday lunchtime, she'd had enough. Byford could go screw himself. As for Jack Pope, she'd given the cheeky sod a lift home from hospital, been sorely tempted by his lech proposal she should be his night nurse. She'd gone back to her place instead, slept for England.

After a late lazy breakfast, the Bullring was calling her name. She'd nipped into town for a bit of retail therapy: books, more bubble bath, earrings, two skirts, three pairs of trousers and a new bra. Needed bigger sizes but hey! Pregnancy's a growth market. She'd finally popped in to break the baby news to her mum and gran. Emmy and Sadie were chuffed to bits. Good mood must've been catching. Bev had raced home, rounded up the girls for compulsory fun at the Crack House. Mind, the wit-smith who'd come up with the club name needed a smack.

Swigging shandy, she gazed round. Décor was cream and sepia and despite the baccy ban smelt smoky-stale. When Mac had said not to expect a lot, he wasn't kidding, though he'd better be any time soon. They'd already sat through five funny men routines. The Highgate posse made up half the audience; the rest looked as if it had strayed in off the street, probably expected Paul Merton or Russ Noble to be on the bill. So not happening. The Crack House (thanks to Mac, she was an instant expert on these matters) was open-spot slots, a gig for unknown up-and-coming comics. Close but not quite comedy karaoke. Eventually, most of the turns wanted to make it big on the circuit. That wasn't Mac's motivation. The stand-up was his antidote to the stress of being a cop. DC Tyler wasn't about to give up the day job.

Timely reminder. It was work first thing. Bev grimaced. Best switch to the soft stuff.

"When's he on, sarge?" Sumi hadn't got the hang of this off-duty lark.

Bev shrugged. "Haven't got a clue."

"Nothing new there then." Frankie smirked.

"Should be on stage, Francesca." Bev made a show of checking her watch. "Next one leaves in ten."

"God. You're sharp." She tilted her glass.

They hushed it when the compère tapped the mic. He reminded Bev of those little rubber trolls that kids used to attach to the top of their pencils: small, pot-bellied, frizzy hair sticking out round a bald spot. Bloke raised a few sniggers though with a sarky take on celebrity boob jobs.

Caz leaned in, confided sotto voce. "Only time I ever had great tits? When I was carrying."

"Carrying what?" Sumi sucked Saint Clement's up a straw.

"Cases. What d'you think?" Caz put her arms round an imaginary bump. Her kids had reached junior school stage. "No shit. Thirty-eight double dee. My old man thought he'd died and gone to heaven."

Exaggerated sniggers. Bev narrowed her eyes. Sumi was a

touch green, not dark vert; Caz had a glint in the eye. Frankie was suspiciously silent. They were up to something.

"Getting pregnant's a bit drastic." Sumi grinned. "Can't see it catching on."

"What do you think, Bev?" Caz, all innocence.

Bev reckoned she'd been rumbled, that she wasn't just imagining the sideways glances going round Highgate, that her expanding waistline was indeed the subject of growing speculation and juicy goss. Hands in mock surrender, she confessed. "OK you got me. I'm pregnant. Couldn't afford the boob job."

Squeals of delight round the table. "Bev, that's brill."

"Nice one, sarge."

Nice two, actually. But she'd not go that far yet. Frankie already had bubbly on ice at the bar. Bev watched as she sashayed back with a laden tray. "Stitched me up good and proper," she smiled. "Didn't even get a sniff."

"Here's to the great detective." Frankie raised a glass.

"Finished, ladies?" Troll Man inquired, eyebrow heading for non-existent hairline. "Next up's a guy who knows his way round the comedy block. A legend in his own north Midlands neck of the woods… the Crack House is proud to host his Birmingham debut." He glanced at something scribbled on his wrist. "Put your hands together please for… Mick Taylor."

Stage name? Or was Troll Man too vain to wear specs? Anyone's guess, but Mac entered through a side door, stepped up to the mic. And the crowd went wild. Well, the Highgate contingent did. Their wave of whoops and wolf whistles almost drowned the sound of Bev's ring tone.

She caught the odd phrase from Mac: observational stuff on crime and the police. They all missed the punch line. Powell was on the phone asking for backup. Major incident in Balsall Heath. Looked as if it could turn nasty.

Mac cottoned on quick. He joined the exodus to the door.

The four people left clapped desultorily. Maybe thought it was part of the act.

21

Blue lights. Braying mob. Balsall Heath. The drama was unfolding as Sumi dropped the others close to the action. Bev, Mac and Carol ran from the car, leaving Sumi to park wherever she could. Wouldn't be easy. Space was at a premium. Five fire engines idled, generators hummed, crews on standby. Ambulances, paramedics similarly primed. Mounted police and foot patrols in riot gear were poised at both ends of the street chomping at literal and metaphorical bits. An angry chanting hundred-plus crowd probably imagined it was keeping the cops at bay. Bev reckoned DCS Flint was actually holding his officers back, afraid of provoking violence. Further violence.

En route, she'd picked up unconfirmed reports via a call to Highgate control. An unknown source had rung police claiming demonstrators had dragged a man from a detached house. The hapless victim had been badly beaten and now lay in the middle of the road.

Bev clocked Powell and Flint in the front line. The DCS had binoculars to his eyes. She doubted he could see much through the wailing wall of protestors. Flint's instinct would probably have been to go in, save the poor bloke from further harm. But as every officer knew, more than one life was at stake.

The detached house, Victorian redbrick, double-fronted, was a probation hostel. Milton Place was one of more than a hundred similar establishments operating in England and Wales. They accommodated around two and a half thousand released cons. Anyone who read the papers knew forty per cent of the hostel population comprised sex offenders. Hand-painted posters suggested the protestors were well read, and in this case two plus two equalled big trouble, potential tragedy.

As well as the stats, the press was wont to run scare stories about sexual predators living in the community. The emotive prose stirred anger among outraged residents. Hostels in other parts of the country and the city – though not Milton Place – had been targeted before. Bev recognised action group acronyms on some of the homemade banners. SOB: Sex Offenders Out of Birmingham; CAP: Campaign Against Perverts; MAD: Mothers Against Deviants.

Previous demos had been generally peaceful. Had saturation coverage of the Disposer added fuel to an ignorant free-for-all fire? Had the protest been hi-jacked by a handful of mindless yobs? Or more sinister activists with vested interests?

Questions for later. She reckoned Flint's current priority was working out how to defuse a rapidly escalating and explosive situation. The mass of bodies had parted to reveal a chilling tableau. Four or five protestors swathed in scarves and balaclavas circled their injured prey. A big guy, almost certainly the ring-leader, goaded the crowd: torch the bastard? Or the building?

Through Flint's binoculars, Bev saw twelve, maybe thirteen forms silhouetted in the few remaining windows that hadn't been smashed. Trapped men. Scared to flee, terrified to stay.

"Both. Both. Both," the herd chorused.

"Bastards," Powell hissed, jaw clenched, fists tight.

"Cool it, Mike," Flint warned.

Bev had never seen the DI so edgy. Unsurprising perhaps. Only four months back a young constable and two other men had been killed in an arson attack on a halfway house in Selly Oak. It happened on Powell's watch, and though he wasn't responsible, Bev reckoned he still carried a heavy burden of self-imposed guilt. She offered a Polo, registered his haunted features, trembling hand.

Curious onlookers were gathering beyond the police cordons. Bev spotted Mac and Carol circulating trying to elicit information.

The noise had probably brought out the neighbours. Or maybe the light show was the attraction. A high-powered beam from a police helicopter intermittently strafed the scene, augmenting the street-lights' orange glow. Two, maybe three TV crews recorded the action. Police cameras captured the evidence. All the cops had to do was catch the villains. Bev couldn't see the bad guys getting away. Vine Street was virtually sealed.

"What now, boss?" Her breath emerged in white puffs. She stamped her feet, rubbed her hands.

"Pray that bloke's got more than one brain cell." He nodded towards the gobby guy goading the crowd. The one-word chant had changed. Still four letters, a world more menace.

"Burn. Burn. Burn."

A mile or so away in Moseley, a young woman in designer track-suit and trainers took a shortcut down an alleyway to reach her Mazda. The passage ran between two rows of shops, brick walls either side were daubed with graffiti, dusty determined weeds struggled here and there through the mortar. The alley was unlit, stinking of cat pee, littered with empty lager cans and junk food cartons. At that time of night most people would walk round several blocks to get to the car park. Jodie Mills was blasé, had no intention of allowing fear of crime or anything else to restrict her life or movements. She also ran self-defence classes in the church hall opposite, held a black belt in judo. And clutched a very large torch.

A bulging black bin bag almost blocked the narrow path. Jodie scowled, mumbled something about bastard litter-louts, kicked out angrily as she passed. The resultant split in the plastic revealed more than household waste. The face was human, and male. One wide-open eye stared as if shocked at the kick in the teeth. But the blow was post mortem. No doubt about it, given the smell.

Mike Powell smelt it first. Petrol. The DI's fraught glance darted wildly as he tried to locate the most likely source. Got it. The gang leader was waving a bottle in the air, taunting the man on the ground. Even from this distance the DI saw liquid splash on the road, inches from the victim. The fumes were growing stronger. Powell couldn't make out the undoubtedly terrified man's features. The picture in the DI's troubled mind was of a young police constable. For weeks after the arson attack, PC Simon Wells appeared nightly in the DI's dreams, featured daily in flashbacks. The visions had become less frequent of late. Now they were back, and emotions threatened to overwhelm him: the shock and fury and sadness at the futile waste of life.

Powell bounced on the balls of his feet, felt adrenalin fizz through his veins. Apart from one brief digression, he'd always gone by the book; never put a foot wrong when it came to rules, regulations, routine. It made him reliable. More than that: rigid. Where Bev sometimes rushed in foolishly, Powell feared to tread. Maybe that's why it took her a second or two to realise who'd broken ranks, who was charging down the street, black coat flapping like wings.

She watched open-mouthed as the DI headed straight for the swaggering gang leader. Surprise element? Delayed reaction? Disbelief? Whatever. The guy was unprepared. Powell's flying tackle brought the scumbag crashing down. Pinioned to the ground, he couldn't avoid Powell's fist in his face. The DI lashed out again. The rock came out of the crowd, smashed with an audible crack into Powell's temple. The stunned near silence lasted a couple of heartbeats. As Powell toppled over, the jeering crowd closed in.

Trembling, Jodie punched three nines on her mobile and paced impatiently as she waited. Seemed no time at all when an unmarked car pulled over, straddled the kerb. Jodie frowned. She'd expected flashing blue lights and two officers. Her worry lines deepened as the driver got out. She recognised Matt Snow immediately. She'd been an avid reader of his column since it started. Jodie was OK – if not happy – about being interviewed. By the time a police patrol car arrived twenty minutes later, the reporter had already left the crime scene. One of the officers blamed an ongoing incident for the delayed response.

Flint's standoff policy had allowed police numbers to swell, tension to increase. But when it all kicked off, Bev reckoned there were probably more uniforms in place than demonstrators. She didn't scare easily, but the sight, sound and smell of approaching police horses nearly made her wet her pants. Several tons of quivering horseflesh, clopping hooves, snorting nostrils, clanking metal was awesome. And effective crowd control.

Screaming, yelling demonstrators dispersed in all directions as the cavalry drew close. Her earlier assumption that the bad guys were virtually corralled proved premature and optimistic. Posters and banners were ditched as protestors fled through gardens either side of the street, officers in pursuit.

With no body armour or baton, Bev held back. Self-preservation? Maternal instinct? Babies were probably the last thought on her conscious mind. Flint had drummed it into the squad that people safety and public order were priorities.

Controlling events and care of casualties was more important than containment and securing convictions. If a few sheep escaped, that was OK. But not the leaders. He wanted them rounded up.

Bev narrowed her eyes. The main man was going nowhere. She weaved her way through what was left of the crowd, knelt by his side. The guy felled by Powell was unconscious, flat on his back, bleeding from the nose and mouth. Powell must've yanked off the balaclava. It was in the road, next to a Zippo lighter. Inches away lay the original victim, curled in the foetal position, hands round his head, whimpering like a baby. So where was the DI?

Paramedics carrying stretchers were heading this way. She left them to it, stood in the middle of the road, briefly took stock. Her heart had stopped banging her rib cage, but the pulse still whooshed in her ears. She took a few steadying breaths as she scanned the rapidly emptying street. Flint had made a good call. Potential tinderbox ignition had been averted. She'd envisaged petrol bombs, missile throwing, general mayhem. Fact that people were being carted off with only token struggles seemed to confirm her earlier suspicion that most of the crowd had been railroaded by a small gang of hard core troublemakers.

Early on, she'd seen officers frogmarching two of the scarf-wearers towards a line of waiting police wagons. In the initial chaos, confusion and noise it hadn't been possible to get the big picture, just clips and cameos. She'd spotted Mac and Caz in the crowd scenes; Flint barking orders through a bullhorn.

But no DI.

Hands in pockets, she walked the street, glance raking from side to side, genuinely concerned. Powell was a jobsworth; the only cop she knew who quoted PACE like it was a party piece. He'd never crossed a line, police or otherwise. Talk about breaking the working habits of a lifetime. Bev twisted rules like Geller bent spoons. But not in front of an audience. And never in front of a camera.

"'Kay, boss?" Mac's face glistened, sweat dripped from his chin. She handed him a crumpled tissue from her coat pocket.

Brisk nod. "Seen Powell?"

"Not since the big fight." He mopped up, mouth down. "What a moron."

Bev shrugged. Was he? She kind of admired the DI's action.

Showing Mac the lighter she'd bagged as evidence, she said, "The moron stopped a man getting toasted."

"Yeah?" Mac said. "What if Super Mike had sparked the riot? Set the whole shebang alight?"

"Didn't, did he?" Bottom lip jutted. Wasn't much of an answer.

They watched as officers escorted straggling demonstrators down the street towards a lift to the station. "Take ages to process that lot," Mac moaned.

"Tell me about it." Mostly they'd be dealing with public order offences, criminal damage. She hadn't heard arrest figures yet but sighed, pictured another rainforest of paperwork. Highgate's cells would soon be awash. Other nicks would have to take the overspill. Vast majority of the offenders would get bail first thing. Magistrates were in for a busy morning. The mouthy minority would almost certainly enjoy a lengthy remand in custody.

"If you two have nothing better to do than…"

Bev spun round, eyes blazing, bit back a mouthful. DCS Flint didn't look as if he'd appreciate any lip. "Go and take a look at this." He handed her a piece of paper. "There's a body. That's all I know."

Still seething, Bev read the address. Saint Mary's Row. Just down the road from her place. She glanced at Flint. She so wanted to tell him to take a flying fuck. Not cause she'd been called in on a day off. Didn't give a monkey's about that – she'd work in a bank if she wanted a nine to five job. It was Flint's arsey sarky attitude. If you've nothing better to do… Like they were swapping lead swinging recipes. Sod it. She'd had enough. "Actually, mate…"

He didn't hear. He was rubbing both hands over weary face. His complexion had a sickly hue. The bloke looked all in. She'd never seen it before: a person aging ten years in two hours. Maybe it was delayed shock. They'd come a gnat's eyelash away from a riot. Maybe he was replaying the crowd's chant: *burn,*

burn, burn. Even so… heat, kitchen, and all that. She opened her mouth.

"Sarge." Mac with his don't-say-anything-you-might-regret-later-expression.

Fine. Flint'd get the benefit of the doubt. Once. Not trusting herself to speak, she gave a mock salute, turned to go, dithered and turned back. "You seen the DI, sir?"

"In an ambulance." Powell had staggered there before passing out. "After treatment, he'll be going home."

"Home?"

"The DI's on suspension pending an inquiry."

22

Mac drove to Saint Mary's Row in a squad car commandeered at Vine Street. Sober but pissed off, Bev felt like hitting more than the road. She drummed twitchy fingers on her thigh, stared through the window, scowled. Must be chucking out time in Moseley. Chucking up, too, going by the charming scene outside the Nag's Head. A teenage girl was bent double in the gutter surrounded by chavs. Binge babes. Morons. The way Mac had described Powell. She sighed, still reckoned Flint was out of order, giving the DI the suspension elbow. No mileage discussing it now. Her DC's views were crystal.

"Reckon you'll get made up, boss?"

"You on about?" Knew he wasn't talking lippic.

"With Powell on gardening leave, they'll need a DI."

"Yeah right." More chance of winning Eurovision.

"Why not? You'd be great. Put in for inspector once before didn't you?"

"Twice." Said it all. Former yes-man Powell had pipped her at the post second time round.

"There y'go then." Like it was a done deal. And Mac had no business to. The DI was in hospital injured for Christ's sake.

"Take a right," she snapped. "It's quicker." Powell hadn't even been sent home yet, let alone packing. Talk about stepping into dead men's shoes.

"Better get his uniform out of mothballs, if you ask me."

"I didn't." Tight lips were tautened. Powell could be a dork. But he'd saved a bloke's life, and there'd been no further casualties. Seen one way, he'd averted a crisis. She hoped some of the brass would look in that direction. Flint certainly didn't.

She stifled a yawn. Great night this was turning out to be.

"Knackered, boss?"

She shrugged. Dog tired. And it wasn't over yet.

Done and dusted, the package was ready for e-mailing to the subs. Matt Snow poised the cursor on send. Light from the monitor cast a pale green glow over his pasty features, a desk lamp was the only other illumination. He was at home, in his study. A shorthand notebook open at his elbow was ring-stained with tea slops from a Take That mug. His fingers tapped against the keys as mixed emotions crossed his mind, creased his forehead.

The prose had flowed; the story had written itself. Or maybe not. The Disposer had lent more than a hand. Snow sipped tea and grimaced. It had gone cold. Unlike the copy. It had everything: name of the Disposer's latest victim, interview with witness who found the body, quotes from the killer. It was ready to go.

So why the hesitation?

The reporter fingered his fringe. He was sitting on a major development in a running story. Had it to himself, big up-yours exclusive. And that was the sticking point. The cops were bound to come sniffing, get really heavy this time. He'd been surprised they'd not turned up earlier at the crime scene. Realised they were otherwise engaged when he switched on the radio driving back. The Vine Street demo was top story on BBC WM. Snow sighed. Not for much longer. Compared with a serial killer, Milton Place was a minor disturbance. The riot-that-never-was made Small-earthquake-in- Chile-not-many-dead sound earth-shattering.

So why was he still dithering? Something niggled. He squeezed a pimple on his chin; face had outcrops of spots. He mused about the free hand he'd had at Moseley while the cops were occupied with a paedo-related incident up the road. Coincidence? Or brilliant timing? Snow shook his head. No way could the

Disposer have orchestrated the protest at paedo-palace. Could he? It'd make no diff anyway. Snow knew he'd no choice other than to file the copy. There was no point covering his back when the Disposer had a knife at his throat. Eyes closed, Snow swallowed hard. Not just his throat. He reached for the pay-as-you-go, opened the picture gallery. The god-awful shock still sent shivers down his spine. His mother photographed at home in Shropshire, grey hair fanned against her pillow. Another shot. Anna Kendall in the Manhattan, Snow's shoulder just in frame. More unwanted gifts from the Disposer.

And the recording the reporter had made the other night? He'd been stupid enough to leave it in the machine. The Disposer had helped himself to the tape. Snow wouldn't make the same mistake twice, but that didn't help now.

If the story didn't appear in print, the killer would deliver on his threats. If it did, the reporter would have the cops on his back. No-brainer then.

He clicked the mouse. The pay-off had better be worth it.

"Chippie on the corner, boss." Mac tilted his head as he locked the motor. The Fry-by-night.

"How 'bout checking the stiff first?" Like there was any doubt.

"Only saying." He glared at her retreating back.

"Saw that, mate." They locked glances in an estate agent's plate glass window. He flashed a toothy grin. Her lip twitched. Impossible to do the tetch with Mac for long: he had one of those cute faces, reminded her of the bear in *Jungle Book*. She was starving, as it happened. Could eat a sodding horse. Equine flashback. Maybe not.

A few doors up, a couple of fresh-faced police constables guarded the entrance to an alleyway: laundrette one side, optician's the other. Mac cracked a line about being able to see if your washing was clean. She cut him a withering look. "So sorry

I missed your act."

She'd not come across either of the PCs before. She'd have remembered, given they looked as if they should be in a boy band. The new kids on the block introduced themselves as Mo Iqbal, Danny Rees. Both had bright eyes, smooth skin. Bev felt old enough to be their mum. "What we got, lads?"

Iqbal cleared his throat. "Body in a bin bag." She exchanged a more telling glance with Mac this time. Wally Marsden's corpse had been covered in black plastic. Iqbal again: "Woman taking a short cut to the car park nearly fell over it."

Bev frowned. Plenty of gobby pissheads around, no woman; probably still in a state of shock. "So where is she?"

Iqbal found the ground fascinating.

"We let her go." Rees chewed gum.

"You did what?" Keeping a steady voice wasn't easy. Key witnesses didn't get to go. Not before they'd talked to a detective.

Rees folded defensive arms. "Stroppy cow said she had to get back to the kids."

"Stroppy cow with vital information perhaps?" Hands on hips.

"We got her name and address." And Bev got a sullen scowl from Danny boy.

"What you want, the Queen's Police Medal?"

Rees spread his hands. "We tried…"

"Not hard enough. See to it, Mac." She barged past, and down the alleyway, shuddered as a rat the size of a cat crossed her path. Another was tearing into the body's temporary shroud with pointy yellow teeth. She screamed at it to fuck off. It gave her a lazy contemptuous glower before slinking into the shadows, tail twitching.

When Bev saw the dead man, tears pricked her eyes. How could anyone treat another human being like that? Trussed like a carcass and dumped in dog-turd alley along with the rest of the crap. She could only make out a profile of the head and shoulders through the split plastic. The body must've been balled and bound to fit inside. Difficult to gauge but she reckoned the victim had to be below average height, weight. Didn't look that old either, mid-twenties perhaps. A single eye stared balefully from the battered face on to a strip of concrete liberally splattered with gum and phlegm like some kind of grotesque artwork. Ditto the walls; brickwork was virtually covered in gang tags and aerosol street murals.

Not sure how long she stood there taking it in before Mac gently tapped her arm. "OK, boss?"

"Whoop-de-do." She sighed, sick to the stomach, sick of dragging her sorry ass round shitty crime scenes, sick of seeing the depths to which some people sank. She watched Mac's gaze follow the depressing route hers had already travelled. Couldn't do much else till Overdale showed.

"Pathologist's on the way, boss." Even the joker sounded jaded.

Bev nodded, knew Mac would've put in the call. She couldn't see the boys from Blue having the nous.

Mac folded burly arms across his chest, continued surveying the scene. "Reckon it's down to the Disposer, sarge?"

"Oh yes." She tilted her head at the wall. Surprised Mac hadn't spotted it. The killer had left a message this time. In among the graffiti, in among the multi-coloured gang tags, crew names, clenched fists, raised fingers. One word: Disposed.

"Had your chips, mate." Mouth down, Bev nodded at the Fry-by-night. A guy in chef's checked strides stood in the middle of the pavement lowering steel shutters.

Mac shrugged, flicked the ignition. "Could be worse."

"Got that right." Ending your life as rat food in a back alley took the biscuit. Bev shuddered. The pathologist was pretty sure vermin had caused some of the damage to the victim's face. Blunt instrument was probably responsible for the rest. Overdale thought maybe smooth stone, hammer, something of the sort. Scene of crime guys were still working under auxiliary lighting, searching for the murder weapon, any evidence they could lay fingertips on.

Bev rubbed a hand over her face; skin felt tight, dry. "Best talk to the woman who found the body, first thing."

"Jodie something-or-other," Mac said. "Lives up in Greenfield Road. I'll grab a word on my way in."

Bev nodded. She'd covered the young uniforms' backs when she'd brought Flint up to speed on the phone. Didn't mention Mo and Danny had allowed the witness to take off. She seriously doubted they'd make the same mistake again. Not given the aural fleas she'd dished out. Both officers had apologised properly, and Mo fetched coffees all round from Subway. Least the kids were now on the learning curve. Flint probably hadn't even taken in the peripheral stuff. Not given the Disposer had claimed his third victim.

Establishing the victim's identity would be a priority tomorrow. Glance at the dash. Make that today. The clock showed 00.05. Her yawn revealed a set of tonsils. Mac must've registered both. He gave a warm smile. "Best get you home, Cinders."

"What's that make you?"

He waggled his eyebrows. "Handsome prince?"

"Is the stand-up that good?" Seemed an age since they'd legged it from the Crack House.

"Better."

"Course it is."

Baldwin Street was next left. Bev could easily have walked, but was shattered, couldn't wait to pull back the duvet. Mac parked outside. She grabbed her bag, reached for the door.

"Not inviting me in for a nightcap, sarge?" He kept a straight face; she could tell it was a wind up.

"Nightshade, maybe."

"Take that as a no, shall I?" He sniffed.

She had one Doc on the pavement before remembering the gift she'd been carrying round all night. She sat back, searched her bag. "Bought your Joe a little pressie." During the Bullring shop athon. She reckoned the lad could do with a bit of cheering up, being stuck in hospital and all that. Still ferreting, she didn't spot Mac's puzzled frown. Yo! She flourished the boy's gift, flashed an almost beautiful smile, trumpeted a triumphant: "Da-da."

Mac peeked. In the bag was a pink fluffy bunny. His boy was called George; an eight-year-old seriously into Transformers. Mac hadn't the heart to tell her. "You'll make a wonderful mum, Bev."

"Yeah, I will, won't I?" She winked then warily searched his face. "You winding me up?"

MONDAY
23

"The victim's Todd Freeman, he was twenty-four years old, lived in Aston." Anna Kendall with an early morning alarm call. "Says here, he was released six months ago."

Hair mussed, Bev was propped on one elbow in bed, cheek creased from where she'd been sleeping on a Jeffrey Deaver. Not that the novel wasn't thrilling, she'd just been too knackered from real life twists to keep her eyes open. They were saucer-wide now.

"What else has he got?" Bev asked. Meaning Matt Snow. Anna was at the subs' desk, reading from a monitor. Sneak preview. Bev swung bare legs out of bed, winced at the temperature, central heating didn't kick in till six. She missed the last few words. "Say again, Anna. Didn't catch it."

It was difficult, she said. If anyone heard the call, she'd be shown the door. "I've given you the top lines anyway, Bev." Sure had. Freeman had apparently served two years in Winson Green for child abuse. He'd been attacked by fellow inmates, and got a load of press after threatening to sue the Home Office for damages.

"Hold on…" There was a frown in Anna's voice. "There's a note here… says Matt's working on a related item… needs to go next to the lead." Bev heard papers rustling, pictured Anna searching for clues. "Nothing obvious here, but it'll all be in the early edition."

"Hit the streets 'bout ten?"

"Yeah," Anna said. "I hope the head start helps."

She smiled. "Sure will." And get her a gold star from Flint. She needed it. She wanted several words in private with the boss

164

later that day; a little leverage might help her case.

Still holding the phone, she slipped an arm into her Snoopy dressing gown. Oz's smell clung to the fabric. She quashed the same thought every morning. "Any sign of Snow, Anna?"

Not so much as a flake of dandruff. Anna said the reporter had e-mailed his copy. She thought the police might find him at his flat.

"You're a star, Anna Kendall. Catch you later."

But Snowie first. Bev hit a number. Minutes later a squad car was on its way to bring him in.

The Highgate jury was split. Picking up the buzz going round the nick, Bev reckoned it was fifty-fifty. Powell was either police hero or dickhead. Wherever two or three cops were gathered together, canteen, coffee machine, corridor, there was only one topic being kicked around, and everyone shooting their mouth. Bev sighed. Shame Vince Hanlon wasn't jury foreman.

"Took guts to tackle that yob." The veteran sergeant had caught some of the breakfast telly footage. "There was no time to pussyfoot around." Vince parked brawny arms coated in silver hair on his paunch. "Now Mike gets it in the neck for thinking on his feet."

Apart from the mind-boggling choice of anatomical phrases, Bev was with Vince hundred per cent. "I was there, mate. You're preaching to the converted." It wasn't as if they could afford to lose an experienced player. Not when it was three-nil to the Disposer. Four counting Gladys Marsden.

"Some nutter running rings round Flint doesn't help," Vince moaned. "I'm not saying he's not a decent enough boss…"

Flint's shiny black lace-ups appeared in Bev's eye-line. Vince was oblivious to the DCS descending the stairs behind. Her sudden coughing fit stopped Vince landing himself in the excrement. She'd got his drift anyway: bad enough being made to look a fool by one of the villains, how much worse when it was down to one of your DIs?

"This it, Vince?" Reason she was there: envelope on the desk with an *Evening News* miniature masthead and her name in copperplate. As Flint exited down the corridor, she grabbed a handful of Vince's humbugs. "Best keep me sweet, big guy." She winked. "Or I'll grass you up to Flint."

The library pic had been couriered from the *News* building, courtesy of Anna Kendall. Bev studied it, coffee in the other hand, as she walked upstairs. Curly black hair, good skin, even white teeth: Todd Freeman didn't look like a paedophile. Doh, Beverley. They don't all look like clones of the devil. She sniffed, elbowed the door to the murder room without spilling a drop. Lucky. It was the inaugural outing for the trousers. Shame bad guys didn't look the part, she mused further, had it tattooed across their forehead. The good guys would be out of a job in no time. Bring it on. Her wry smile faded fast. Either way Freeman hadn't deserved to end up as rats' takeaway. The bleak thought unlocked last night's bad dream: bared teeth, babies, bin bags. She shuddered, censored the unwanted images fast.

Cup keeping a chair warm, Bev searched a drawer for Blu Tack, fixed the print to the latest in a lengthening line of white-boards. Gruesome shots from last night's crime scene were already displayed. Hands on hips, she focused on the latest exhibit. Ante-mortem, Freeman was definitely easy on the eye.

"Wotcha, sarge."

"Daz." She fluttered fingers in distracted greeting before taking her front row pew. Squad members not already working scenes drifted in. Fifteen men, seven women. Doubtless Flint would be asking for more officers, more resources, assuming he was still senior investigating officer. Rumour had it the brass wanted to hand overall control for Operation Wolf to an assistant chief constable. Smart money was on Les Nixon, ACC Operations. Speculation was also rife as to who would head up the Milton Place inquiry. It'd be a right slap in the face if Flint were shifted sideways. Mind, Highgate was riddled with rumour mills.

Bev sipped coffee, earwigged Daz's banter with a couple of DCs. Sounded as if he was running a sweepstake on the duration of Powell's suspension. She tutted, shook her head. Despite more run-ins with the DI than a racetrack, she felt sorry for Powell. Much as anything, she didn't think he had a lot going in his life apart from the job. Still... "How much, Daz?" She reached in her bag, handed him a couple of quid, took a folded piece of paper.

"OK, boss?" Mac parked his bum on the next seat. Bacon fat fumes wafted from the lumberjack shirt. No prizes for guessing he'd graced the canteen with his presence.

"Dandy. Sauce round your gob, mate."

"Ta." A glint in the eye meant he was honing a comeback line. It wasn't delivered; Flint's brisk entrance saw to that. The DCS strode in waving a tape in his hand. Came to the point before reaching the front. "I'm not saying it's the break, but it's a lead."

The squad's body language altered in an instant, sprawled legs were drawn in, slumped bodies straightened. Flint talked as he inserted the tape into a machine. "Woman called the hotline this morning, wouldn't give her name." He lifted a finger for hush; superfluous given the room was pin-drop silent.

The husky voice was local, maybe middle-aged. It described a strange man hanging round the perimeter fence at Lidl's car park on the day Philip Goodie was attacked: short, skinny, blond hair, sticky-up fringe, brown suit, shifty-looking. "Must've been there forty minutes at least," she droned. "Saw him when I arrived, still there when I'd done me shopping."

So why not come forward earlier, lady? Bev frowned. Trouble

with anonymous calls, you couldn't put a supplementary or six.

"Sound like anyone we know?" Flint's lips formed a thin line.

Rhetorical question. Everyone in the room knew the tape pointed a finger at Matt Snow. Make that two fingers. Seeing as word got round here faster than MRSA, they'd also heard that Mac had phoned in from Moseley. He'd caught last night's eye witness – Jodie Mills – just as she was leaving for work. Ms Mills had placed Matt Snow at the Todd Freeman murder scene.

The news hadn't particularly excited Bev. The fact he'd been there was sure to emerge when the reporter's articles hit the streets, it didn't necessarily follow he was in the frame. Flint saw it differently. Either way, they'd soon be asking Snow for his version. The patrol had dropped him off at the nick twenty minutes ago. He was downstairs waiting to be interviewed.

Jotting a few ideas on a pad, Bev kept half an ear open as the DCS assigned tasks to the rest of the squad. The poster campaigns on the Churchill and Small Heath park were still prompting calls; the Eddie Scrivener news coverage had led to half a dozen sightings. Both meant a mountain of follow-up work. As for the latest murder, Flint was dispatching more detectives to join those already in Moseley. Loads of people lived in flats over the shops, and houses bordered three sides of the car park where the alleyway led. Lots of doors needed knocking. When Flint said Milton Place would now be treated as a separate inquiry, Bev tuned out momentarily. Operation Wolf contained more than enough to exercise her brain cells. Mulling it over, she tapped the biro against her teeth, pricked her ears at the word rumours.

Oops. She'd missed something. She glanced up, reached for her coffee, as Flint swept a searching gaze over the troops. "Whatever you may have heard, I can say categorically that ACC Nixon is not being called in. The Chief Constable sees continuity of command as vital in a case as complex as Operation

Wolf. So you'll be putting up with me for a while yet." The smile reached a corner of his mouth this time. "Piece of news you'll not have heard. Hot off the press as you might say." Get on with it, thought Bev. "It concerns SIO for the Milton Place inquiry. Obviously it depends on the medical, but lead detectives don't get much better than Bill Byford."

Coffee sprayed everywhere. She used her free hand to dab at the new trousers. Mac handed her a crumpled tissue, ran a finger round his top lip, mouthed, "Coffee moustache."

"OK now?" Flint asked.

Just perfect.

"A mention woulda been nice," Bev hissed. The loos at Highgate were deserted but it wasn't the best place to make a phone call.

"Can you zip it for two minutes?" Byford, just about keeping his cool at the other end of the line.

Considering she'd ignored him all weekend, she couldn't exit the brief fast enough to give him a piece of her mind. Seated sulkily on a down-turned toilet lid, she had her back against the wall, knees drawn up, berating him for keeping her in the dark. She was keeping an eye on the time – there was just ten minutes before her rendezvous with Flint in Interview One.

"Look, Bev," Byford soothed, "me coming back to Highgate's been on the cards for a couple of weeks. Nothing to do with Milton…"

"A coupla…" Her voice hit the ceiling, bounced off the tiles.

"Pipe down, will you?" She heard a deep intake of breath. "Why do you think I've not said anything?"

"Told me to button it a minute ago. Make your mind up."

He gave an exasperated sigh. "I didn't want anything coming out until it was definite. How do you think I'll feel if the doctor says I'm not fit enough?"

"Course he won't."

"She."

"Same diff." Her bottom lip jutted. "When you seeing her?"

"This afternoon." A tap dripped in the silence.

"Shit, guv, you could've told me." She stressed the *me*. Surely she was more than just another colleague if not – in every definition of the word – a mate. Or maybe not. Maybe the fact they'd come so close to getting it on was the reason he'd pulled out, stood her up. Despite what they'd shared over the last few months, he was still the boss. So he was putting in the distance before the big comeback.

"Now you know, what's your thinking?" That the cajolery in his voice meant he was trying to get round her. Like that would work. Professionally, having the guv back in business was the best news she'd had in ages. Finest cop she'd worked with. Personally, she no longer gave a toss. "Can't wait. Sir."

Byford interpreted the delivery not the content. "Are you still pissed off?" Swearing. Not like the guv she knew and loved. Once upon a time.

"Pig in shit, me. Sir." She pulled a face. Not the smartest remark given the location.

"Pity's sake, Bev, even when I worked there you didn't call me sir. How much longer are you planning to keep this up?"

"Coulda told me face-to-face." Stead of leaving the equivalent of a Dear John letter on the answerphone.

"I'd no idea Flint was going to shout his mouth…"

"Not work. The weekend. You. Having better things to do." She scowled, reckoned maintenance ought to fix that tap.

"Is that what this is all about?" He took the silence as a yes. He came close to hanging up; she was wearing his patience thin. Then he realised that for Bev even to make the call, let alone reveal the vulnerability, was a massive step in Morriss-world. And he owed her an explanation.

"If looking out for my son was a better thing to do then…

guilty as charged." She heard the stroke of an eyebrow, listened as he talked her through Rich's call, how he'd spent the weekend trying to help. "He needed me, Bev."

And I didn't? She thought it through, recognised the guv had a strong case, realised she'd probably always put her kids first. So busy cogitating, she almost missed the best bit. "And… God help me, Bev…" He paused, maybe to let her catch up, or let it sink in. "I need you."

She closed her eyes, chewed her bottom lip. Maybe she'd been a tad hasty. "'Kay." She dragged a sleeve across her nose. "Just don't start bossing me round when you get back." Her face was one big smile. "Joke."

24

"Tell me, Sergeant Morriss, did I say something funny?" Flint sounded genuinely baffled, but affected bewilderment creased his face. Cops were good actors, great at dissembling. Must be the bad company they keep. In this case: Matt Snow.

Bev, seated behind a metal table at Flint's right, ostentatiously checked a notebook. Not that she'd written anything. No point given the exchange was being recorded. Snow wasn't to know she hadn't taken down his every word.

"Nope." She traced a virgin page with her finger. "Here y'go, chief. You informed Mr Snow he'd been placed at the scene of a crime. Can't say it has me rolling in the aisles."

It was pushing the veracity envelope a tad but hey, Snow hadn't heard what the anonymous caller had said. Not that he looked moved either way. Sprawled in a hard chair opposite, the reporter chewed a hangnail on his thumb. He was getting to be an old hand at this lark: this was his third police interview under caution. Again, he'd eschewed a brief. "When is it? I'll see if I can get an hour off work."

Flint's bafflement wasn't faked this time. Nor Bev's. "What?" she asked.

"ID parade." He spat a tiny piece of flesh on to the cracked lino. "The eye witness who can pick me out?" The smirk hadn't altered an iota. "Bring it on."

Bluff or bullshit? Either way a husky female voice on the phone didn't add up to a bean, let alone a row of the things.

"Are you denying you were in Lidl's car park around the time of Philip Goodie's murder?" Flint asked.

"Dunno." More nail nibbling. "When'd he die?" The nail stuff couldn't just be a gesture to convey insouciance, as Bev first thought. The skin round his fingers was raw, every nail bitten to the quick and beyond. And one skinny leg encased in crumpled brown polyester, pumped like a piston. He straightened slightly, loosened his tie. "Anyway, since when's shopping at Lidl's been a punishable offence?"

"So you were there?" Flint said.

"Nah. Cheap gag."

Flint rose, walked round, perched on the desk, invaded Snow's space. The flicker of unease across the reporter's face was fast; so fast Bev wondered if she'd imagined it.

"Could cost you dear, Mr Snow."

The reporter looked away first. "I wasn't there, OK. It's his word against mine."

"Hers," Bev corrected.

"Whatever."

Flint and Bev exchanged brief glances, a nod to step up the pressure. "What is it with you and crime scenes, Mr Snow?" Flint ticked them off on his fingers. "Wally Marsden. Philip Goodie. Todd Freeman." Was there shock in the sudden silence? Naming Freeman should've knocked Snow for six. Local radio's top line on the story was that a man found murdered had yet to be identified. The *Evening News* hadn't hit the streets yet. The reporter opened his mouth; changed his mind.

"What is it, Mr Snow?"

"Nothing."

"Surprised we're up to speed? That we haven't had to 'read all about it'." Flint's voice snarled with contempt. "See, here's the thing." The DCS glared, folded his arms. "If the Disposer just wants you to write his story, if he feeds you the information, if he tells you what to say, why do you go to the crime scenes at all? Let alone get there before anybody else."

"I'm a reporter. It's what I do."

Flint raised a sceptical eyebrow. Snow's were knotted in concern.

173

Bev reckoned it was the first genuine emotion he'd failed to hide.

"Is it, Mr Snow?" He sniffed. "Is that all you do?" The eye contact lasted seven, eight seconds before Flint rose, walked back to his original seat.

"Hold on a minute," Snow asked. "Where's this going?"

Flint ignored the question, leaned forward, elbows on desk, gazed at Snow as if he was an exhibit in a freak show. "Would you say you're a violent man, Mr Snow?"

The pale blue eyes darkened. "Meaning?"

"Ever glassed a bloke," Bev said helpfully. "That clear enough?" He mumbled something that sounded like *bitch*. "Didn't catch that, Mr Snow." Bright smile from Bev. "Once more for the tape, please." He leaned back, arms folded. "Mr Snow refuses to repeat his statement."

She leaned forward, lowered her voice. "Son-of-a-bitch." Spat out. "Jack Pope could've lost an eye."

"It was self defence. Pope was off his face."

"Liar. Unprovoked attack is what it was." Normal volume now. "So to answer DCS Flint's question…?" Flint cocked an expectant head.

"I need the loo. I want a break."

She curled a lip. "Locking up's what you need."

Flint twirled a pen in his fingers. "Ever met him?" The sudden change of tack was pre-arranged. Bev scanned Snow's face for the slightest tic, the tiniest signal that might say more than words. The reporter's face was frozen. The piston leg had stilled too.

Recovery came, but not quick. He licked dry lips. "Met who?" As if he didn't know. Snow was playing for time.

"Your psycho pen pal," Bev sneered.

The reporter's gaze flicked between his interrogators. Bad cop. Worse cop.

"Well?" Flint prompted. "Have you?"

Snow's head dropped to his puny chest. "No."

"Didn't catch it, Mr Snow."

"No!" Snow shrieked.

"Let's see if I've got this right." More ticked fingers. "You've never met your informant, you don't have a name, a number, or any means of contacting him."

"Like he's going to tell me," Snow snarled.

"Hear that, sergeant?" Flint turned his mouth down. "Mr Snow appears to be the official mouthpiece of the Invisible Man."

Bev sniffed. "That the same as non-existent?"

The reporter nodded slowly, ashen-faced. "I see what you're doing. I get it now. You bastards aren't gonna shoot the messenger. You're gonna stitch me up and throw away the key."

"I'd say that's another one of your little fantasies, Mr Snow." Flint stood, signalling the end of the session. "I'm giving you some time to think about what you're doing. I strongly advise you to consider your position. Sort the fact from the fiction."

Mid-morning. The canteen at Highgate was quiet. Couple of traffic wardens quaffing tea, and a pair of community support officers at the counter. The plastic plods were stocking up on Penguins and bottled water. Bev sat at a window table in a shaft of strong sunlight, picked a hair from a corned beef and tomato bap. Flint had stumped up for the coffees. She suspected the DCS thought there was a crack in the case, and they'd soon be celebrating with more than Nescafé.

"Reckon he's up for it?" Bev asked, pulling a face as she extracted another hair. Maybe one of the caterers was moulting.

"Up for something. Wish I knew what." He pursed his lips. "He's either devious or dangerous."

"Dickhead or dupe." She sniffed. "Make that both."

"You don't see him as a killer?" He popped a couple of sweeteners into a steaming mug.

Mouth full, she waggled a wavering hand. She and Snow went back a fair few years. Her instinct said no. Then again, she'd never have envisaged him taking a bottle to anyone. Jack Pope had definitely not been drunk. Snow had played fast and loose with the truth there. She wondered if his grasp on reality was any stronger. Either way instinct wasn't evidence. If Snow's hands were dirty with something other than newsprint, they needed to find out what – and stand it up in court.

"Dunno," she said. "Think we've got enough for a warrant?" Search of Snow's home, motor, might uncover proof one way or the other. That the so-called Disposer existed or was a figment of what Flint clearly saw as Snow's fevered imagination.

The DCS leaned in, held her gaze, lowered his voice. "Not with what we've got."

"Best get some more then." She frowned. Was Flint talking cutting corners? Bending procedures? Dangerous territory given Snow's accusations of police embroidery. She'd stitch up Snow like a shot, but only because the bloke was falling apart. As well as the state of his nails, he smelt as if he could do with a wash, his clothes were none too clean and his face was the colour of lard except for the pus in his spots.

Bev chucked what was left of the food on her plate. Couldn't stomach it any more, nor, if she'd read it right, Flint's innuendo.

"What about the headaches?" It was another box to be ticked or not on the doctor's clipboard. Jo Esler looked more media woman than medico. Early thirties, casually dressed, blonde hair in sleek ponytail; her regular features were usually set in a smile. No white coat syndrome in Doctor Esler's consulting room. Byford still felt apprehensive. The detective slipped an arm into a crisp white shirt, took a quick peek at how he'd scored so far.

Blood pressure. Heart. Chest. Reflexes. Looked like a clear round.

"Headaches…?" Byford fastened the top button. "Remind me…" He hoped what Bev called his George Clooney smile would conceal the barefaced lie. The searing pain was unforgettable, but they struck much less frequently now, and his balance was virtually back to normal.

Doctor Esler rolled her eyes. She'd treated Byford since the night of the attack, almost certainly saved his life. She'd come to know and respect the big man. She was also wise to his little ways. "How many a week, Bill? And let's have the truth."

Byford resumed his seat. "Maybe one a fortnight." Esler's eyebrows were almost as eloquent as the big man's. "OK, OK," Byford ceded. "Two."

"So that's twice weekly." She made a note. "Do they respond to pain relief?"

Occasionally. "Sure, and they're nowhere near as intense." Esler applied her visual lie detector test. Byford held the diagnostic gaze, managed not to shift in the seat. The detective wasn't being foolish. There was no point trying to swing the medical if he wasn't ready to go back to work. Physically, he reckoned he was eighty, eighty-five per cent fit, and resigned to the fact that was it for the foreseeable. The thought of early retirement was appealing, too appealing. If he didn't go back soon, he never would. And though tempted, he wasn't ready for that.

Esler ticked another box. Her grateful patient breathed a mental sigh of relief. "How do you feel about three days a week, Bill? See how it goes."

Byford saw a part-time lame duck with two Achilles heels. "No way."

"Glad you thought it through." Esler smiled. "Can't say I'm surprised. You're stubborn as a mule."

Byford reached for his jacket. "Clean bill of health, then, doctor?"

She turned her mouth down. "Slightly soiled, I'd say. But probably in excellent working order."

Bev had worked through more lunch breaks than she'd had hot dinners. Not this one. She fed coins into a hungry ticket machine, swallowed the last bite of blueberry muffin, checked her watch. Given the twenty-minute drive across town, she calculated she had quarter of an hour at most. Why'd hospital car parks cost an arm and a leg?

A steroids 'r' us security guard patrolled the General's main entrance. She flashed a warrant card. The gorilla searched her bag anyway. Cursory check though or it would've taken a month.

"Health hazard that," he snarled. Cheeky sod wiped a hand on his trousers, pointed to the right. "Reception's..."

"I know." The General was second home to a lot of cops. Mostly on account of crims. She grabbed directions from the desk, headed for the lifts, halted halfway down the ward. No sign of Powell. "Buggery-bollocks."

"I beg your pardon?" It was an admonition, not an apology. Bev turned. A matronly sister stood there, lips puckered, hands buried in surplus hip flesh.

Bev couldn't be doing with the aggro. "Running late, love. Visiting Mike Powell. Know where he is?"

"Outside regular hours, you're not." Sister Smug folded her arms, tapped a foot. "Unless you're next-of-kin."

"Wife." Blue eyes blazed. "That kin enough?"

"Babe." Powell in grey silk PJs, wrapped an arm round Bev's shoulder, pecked her cheek. "I didn't know you cared." Fatso was clearly sceptical. He confided sombrely, "We're estranged, you know." Bev wanted to strangle him. He planted another peck. "Good to see you, chicken." She itched to wring his neck. "Excuse us, Mary." He smiled. "Bev and I have so much catching up."

The DI led her to relative safety. "Mrs P, eh?" He grinned, lying on his side, blond hair ruffled for what must be the first time in history. Bev slumped into a visitor's chair. "Breathe a word, ever," she hissed, "and you're dead."

"Feel better already." His lip still twitched. "So what you doing here?"

"That's nice."

"Surprised to see you that's all."

Bev was surprised, too. Apart from the bruise on his left temple, Powell looked fit as well as fairly tasty. The casual look suited him better than the customary sharp tailoring. Mind, dressing down didn't get much lower than jim-jams. "Not at death's door, then?"

"Nah." He stroked the side of his head. "Observation mainly. Should be out tomorrow. Where's my grapes?"

"Tesco?" She suspected he was trying to keep the chat light, noticed a slight tremor in his hands. Lonely places, hospitals. Especially for someone who never talked about family, whose wife had buggered off years ago, and whose professional life hung in the balance. No time for social niceties though.

"What you did was freaking stupid." His knuckles turned white. She looked him in the eye. "And I'd've done exactly the same." If she were Powell. And felt guilt for losing a young officer in a fire. "It got to you, didn't it?"

"What you on about?" Seemed to her the snarl was token.

"I was there, Mike. I saw it." The use of his Christian name was a first. Maybe it was that, maybe the warmth in eyes as blue as it gets. Still he hesitated. She sat forward, reached for his hand. It took more than quarter of an hour for it all to spill out. He told her about the trauma he'd gone through when Simon was killed, the continuing night terrors, the torment he'd felt watching impotently as events unfolded outside Milton Place.

"Had to do it, Bev. No choice." He searched her face for approval.

"Saved a life, Mike."

"Yeah. And lost a job."

"Don't know that." Nor was he aware of the leverage she might now have with Flint.

"Guy's in here you know." Powell had been visiting the sick when she arrived. Apparently the young victim was in the next ward. "Shattered nose, jaw, cheekbone, detached retina."

"Live though, won't he? Why'd they go for him?"

"He's no idea. No convictions for sex offences. No one said anything, just dragged him out."

"Mistaken identity?"

Powell shrugged. "Who knows?"

Briefly she told him how it was panning out: twenty-two arrests, eighteen remanded on bail, four blokes in custody refusing to give more than their names. The DI was still thinking about the guy he'd saved. "He thanked me for helping him, Bev."

She smiled. "Deserve it, mate." No wonder he'd been in high spirits earlier. "Best hit the road." She reached for her bag. "You like blueberry muffins?"

"Yeah."

"Me too. Next time maybe. Ciao."

She was four beds away when he shouted. "Hey, babe, I want a divorce."

"Bite me."

25

"Much as it grieves me, I think we'll have to let him go." It was Flint's verdict after the day's second session with Matt Snow, the latest with his brief banging on about rights. Early evening now and Bev was in Flint's office reviewing the interview and the evidence – lack of.

Forensically, nothing linked Snow to the murders. No prints, hairs, skin cells, fibres. On the witness front, one anonymous phone call did not a conviction next summer make. As to motive, whatever Flint's opinion, Bev thought it was questionable, if not risible. Killing as a career move? I don't think so. One thing she was sure of: Snow had vital information, and he wasn't sharing. They could probably hang a police obstruction charge round his scrawny neck, but...

"Know what they say about giving people enough rope?"

"If we release him... he'll incriminate himself?" Flint was chucking balls of paper in the bin.

"Guy won't do diddly in custody." Set him loose, he might slip up. And they only had Snow's word that he'd not got up close and personal with the Disposer. Assuming the bastard existed, surely there'd be physical contact at some stage?

"We'd need a tail." Flint's missile went wide.

"Natch."

"Twenty-four-seven. Doesn't come cheap. I'll give it some thought." Another wide ball.

Bev shrugged. What price a life? Thank God Anna Kendall wasn't charging for sleuthing on the side.

"What do you make of this?" Flint turned a newspaper to face her, *Evening News,* late edition.

She'd already seen it, still couldn't work out why Snow had

messaged the desk to hold the front page. "Ain't gonna set the world on fire, is it?" The sidebar wasn't much more than a re-run of the Disposer's first letter: I am our children's saviour. Paedophiles are scum. Paedos are vermin, yada yada. Bev narrowed her eyes, envisaging a cat among the pigeons. Make that a feather-ruffling pig. "Why don't we write to him? The Disposer?"

Flint's ball hand stilled mid-air as he stared at her. "Saying?"

She leaned forward, elbows on knees. "The guy thinks he's smart, right? Leading the dance, calling the tune, writing the script…"

"I get the picture."

"'Kay. So we ask him something only the killer could know." While Flint thought that through, she ran a mental checklist of some of the information they'd withheld from the media. "What about the spray paint in the alley? No one outside the squad knows about that."

"And?" He was prepping another missile.

Just let me get my crystal ball. "Depends what we get back." She sniffed. "It could prove whoever's writing's genuine."

Flint shrugged. "There's no doubt the killer was behind the first letter. There's privileged information in it."

"Yeah. The first." She let that sink in. "What if there's a copycat clown out there?"

He threw the ball from hand to hand, four or five passes, then laid it on the table, game over. "We'd have to run it past the lawyers. Police using the press to correspond with criminals raises all sorts of issues, ethical questions." He gave her a fleeting smile. "Joined-up thinking though, Bev. I like that."

Ain't gonna like this. "Not my baby, boss."

"Oh?"

"DI Powell's. Saw him in hospital. Lunchtime." She was taking his name in vain: Powell wouldn't have a clue what she was on about. Bigging up the DI was more leverage in her one-woman campaign to get him back in harness. Fact that so far there'd been no media mauling helped; the DI was a hero according to the *Post's* leader column.

Flint's thin lips almost disappeared. "Powell's not on the inquiry." He reached for a file: case closed.

No one said it'd be easy. She straightened, aimed for gravitas. "Mike Powell saved a man's life out there, sir."

"Potentially jeopardising the entire operation." Chipped ice.

"It was a calculated risk. You ever taken one?" Supplication? Insubordination? Knew she was treading a fine line.

"He disobeyed an order, sergeant."

"An order issued before the immediate threat to a man's life, sir." God's sake, Bev, tell it like it is. She spread her hands. "That bloke was toast any second." Waited till he made eye-contact. "Powell couldn't stand idle and watch a repeat performance of Monk's Court." She put some spin on what the DI had confided earlier. That he'd acted on instinct, initiative; doing nothing wasn't an option. Flint listened, nodded a few times. Bev thought it was in the bag.

"Thanks for that, sergeant." The DCS picked up a slim gold pen, started writing.

Bev closed her gaping mouth. "And?"

"I'll bear it in mind at the inquiry."

OK. Bull by the bollocks. "We need senior officers like Mike Powell, sir." Again she waited. Her eyes held more meaning than the words. Was Flint up to the interpretation? "The DI wouldn't bend a rule if it bit him in the bum. He's as straight as a die." She couldn't afford to query Flint's integrity straight out. If mistaken, it would be professional suicide.

Cold stare. "Is that why you're still sergeant?" If attack was the best form of defence, he'd got her drift. And like Bev, he was treading carefully. Maybe they had the measure of each other.

"Nah." She gave a brittle laugh. "Too lippie for the men in

grey, me." She'd never get further than DS cause she didn't lick arse, and didn't stay in line. Never crossed an important one though.

Flint leaned back, crossed his arms, looked her over. "Yes." The word had three syllables.

Waste of sodding time. She gathered her bits, grabbed her bag. Gobbing off had done squat for the DI and now she'd made an enemy of Flint. Great day's work.

He reached for the paper ball, played it between his hands. "Pick your battles better in future, Bev."

She rose. "Sir."

"Soon as he's fit, I'll ask Powell to take on admin duties pending the inquiry." The bin pinged as the ball went in. "I'd already made the decision."

Bev could barely speak her teeth were clenched so tight. He'd let her bang on like a drum kit. "So all this…"

"Was very revealing. It taught me a lot about you." She so didn't like the sound of that. Nor Flint's thin smile. She didn't trust the man. He might know more about her. She was kidding herself thinking she'd got his measure.

Quit while you're not ahead, Beverley. She turned at the door. "Hope it taught you I don't jump hoops. Not for you. Nor anyone."

"Oh go on, sweetheart." The plea was from Bev's mum asking her to Sadie-sit. Emmy rarely asked a favour, but she had tickets for a Cliff Richard concert, the regular sitter had pulled out and Bev's gran was throwing a wobbly. Mobile tucked under chin, Bev was rifling her knicker drawer. She'd only just chilled since the Flint altercation. The drive home helped, as had the passion fruit smoothie.

"Any other night, ma, I'd be there in a flash." She'd already said no, twice. She heard a querulous Sadie kick off in the background, pictured her mum's lovely face, saw the disappointment. Bev tightened her lips, knew the scumbag who'd attacked Sadie was to blame for all this. Three years on and her gran's nerves were worse. The old lady rarely ventured out, was petrified staying in, especially on her own.

"'Kay, love. No worries. What are you up to? Something exciting?" Pollyanna Emmy versus Bev-the-heel-Morriss. No contest. Her mum reckoned Cliff was the bee's bollocks.

Bev closed the drawer. "Time you want me, ma?"

It was Byford's fault. He'd phoned earlier, said he'd try to book a table this evening at San Carlo to celebrate passing the medical. Hadn't phoned back to firm anything up. She was pulling faces in the mirror a minute later when Frankie strolled in with the phone.

"Good God, Bevy, you're never gonna wear that, are you?" A pink leopard print thong dangled from the drawer. She took the phone, gave Frankie the finger. "Hey, guv. Sorry 'bout this…"

Not tonight, Joseph.

"Don't turn round. Do exactly as I say." The crap line in a Marlon Brando mumble was from a B-for-bad movie. Matt Snow had more sense than to show his derision. But he'd expected something original from the Disposer. The reporter shot an involuntary glance in the driving mirror. And froze. That was original all right. No wonder the voice was muffled. Dark eyes glinted beneath the grille of a burqa. Snow looked away but not before split second eye contact in the glass.

Almost midnight now, the reporter had hit a few dives after the cops let him go. Hadn't been too hammered to spot a back seat passenger in the Fiesta as the cab dropped him outside the flat. The reporter had no doubt who his uninvited guest was. No point walking away from it, they had to deal sooner or later. Didn't stop Snow cacking himself though. In a weird way he was partly relieved. During the latest police grilling, he'd begun to doubt the killer's existence himself.

"I think we need to talk, don't you, Matthew?" Less muffled this time. Male. Educated.

"Sure. That'd be good." It sounded as if Snow had a pond of jumpy frogs in his throat.

Rustling from the back, sudden movement. "On edge, Matthew?" Snow felt cold steel at his neck, hot breath in his ear.

Jesus Christ. No. Not like this. Whirling thoughts. Darting fears. Body immobile. Warm blood trickled already where the blade bit into skin.

"I'm not going to hurt you, Matthew. We still have work to do, don't we?" Terror and the knife's pressure paralysed Snow. The Disposer used the blade to underline the point. "Don't we, Matthew?" Snow winced. "I'll take that as yes. When I remove the knife, don't open your mouth unless I tell you. If you turn round, I kill you. Clear?"

Another wince. The pressure eased. The fingers Snow ran round his neck came back sticky, stinking of blood. "Flesh wound, Matthew. Nothing to worry about." An opened box of tissues landed on the passenger seat.

Snow cut another glance in the mirror. Imagined the bastard had a sly grin under the headgear. Not that he could tell. He could stare at the reflection until the cows left home, and still be unable to provide a decent description. Shame that. Because this time the psycho had gone too far.

"So... current state of play? I'm pleased, Matthew. I think I can trust you." Snow clenched his fists. "Between you and me, the mission's almost over and as we know, that's when your work really begins." Snow's frown deepened. "Come, come, Matthew, you must have realised that once the project's complete my part is over. I've no intention of getting caught, going to prison, being punished for doing the world a favour. The plan was always to kill myself. Don't look like that, Matthew! I'll make sure you have everything you need: the biographical material, the photo albums, we can still tape the interviews. You were always going to be the writer." He paused. "Think of me as the ghost."

He talked for five minutes. Paedophiles had destroyed his childhood, he told Snow. Gave chapter and stomach-turning verse. There were two monsters he still wanted to kill, then he'd take his own life. When he named names, Snow would realise just how big the story was. As well as the glory, he promised the reporter a cool half-million.

A brown envelope appeared at Snow's shoulder. "A little advance, Matthew."

Bloodstained fingers trembled as he tore the envelope. Snow gasped; beer-laced bile caught in his throat, tears stung his eyes. The photograph showed Snow's mother, naked, stepping out of the shower.

"Advance warning, Matthew. Fuck with me." The blade appeared, skewered the print. "I fuck with her."

Snow dropped his head in his hands, bony shoulders shook as he sobbed. Any idea of talking to the cops vanished in that instant. He was way out of his depth. It had been a dangerous game. And he was no longer playing.

TUESDAY

26

"Matt's phoned in sick." Anna Kendall's opening words. Bev had put in the call from her office hoping to arrange a newsroom snoop, keep up the pressure on Snow if only for an hour or so. There'd be no round-the-clock tail. Flint had vetoed it at the early brief, couldn't get it past the bean counters. Brief's only bright spot had been Flint's announcement that the guv would be back at his desk tomorrow. Bev knew already, didn't stop her cheering with the rest of the squad.

"What's up with Snow this time?" Feet on desk, she was checking her hair for split ends, decided to book a trim.

"Dicky stomach, I think."

Knew how he felt. Twice she'd thrown up in the middle of the night; so much for thinking the baby barfing was over. How much longer did it go on, for God's sake? She sniffed. Pigging out on Belgian chocolate and Bailey's with Sadie last night probably hadn't helped.

"Why the call?" Anna was breathy, expectant. "Is it the interview? Are you coming in?"

Anyone would think it was a royal visit. Telling Anna it wasn't worth the trip without Snow's presence wouldn't be the smartest move. "Love to, Anna. Bit tied up at the mo."

"Stupid of me. You must be so busy right now..." She tailed off uncertainly. Her question unanswered. "So why..."

The call? Feet. On. Think. Beverley. "Fancy a drink, tonight?" Shit. Sounded like she was hitting on her. "Be useful, like, before getting down to business." Another double entendre. Double shit. "God, that sounds..."

"A great idea." Anna laughed. "You're right. When it comes to big interviews, it's dead useful to feel you know someone a little beforehand. There's hardly ever time in this business, but on the odd occasion I've gone down that path, it's really paid off."

Time and bar sorted, inspiration struck. "Anna? One other thing you might be able to help with..."

"Call for you, boss." Mac Tyler waved a phone in the air. Bev had been prowling the squad room, pacing up and down in front of the whiteboards, gazing into dead men's eyes, rueing another dead-end day. Follow-up calls leading nowhere, run of unreturned answerphone messages and e-mails, same old. Most of the afternoon had been spent on what she un-fondly called recycling: rereading police and pathology reports, reviewing key witness statements, rewinding video footage. Trying to join the dots – see the picture. They weren't even close: dots or cops. Hundreds of officer hours, shed-loads of shoe leather, so much graft, so little to show. Make that nada.

"Who is it, mate?" Better be good. She'd been necking Red Bull, dying for a pee now.

"Bad line, sorry, boss." Could be something to do with the wire dangling from his ear. She scowled: probably listening to Five Live.

"Bev Morriss."

"Sergeant... you said to phone..." A woman's voice petered out. Bev frowned, couldn't place it. Not surprising. She'd given her numbers out more times than Directory Inquiries.

"Yeah?" Pained expression, crossed legs.

"I'm sorry to bother you, sergeant." Sounded like she had a cold. "It's Mrs Graves. Madeleine Graves."

Bev's mental Google came up with: swanky pad, husband topped himself, brownies to die for. "Mrs Graves. Thank you for calling. How may I help?" The simper turned heads with incredulous faces:

Mac, Darren New and Caz Pemberton's.

"So sorry… I'm still not thinking straight. It's such as shock."
Another anonymous letter? The widow didn't have a cold. Bev
heard it now: she'd been crying. "Slow breaths, Mrs Graves. Take
your time."

In the background, a grandfather clock chimed the half-hour.
Bev's watch had 5.20. Snuffles and sniffs then: "I discovered it
when I returned home. I just don't understand how anyone
could do such a thing."

Break-in? Place trashed? Stuff nicked? There'd been a fair few
valuables knocking about, family obviously worth a euro or two.
Bev ran her gaze down a list of local cop shops stuck on the
wall. Tudor Grange was Handsworth's patch. "Mrs Graves, best
thing…"

"I wouldn't ask, but… you were so… kind." Catch in the
throat. "Please, dear, please can you come round? I'm on my
own. I don't know what to do."

Quick calculation. It'd mean missing the late brief. She
scowled. More barely disguised flak from Flint. On the other
hand her time sheet was in rude health. And the woman was in
obvious distress. "With you in…" She frowned. Click on the
line. "Mrs Graves?"

Pensive, she dropped the phone back on its cradle. Mac was
mangling a keyboard with two fingers. "OK, boss?"

Not if she didn't get to the loo. "Gotta dash." She turned at the
door. "Mac, tell the chief I'm out interviewing witnesses."

"Straight up? Someone seen something?"

She waggled a hand. Madeleine Graves must've seen something.

Madeleine Graves stared at her late husband's portrait. Her face
was a wreck of mascara and tear tracks; his was obliterated by a
recent coat of red gloss. The stink of paint overpowered any

lingering pot pourri.

"It's completely ruined," Madeleine sobbed. "Who would do such a thing?"

Bev turned her gaze from the painting. "Did your husband have any enemies, Mrs Graves?" One. Obviously.

"Everyone loved Adam." She shook her head, dabbed her face; the handkerchief had an embroidered A. The widow's make-up was patchy now. Like her recall. Chucking a can of paint over a portrait was hardly a loving act. Loathing maybe.

Especially since nothing else appeared to have been touched. Madeleine had been at a friend's house playing bridge, arrived back around five pm, found a side door forced, fumes hit her soon as she stepped inside. Couldn't believe her eyes when she saw the damage. Not just the paint. The canvas had been badly hacked about with a blade of some sort.

"Sure nothing's missing?" Bev asked

"Of course I'm not sure." Snappy. Bev waited out the silence. Madeleine took a deep breath. "Forgive me, dear. I'm still in a state of shock."

"You had a look round?"

Brisk nod. "As far as I can tell nothing's gone, but…" She held out empty palms. "I may have missed something, I'm not…" Herself. Not with trembling hands and shaking knees.

"Sit down, shall we?" Bev tucked an arm under Madeleine's elbow, steered her gently to the kitchen. "Hot drink?" Small rituals. Big comfort. It would give the woman something to do, help her focus.

"Coffee. Thank you, dear." The widow struggled on to a stool, lavender silk skirt riding up her thighs.

Bev gave a lopsided smile. The latte machine was beyond her. She fixed instant, kept the voice casual. "Noticed any strangers hanging round? Anything suspicious?" Had to ask though they always struck Bev as daft questions. If someone clocked something iffy, surely they'd call the cops? Or maybe not. According to the tabloids, the police can't put a flat foot right these days. Any days.

"No, dear, nothing." She twisted the hankie in her hands.

"Burglar alarm on?" Madeleine's face was answer enough. "Sugar?" Bev added two spoons. "Was your son home?"

"No. Thank God." That was heartfelt. Scared Lucas might've been attacked? Or that he'd have a go? Could mean trouble either way. Ask Tony Martin. "He's staying with a friend from college." Mrs Graves stared into space, still fiddling with the hankie. "Bristol, I think he said."

"Here y'go." Bev smiled, pushed the Gold Blend Madeleine's way, hopped on to the next stool. "I know this is difficult, Mrs Graves…" Sure was. Asking a grieving widow if her bloke had any dirt on him. As well as a can of Dulux. "Did your husband have any problems at work?" Medical profession attracted lawsuits like moths round candelabra. Maybe a whingeing patient…

"Nothing." Lipstick had bled into the fine lines round her mouth. "Never."

No ambiguity. Unless he hadn't told her. People went to extraordinary lengths to keep secrets from their partners. Mind, suicide was a tad over the top.

"We told each other everything." Fond smile. "It's why our marriage was so strong."

She gently patted Mrs Graves's arm. "Sure." Sure she'd put in the checks. If litigation had been pending, presumably paper-work would still be in the system. Assuming the problem was professional.

Bev cleared her throat. "Attractive man, your husband, Mrs Graves." Posh for totty magnet.

"Yes. He was." The smile vanished as the implication sank in. "What are you saying?"

Maybe some besotted patient had read too much into his bedside manner. Hell hath no fury like a stalker scorned. Or maybe Dr Graves had a habit of stringing women along. Delicate territory. Best tread carefully. "Was he having an affair?"

Colour drained from the widow's face. For a second or two it looked as if she might keel over. "Women tended to throw themselves at my husband, sergeant." Cold stare. Yes. And? "Adam never gave them a second glance."

Not talking quick looks. "Fine." Bev smiled, made mental notes. Mrs Graves was in the dark or in denial. Or the doc was pure as the driven snow.

Every breath you take… every move… Bev's favourite track. She was driving back from the Graves's place, helping The Police with the chorus, volume almost loud enough to drown out the Nokia's ring tone. She glanced at caller ID. Penalty points or pull over to take it? Points she'd risk but not the ensuing bad press. She parked the Midget near a hole in the wall on the Alcester Road. Needed cash anyway to get in a round or two with Anna Kendall.

"Guv. How's it going?" A rocket lit up the night sky, stars cascading like a mini Niagara. Firework season started earlier every year. They'd have Easter eggs attached soon.

"Milky Bars are on me, kid." She heard the smile in his voice.

"Miss your mouth again?" Her lips curved.

"Oh, how they laughed. Table's booked. San Carlo. Seven o'clock."

"For?"

"Tonight."

Shit. Silence. Broken by Byford. "I thought we said…"

"Sorry, guv, something's come up." She told him about the meet with Anna Kendall. More silence suggested the big man was underwhelmed. "Problem with that?" she asked.

"She's a journalist, Bev. Can you trust her? Are you sure she's on your side? Not sniffing for a story that'll drop you in it?"

"Gee, guv, never thought of that." Course she'd considered it. Like she'd considered the strict guidelines on evidence gathering. She wasn't brain dead. "What you take me for?"

"Not for dinner, that's for sure." The joke, like the laughter, was weak. The warning was implicit. Sure no one's taking you for a ride?

The cab dropped Bev in Broad Street just after seven. Lights were bright, buzz was muted; in a couple of hours the area would be heaving. People out for a good time on cheap booze in noisy bars. Some ending the night behind bars on drink-related charges. Yep. Quick check. Police surveillance vans parked in the usual places.

Bev dug gloved hands in pockets, glanced at the sky. Starry starry night. No wonder it was parky. Glad of the winter coat, she headed for the Hard Rock café. Glad too she'd nipped back for a quick shower and costume change. She'd eschewed the blue look for a loose-fitting, long-sleeved blackberry frock. This was its first outing. Doubtless she'd grow into it.

A group of lads gave her the eye *en passant*. She masked a smile. Go, girl. Not lost it yet. Jack Pope once said, you scrub up good, babe. His subsequent limp only lasted an hour. Still smiling she arrived at the bar, without thinking ordered Southern Comfort. Force of habit. Used to drink here with Oz. The smile faded slowly. Fled completely when she clocked Jagger strutting his stuff on the wide screens. More Oz memorabilia. He was a Stones' groupie, knew the words to every song, and the moves. Painful memories. She didn't want to go there.

A hand waved gently in front of her. "Come in, Captain Bev."

She turned, forced a smile. "Anna. Hi. Miles away."

"Never?" She shucked off a black trench coat. Looked great in a purple smock and pixie boots. The gear wouldn't do anything for Bev. She'd resemble a club-footed aubergine. "Drink?"

Anna asked for orange juice, wandered off in search of a decent table. A few guys followed her with lecherous eyes. Kendall was sexy without being obvious.

Glasses in hand, peanuts in pockets, Bev made for the corner. She reckoned they'd be in for some preliminary small talk. Be a bit unsubtle asking the girl straight off if she'd struck oil.

"I found them." So much for preamble. Bev sat down. "Thing is," Anna continued, "there's boxes of the things. Wasn't sure how far back you wanted to go."

Neither was Bev. Her thinking was that Snow's work had almost certainly played a part in landing him in the excrement. Odds were something he'd written had got him noticed. Or someone he'd interviewed had singled him out. Or she could be barking up the wrong redwood. She'd started scouring back copies of Snow's greatest hits; the columns alone could take ages. Even then she'd only be covering what had appeared in print. What about the material that hadn't made the cut? Detail that hadn't seen the light of day? Which is where the shorthand came in. As in notebooks.

"How many you reckon are there?" Bev offered a pack of nuts.

"Cheers." She tore the wrapper with her teeth. "Hundreds."

"Oh joy." Needed narrowing down. Wheat from chaff, sheep from goats and all that. "Any stories given him a load of grief this last year or so, say?"

"Not that I know of. I could ask round if you like." She licked salt from her lips. "Don't worry. Discretion's my middle name."

Bev tilted her glass. "Cheers."

"Thought I'd bring you a dozen at a time? Not so obvious then. Not that Matt would notice."

"Oh?" Bev tore her glance away from the in-house entertainment; a bare-chested Marc Bolan was now cavorting on the screens.

Anna took a sip of juice. "Apart from the fact he's hardly ever in? I think he's got enough playing on his mind." Snippy for Anna.

"Like?" Bev asked.

She popped in a nut, chewed slowly. Thinking time? Wondering how far to go? "OK. Here's the thing. I like the guy, right?" Nod from Bev. "But I'm not sure I know who he is any more. It's like there's two of them. One minute he's Matt of old, the next he won't give you the time of day. He's pissing people off mightily. Going round the newsroom playing the big I am. Dropping hints about book deals, film rights." She paused, tapped the side of her head. "I think he's losing it."

"As in crazy man?" The thought had crossed Bev's mind a couple of times.

"As in I think he needs help." The writer reached into her case. "This lot covers the last six months or so."

"Appreciate it, Anna." Bev took the first notebook, flicked through page after page of surprisingly neat squiggles. It could've been ancient hieroglyphics to Bev. Fortunately she wouldn't be doing the deciphering.

"When you've finished, I'll get the next lot." Anna gathered the glasses. "Ready for another?"

And another. And another. Shoptalk segued into small talk, relaxed, easygoing. Drinkers and diners drifted in, as Bev and Anna touched on music, movies, books, holidays. The girl was good company. They only stopped to grab a menu, order food. Burger and fries for Bev, Caesar salad for Anna.

"God, I'd love a chip. I can't touch greasy foods at the moment." She pointed ruefully at her bump. Bev sucked hers in. Shame she'd didn't have the same problem. In six months, she'd be the size of a housing estate. Bev reckoned Anna's gesture was an unspoken no-pressure invitation to talk babies. So far, she'd studiously avoided the subject with everyone. But Anna was in the same antenatal boat. Duck the offer or dive in?

"When d'you stop being sick in the mornings?"

"Stop?" Anna smiled. "What's that?" They swapped stories,

shared fears, laughed a lot.

"Had any cravings yet?" Bev asked. She lusted after dark chocolate and cookie dough Häagen-Dazs but then she always had.

Anna pouted. "Does David Tennant count?"

"Who?"

"Doct…"

"Joke." Bev flapped a hand.

Anna rolled her eyes. "What about you? Cravings?"

Unbidden Oz's image popped into her head. "Nah. Bit early yet." She blew her cheeks out on a sigh.

"Will you stop working?"

"God, no," Bev said. "I'd go doolally. You?"

"Not an option."

"How's your partner feel about that?"

Anna dropped her gaze. "We don't see each other any more."

Foot. Mouth. Bev lifted a palm. "Sorry. No business a mine."

"Don't be." She smiled. "I'll manage. Great family. Good mates. What more does a girl want?"

Bev raised an eyebrow. "Doctor Who?"

WEDNESDAY

27

A squidgy blueberry muffin had taken squatter's rights on Bev's keyboard. Smiling, she closed the office door, strolled over for a closer look. The tiny flag stuck in the sponge read: Bite me. She shook her head, still smiling. Powell must be back in admin action. Must remember to collect her sweepstake winnings off Darren. Byford was in the building too; she'd spotted his Volvo in the car park.

Coat hung, bag slung, she took the weight off her feet, added avoirdupois with every mouth-watering calorie. Body must be telling her it needed blood sugar. Her brain certainly was. Last night's Southern Comfort was this morning's all-over ache. She made a mental note to knock the booze on the head. Bet Anna Kendall hadn't woken with a mild hangover.

Matt Snow's notebooks would soon be getting the treatment. Bev had detoured to the incident room, dropped them off with Caz Pemberton. Pembers had brilliant shorthand and was clued-up enough to know what to look for. Bev had again flicked through a few pages, apart from proper names it was still ancient Egyptian. She chucked the cake paper in the bin. Grimaced. It was a long shot anyway.

"Missed again, boss." Mac hovered in the doorframe.

"Tyler," she snapped. "Don't you ever knock?"

He shrugged, sauntered in. "Take a look at this." Handed her an overnight report.

Frown lines appeared as she read. "So?" Struck her as a bog standard mugging that went wrong. Or right. A passer-by gave chase. The attacker fled before too much damage to person, none to pocket.

"The victim," Mac said.

She glanced at the paper in her hand. "Roger Doyle?"

"Rang the squad room this morning. Reckons he had a lucky escape. Thinks he might've been the Disposer's next target."

Bev scratched her neck. "Doyle's a paedo?"

"Yeah. But he did the decent thing calling it in."

For sure. If Doyle hadn't put himself on the line, the crime wouldn't get a second look. Street robberies were two a penny. An attempted mugging wouldn't even have hit CID radar.

"Can he describe the attacker?" Bev asked.

"That's what Flint wants to know." He held her coat open.

The greying beard gave the lie to Roger Doyle's coal black mullet. Bev reckoned it was a rug anyway. She didn't give a toss if the hair was fake as long as his story stood up. Doyle examined their warrant cards closely, compared photos with faces. His was scarred by a jagged line running from the corner of the left eye. He handed back the IDs. "Can't be too careful these days, can you?" The fat man's smile revealed small crooked teeth.

Doyle's huge buttocks swayed under baggy grey slacks as he led them down a narrow hall. The bungalow smelt of baking cakes and boot polish. Bev loosened her coat. The kitchen was too hot, could do with a window being opened. One pane was boarded up with wood, sunlight showed streaks of dirt on the others.

Doyle ran a damp cloth over a spotless work surface. "Please sit down." There were two chairs round a pine table. Mac leaned against a wall. "I thought long and hard before dialling the number." His hand was steady as he poured boiling water into a teapot.

"What tipped the balance, Mr Doyle?" Bev folded her arms. Darren New had run a record check, phoned details as they drove over. Hadn't been easy listening. She felt uneasy now. It was difficult to marry the inoffensive-looking bloke making tea with a man who'd committed indecent acts against kids. Doyle had been sent down three times, seven years in total.

"I've paid my debt to society, sergeant. With interest. Justice executed inside was rougher than anything meted out by the court. Prisons are dangerous places for paedophiles." He traced the scar, left them to draw their own conclusions. Bev doubted the gesture was unwitting. Without eye contact it was difficult to be sure. Doyle was doing anything to avoid looking her in the face.

"I've been punished enough. I'm dead as far as my family's concerned. They cut me off completely after the first prison sentence. I've rebuilt my life. I have a reasonable job. The therapy's ongoing. I know what I did was wrong. I'm sure it won't happen again. As sure as I can be. But still I'm persecuted." He flapped the cloth at the broken window. "Dog mess through the letterbox, hate mail, I live with it. I have to. But last night a man tried to kill me."

That was well over the top. "Kill?"

"He had a hunting knife, sergeant."

Eyes widened. Not seen that in the report. "Did you mention…?"

"I made light of it last night. Didn't want any fuss. I told the officers I just wanted to get home. Forget about it. But I couldn't." Doyle was still rubbing at non-existent stains. "I couldn't stop thinking about the men he's killed, how many more victims there might be. He has to be stopped, sergeant."

"How'd you know it was the Disposer?"

Doyle met her eyes for the first time. "Because he told me."

Joshua Connolly was not helping police inquiries. The protester had been in custody at Highgate since Sunday night. He'd be enjoying the hospitality for at least another twenty-four hours.

Magistrates had granted the extension so that Connolly could be questioned further about his part in the disturbance at Milton Place. In four sessions over two days, he'd shared not much more than his name with previous interlocutors. The interview baton was now with a suited-and-booted Byford. Baptism of fire on the first day back. Interview Room 1 was stuffy and smelly: stale sweat, cheesy socks. Byford loosened his tie a touch.

"Why did you join the protest, Mr Connolly?" The detective was up to speed. He'd studied reports of the incident, spoken to officers who'd attended, had a detailed briefing from Flint, plus Bev's take on events. DS Frank Knox sitting alongside the guv would try to fill any gaps. Knox, a tall lanky redhead, had been one of the first on the scene.

Connolly's open-mouthed yawn revealed several fillings and complete contempt for the proceedings. The twenty-nine-year-old had history. Checks revealed he'd been a student activist at Leeds, graduated to professional pain-in-the-arse-dom. Pro-environment and animal rights, he was against abortion and the Iraq war. He'd been filmed shouting his mouth off at rallies all over the country. Convictions included criminal damage and assault. He lived in housing association property in Kings Norton with a woman and two kids. Not a silent partner, she'd turned up twice at the nick, banging on about police brutality.

Maybe action man was getting bored, wanted to stir things a bit. He unfolded his rangy denim-clad frame from the metal chair, touched his trainer-encased toes a few times then sat cross-legged on the floor. Pink flesh was visible through raggedy holes in the knees of his jeans. Connolly ran derisory green eyes over Byford. "Not seen you before, old man."

Byford shrugged a so-what? "What about Andrew Leach? Had you seen him before?"

He tossed a mousy fringe out of his eyes. "Who?"

"The man you were set on torching."

Complacent shrug.

"Just offering him a light, were you?"

"Don't smoke. Filthy habit."

"Your prints on the Zippo."

This part of the interview was academic in a way. Though Connolly had tried hiding his face under a scarf, they had enough forensic and photographic evidence to secure a conviction on the assault charge. Video footage had captured Connolly kicking Leach as he lay in the road. Fibres from Connolly's clothing had been transferred to the victim's. And vice versa. Connolly knew all this. Knew he'd go down for the attack. As to the charge of incitement... what the cops wanted to know was why Connolly had hijacked what had started out as a peaceful demonstration.

"You didn't answer the question," Byford said. "Why did you join the protest?"

He used a matchstick to pick his teeth. "You got kids, old man?"

Byford rolled his eyes. "Your point being?" As if he didn't know.

"Kids need protecting."

"Setting fire to a man will do that?" As if it was a serious question.

Knox snorted, folded his arms.

Connolly's fringe flopped; this time he let it. "Scaring the shit out of him might." It was the story he'd maintained throughout: fear not fire; he'd no intention of killing anyone.

"Got the wrong man though, didn't you?"

"They're all vermin." He spat on the lino.

"Andrew Leach served nine months for fraud. Wipe that up. Now." The order was softly spoken. It was Byford's way. The lower the volume the more menace it held. Connolly picked up on it. Sullen-faced, he dug a crumpled tissue from his pocket and complied.

Byford rose crossed his hands behind his back, silently

circuited Connolly a couple of times then, casually: "How did you meet him?"

Slight pause. Was it significant? "Who?"

"The killer." The guv's flared nostrils suggested a rank odour. "The maniac who calls himself the Disposer." Not that there was proof of a connection. It was Byford's gut instinct. Logic held that Sunday's protest was a backlash to the saturation media coverage, the countless column inches and airtime devoted to the Disposer and his killing campaign. Had Connolly hopped on a bandwagon? Or was he co-driver of a battle-bus steered by the Disposer? Had they infiltrated the demo to distract attention? Was it an elaborate sleight of hand as a young man's body was dumped in a filthy alley?

Connolly circled a finger at his temple. "Where'd you lose them?"

He meant marbles. Byford sighed. Wished he had a pound for every time he'd heard that one in an interview room. "Not very original, Mr Connolly. But you're not, are you?" He perched on the desk, a size ten brogue swinging inches from Connolly's flushed face.

"Meaning?"

"Work from a script, don't you?" He quoted lines from the killer's letter. "'Our children need protecting. Paedophiles are vermin.' Words courtesy of the Disposer. How did Mr Connolly put it, Frank?"

Knox chewed gum, stared at the protester. "'Kids need protecting. They're all vermin.' Then he gobbed on the floor, sir."

Close but no gold star. Byford tutted. "Not perfect then. Six out of ten? Are you a slow learner, Mr Connolly?"

Connolly was quick, but Knox was faster. By the time the protestor was on his feet, Knox was in his face, restraining Connolly's clenched fists. Outwardly cool, Byford's heart raced; he'd not seen that coming. Losing his touch or rusty technique after three months' thumb-twiddling? "Bad move, Mr Connolly." He pointed at the chair. "Sit."

Connolly slumped, arms folded, legs crossed. Byford hid his frustration. He'd got a rise out of the guy. So what? Most people thought paedophiles were vermin. Who didn't think children needed protection? Fact that Connolly had used a similar form of words to the Disposer was proof of very little. His instinct still told him there was something more tangible.

"Todd Freeman. What do you know about him?"

"Another dead pervert." Connolly sneered then clamped his lips. Too late. Byford pounced.

"Clairvoyant, are you?" The protester had been in a police cell since Sunday evening, room service didn't include newspapers. "How do you know that?"

"I'm not deaf."

It was just possible Connolly had heard about Freeman through the police grapevine, listened in on officers' conversation. Byford observed Connolly closely. The man was aggressive, hot-headed and truculent, but the detective saw him as a minor player. He also thought it unlikely the Disposer was acting alone. But did that make Joshua Connolly his accomplice?

"How much is he paying you?"

"Put your rod away, Mr Policeman. I'm not biting." The posture, the tone reinforced the words. Byford's experience told him he'd lost Connolly; he'd get nothing more this session. The detective walked round the desk, gathered his papers. "I'm after bigger fish than you, son. You're already in the net."

28

"It's a voice I'll never forget." Doyle had finally been persuaded to abandon the cleaning and park his bulk. His flabby thighs spread over the sides of the kitchen chair, podgy hands rested on the mound of his belly. Bev hid her distaste. For the second time in recent days she found the sympathy shop sold out. She didn't give a sod about the voice.

"What about the face?" she asked. "Did you get a good look?" Bev studied Doyle's as if it was an exam subject: the jagged scar, the full beard, pale watery gaze currently fixed on the shiny tabletop.

There was a rasping noise as he scratched the greying bristle. "I suppose he disguised it. But I'll always remember the tone, the loathing, the hatred. Hissed in my ear."

Yeah, yeah. "And the face?" She exchanged glances with Mac.

Doyle fingered the scar. "I am the Disposer and you're going to die, fat man."

Brimming tears finally skied down the slopes of his cheeks, his massive shoulders shook. Bev itched to shake the rest of him.

"The face, Mr Doyle. Can you give us a description?"

"It was all over so quickly…"

Her heart sank. The one person who'd been in spitting distance of the killer, and it looked as if he hadn't got a clue.

He dashed moist cheeks with the heels of his hands. "But by God, I'll give it my best shot."

Late afternoon and Bev perched on the edge of her desk holding Roger Doyle's best shot in both hands. As e-fits went, it wasn't bad. The male subject couldn't be taken for fifty per cent of the population as was sometimes the case. Nor did it appear to be the wild-eyed loony of an over-eager witness's febrile imagination.

A patrol car had picked up Doyle as Bev and Mac were leaving the house. The fat man had spent a couple of hours at Highgate alongside Al Copley, the imaging unit's sharpest operator. Copley had listened and elicited carefully, painstakingly laid out images, tweaked, honed, fine-tuned, cropped and finally come up with: white male, average height, thin, late-twenties-early-thirties, collar-length dark blond almost mousy hair, almond-shaped eyes, high cheekbones, bar piercing through the left eyebrow.

Whichever way she turned it, however hard she looked, Bev just couldn't see it. Until last night, the Disposer hadn't put a foot wrong – why run headlong into trouble now? "What you reckon?"

Mac's copy was on the windowsill beside him. He glanced down, shrugged. "Who knows? Might hear something soon."

The likeness had been issued to the media just after lunch via a hastily arranged news conference. Bev had leaned against a back wall as Flint read a statement, ducked a few pointed questions. It was a difficult pitch. However the DCS played it, the press would put on its own spin. A routine 'Have you seen this man?' appeal was too bland. But 'Is this the face of the Disposer?' was well over the top given nascent doubts about Doyle's integrity.

Bev sighed, moved to the chair, picked up a biro. The attack had happened around midnight in a badly lit street, round the corner from Doyle's Stirchley bungalow. He claimed to have yanked off his assailant's hood, but admitted catching only a fleeting glimpse of the face. How come Doyle had recalled so much detail? As for the passer-by who allegedly gave chase, he hadn't come forward despite an appeal on local radio. Bev's scepticism wasn't restricted to the scenario. She had the fat man down as a flaky, self-pitying shit.

Mac glanced over her shoulder, shook his head. The doodle taking shape looked like a cross between two Jags and Jabba the Hutt. "Come on, boss. Give the bloke a bit of credit." He paused deliberately. "It's not just Doyle's best shot."

Got that right. It was the cops' as well. "Fair dos." She screwed the paper, lobbed it at a bin already ringed with apple cores, crisp packets and sweet wrappers. "But why'd he do it, Mac?"

"Lost me, boss. Why'd who do what?" He pushed himself off the sill, bent down to pick up the rubbish.

"The Disposer." She took several slugs from a bottle of Malvern water, wiped her mouth on a sleeve. "He's run rings round us. We ain't got a skin cell to go on. Suddenly he's leaping outa bushes, wielding a knife, telling Doyle he's in for the big sleep. That's a hell of a risk."

"Maybe he's losing it?" Mac stood hoisted his jeans. "Pressure getting to him?"

What pressure? She scowled. "Yeah right." Or maybe Doyle was a fantasist. After all the fat man had engineered the attention, seemed to revel in the spotlight. "Doyle's wallowing in it, if you ask me." Mac didn't need to. He'd heard it before. "All that fingering the scar," she sneered. "Blubbing like a baby. Talk about diva."

Mac sighed. "Cut him some slack, boss."

"Why?" The eyes held a warning he habitually ignored.

"You get an idea in your head and sometimes you won't let go."

"Called having the courage of your convictions, sticking to your guns."

"One way of putting it," he muttered.

"Meaning?"

"What if your aim's wonky?"

"Nice line, mate." She turned her back, started typing. "Shame it's total bollocks." She heard his strut to the door, sensed him loitering with intent in the frame.

"Yeah. Well you're off beam with diva. That'd make Doyle female." He shoved a hand in his pocket. "As in the fat lady sings. Must've heard that one, boss."

"Only hearing bum notes, me, mate." She frowned; caught the innuendo. Cheeky sod. "Saying I'm fat?" She glanced round. Into empty space. Going by the volume, he was halfway down the corridor. She recognised the song he was mangling. Even though Mac had changed the lyrics. She doubted Sinatra had ever done anything Her Way.

By the late brief, they had a name. The e-fit of Roger Doyle's attacker had gone out on network TV bulletins. The *Evening News* front page looked like a wanted poster, Matt Snow's by-line conspicuous by its absence. Pensive, Bev shoved the paper in her bag as Flint strode in with an update. Among the calls to the hotline, he told the troops, three people had now come up with the same ID: Wayne Pickering. The latest tip-off had come from a neighbour; a squad car was on its way to a house in Acocks Green to bring Pickering in. The murder room buzzed like a honey farm. Jubilant, Flint stood centre stage. Bev wouldn't be surprised to see him take a bow. Final curtain? Somehow she didn't think so.

"We got anything on him?" she asked.

"Nothing criminal." Flint licked his lips. The but was tacit. "According to one of the callers, Pickering told anyone who'd listen how he had a cousin who'd been serially abused by a neighbour. Not here. Up in Burnley. He was very close to her apparently, more like brother and sister."

Mac asked Flint if the caller had left a name. Bev turned a snort into a cough. Course they did. Flint cut her a glance it was probably best she didn't see.

"And an address. Darren New and Sumitra Gosh are there now seeing what else he can give us."

Bev swung a foot. "When's this abuse supposed to have happened?"

Flint folded his arms. "Twenty years back. They were just kids." Her downturned mouth said it was a hell of a long time to bear a grudge. Flint must've read the message. "The cousin killed herself six months ago."

Bev nursed a solitary hot chocolate with extra sprinkles. Coming up to seven, she was in the canteen waiting for the guv to clock off. The late shift was on digging duty, delving into Pickering's background, uncovering anything that might tie him to the other murders. Two squad members were en route to re-interview Doyle. They needed to establish if there was history between the fat man and his assailant. And if so, why he'd not mentioned it. Thank God she was on days. Doyle gave her the creeps.

Bev had been flicking through Carol Pemberton's copy of *heat,* but fatuous anorexics and C-list nonentities weren't doing it for her. The dog-eared mag lay open on the table as she gazed at the night sky. No stars there either. Dark and stormy wasn't in it. Rain hammered the glass, windblown leaves skittered the surface. Winter was on its way. All they needed was snow. You can say that again. Matt Snow.

She licked chocolate froth off the spoon. The reporter's sick note had turned into a journal. Snow had gone to ground. Again. Only upside was it'd be easier for Anna Kendall to swap short-hand notebooks. The first batch was ready to go back. Pembers had dropped them off; sorry for not coming up with anything.

"Cheer up, sunshine. Might never happen." Powell loomed carrying a sausage roll and a steaming cup of Bovril. He looked remarkably perky.

"Dog died last night."

"Shit, Bev." A picture of concern, he perched tentatively in case she wanted time to grieve. "Sorry. I'd no idea." He must've clocked the curve of her lip. "You haven't got a dog, have you?"

"Nah. Worth it for the look on your face though." Keira Knightley in a backless strapless number stared up from the centre pages. Bev closed the mag, added a couple of sweeteners to the chocolate. Probably time to cut back.

"What you doing here, then?" He took a slurp. "Thought you'd be on the Wayne Pickering reception committee."

Sore point. Flint had made it clear that when Pickering was brought in he wanted Mac as number two on the interview. She'd not asked why; the DCS hadn't explained. She suspected he didn't appreciate her scepticism. Tough. No sense getting further up his nostrils though. With a bit of luck when Operation Wolf was history, he'd bugger off back to Wolverhampton.

She tapped his mug. "Acquired taste, Bovril. Like me with Flint."

"Not flavour of the month, then?" He bit into the pastry.

She snorted. "On Planet Flint, any month." The doors opened. She glanced round. Just a brace of uniforms. Where was Byford? She was hoping for dinner *à deux*.

Watching Powell wolf the sausage roll was giving her stomach ideas.

"Sure about Flint?" he asked.

"Does poo pong?" She ducked flying crumbs; caught something in the DI's delivery. "What?"

"He told me how you lobbied on my behalf. Didn't have a bad word to say about you, Bev."

News to her the DI and Flint had exchanged any words on her – or the lobbying. She'd assumed her conversation with the chief had been confidential. Open-mouthed she watched as the DI dunked the last inch or so of sausage roll in the Bovril. "He told me you showed loyalty, integrity, discretion…"

"You winding me up?"

He flashed a grin. "Said I'd no idea there were two Morrisses knocking round Highgate."

"Don't tempt me," she warned. "I could double that." She nodded at the damson bruise yellowing round the edges at his temple.

"Chill, Bev. He rates you. Just doesn't show it the same way as…"

Line. Cross. Don't. She narrowed her eyes. "Watch your…"

"Just like old times, you pair cosying up." A Fedora appeared on the Formica. She'd not seen the guv in his trademark head-gear for months, nor the suit and tie. Mind, the hat looked spanking new. The old one had that battered look. Right now so did Byford: mauve smudges ringed tired grey eyes, lines there she'd never noticed before. Maybe they should just grab a pizza. Get an early night.

"The DI was just leaving actually," she said brightly. "Weren't you?"

"Was I?" Couldn't the guy take a hint? "Oh yeah. Have you got my cut?"

She narrowed her eyes. "What cut?"

"The sweepstake."

Shit. Daz must've ratted on her. She scrabbled in her purse, pulled out a note. "Only got a twenty. Sorry, mate…"

"No worries." He plucked it, gave it a twirl. "I'll get some change."

Her eyes were slits, teeth clenched. "Tomorrow'll do."

"You bet." He winked, backed away. "Mañana, right?"

Byford ran the hat between his hands. "What was that all about?"

"You don't want to know." She slipped her coat on. "I'm famished. I'll eat anything. What you fancy?"

"Is your car out back?" It was no answer. They talked in the lift, chatted in the corridors. She asked about his day, heard the top lines on the Joshua Connolly interview. Chewed over everything but the topic of food. As they hit the stairs and he started spouting about the foul weather, she knew dinner was a no-no.

"Sorry about this, Bev. Rich is down for a few days. I said I'd meet him for dinner."

She forced a smile. "That'll be a rain check, then."

Kids? Who'd have 'em?

The MG smelt like a chippie. The fish supper from Oceania was on the passenger seat sending out wafts of vinegar. Bev was in a line of shuffling traffic on Kings Heath High Street. Rain was still sheeting down. She flicked the radio, caught the eight o'clock news. The Wayne Pickering angle led the bulletin. *West Midlands police are seeking a twenty-nine-year-old Birmingham man in connection with...*

Simultaneously the e-fit was on a bank of TV monitors in a showroom on the left. Surreal. How weird was that? Fingers tapped the wheel. Almost as weird as Flint's decision not to use her on the Pickering interview – whenever that might be. The officers sent to bring him in had found the Acocks Green bedsit empty; neighbours hadn't set eyes on the so-called, self-proclaimed Disposer for twenty-four hours.

Fifty miles away on the outskirts of Shrewsbury, Matt Snow had the Disposer in his sights. The reporter couldn't tear his gaze from the TV screen. Flicking through channels, he'd caught the D-word on News 24. As in...

Police say the man is wanted for questioning in connection with the so-called Disposer killings...

"Are you all right, Matthew?" Lydia Snow sat in a chunky armchair near the coal fire, knitting needles clicking. She'd been keeping a closer watch on the son she rarely saw these days than what she considered the rubbish on television. Tall and elegant with an immaculate silver chignon, she lived in rural chic on a teacher's pension and her late husband's life insurance. The old farmhouse, surrounded by Shropshire countryside, was low-beams-meets-Laura-Ashley. A touch twee for Snow's city tastes.

He lifted a shushing hand. "Fine, ma, absolutely fine." If the bastard on the news was the Disposer, Snow was more than fine. If an arrest was imminent, his mother was safe. The flying visit to drop subtle warnings looked as if it was a wasted journey.

He hunched forward, knuckles white round a tumbler of Grouse, took in every detail of the psycho who'd broken into his flat, lain in wait in the motor, fucked with his head. The smirking face beneath the burqa; the evil eyes that had scared Snow witless.

"Is this a story you've been working on, Matthew?"

He gave a thin smile. "You could say that, ma." He upped the volume but the voice-over was journalese meets police-speak. He'd ring the desk in a while, get the inside story.

Sighing, his mother rose, stowed the knitting. "Can I get you anything, Matthew?"

"No thanks, ma. I'm cool."

She stooped, pecked him on the cheek. "Good night, darling. If you're gone before I get up, take care." She turned at the door. He was reaching for the remote. "And Matthew. Don't work so hard. No one's indispensable."

He wasn't listening. Reckoned Sky News could be carrying the Disposer story as well. He hit the button. They were teasing the item in a strapline running across the bottom of the screen. The reporter sat through packages on climate change, teenage pregnancies, latest figures on obesity. Barely took in a word, trying to work out the ramifications. Would he lose out if the Disposer were sent down? Where was the mad bastard now?

Right in front of the reporter, his face full frame on screen. Snow narrowed his eyes, shuffled further forward. Didn't look like a psycho: Average Joe – apart from the eyebrow piercing. Snow scratched his ear. Please God let it be over soon. The e-fit was running on all channels, it'd be in every newspaper. The psycho couldn't hide forever; a collar couldn't be far off.

For the first time in days, Snow felt a slight ease in the tension. When the picture cut to an easy-on-the-eye blonde, he sat back, stroked his neck. Blondie was urging viewers to ring the number on the screen if they had information. "Police say the man could be dangerous. They're warning people not to approach him."

As if. Snow sucked the scotch between his teeth. A smile spread slowly across his pasty face. It had barely reached his eyes before the pay-as-you-go vibrated against his chest.

29

"Hello, Matthew."

Snow's heart pounded, the phone shook in his clammy hand, his mouth so dry he could barely speak. Apart from his mother, only one person in the world called him by his full name: a homicidal freaking maniac. "Where are you?" Nervous glance over his shoulder, half expected to see the bastard lurking behind the settee.

"Wouldn't you like to know?" Calm, cool. "Have you been keeping up with the news, Matthew?"

Snow rose, padded to the window, drew the heavy damask curtains tighter. Stupid. Irrational. What good would that do? Close to tears, he raked fingers through his fringe. "Look, mate, I think the game's over. If I were you, I'd give myself up."

"Would you?" Amused sneer. "Why's that, Matthew?"

"It'll go easier for you. The cops might cut a deal." Like hell they would. "I'll come with you if you like. I know how to talk to them. Give you a bit of support." He knew the gabbling made him sound nervous. He was.

The disembodied laugh was loud in Snow's ear. The fact it sounded genuine made it more unnerving somehow. "I suppose I should be flattered." Superior. Insouciant.

Snow paced barefoot in front of the open fire. "I mean it, mate. I know most of the cops at Highgate. Pally with quite a few as it happens. If you want, I could meet you there."

"Still after the scoop, Matthew? Silly question. Don't answer." Sly snigger.

Snow crept into the hall made sure the door was locked, bolts drawn; set the alarm.

"I'd check upstairs as well if I were you, Matthew."

His bowels loosened; his voice a whimper. "Please… don't…"

"Joke. I know you so well, you see. I bet you just set the alarm, didn't you? Don't worry, Matthew. Right now, I've got better things to do than amuse myself with your old lady."

The reporter bit down on his knuckles, drew blood. "What do you want?" A drink. Snow craved a stiff drink.

"What I've always wanted."

What the hell? The mad sod's cover was blown. Like as not he'd be recognised soon as he set foot on the streets. "How'd you mean?" Hands shaking too much to pour, Snow swigged from the bottle, scotch dribbled down his chin.

"To complete the mission, of course. Don't you remember what I told you, Matthew?" Kindly head teacher to dense boy.

Every word was branded in Snow's brain. The bastard said he'd take out two more paedophiles then top himself. "But… this guy… Doyle… he…"

"You really didn't get it, did you, Matthew?" Get what? "When I said I should be flattered?"

Ice in the spine. Acid in the throat. Snow clamped his mouth with a hand. Holy Christ. The cops had cocked it. "This guy, Pickering…?" The nutter who claimed he was the Disposer.

"They say it's the sincerest form, don't they? Imitation." He paused, making sure Snow comprehended. "Know what I call it? I call it a fucking infringement by a fucking impostor. A useless amateur." Shrill sharp tone suffused with menace. "I don't make mistakes." Silence. "What don't I make, Snow?"

"Mistakes."

"Precisely. I want a correction."

"Sorry?"

"Your hearing fucked?"

"No." Snow frowned. Slang. Swearing. Pickering's claim must've really rattled the psycho's cage. Bad news if a serial killer was losing it.

"Tomorrow's front page. I want you to write the lead. Give readers the real story. The prick in the media's a pathetic copycat. The police have screwed up again."

How to piss off the cops in one easy lesson. It was an exclusive he could live without. "Thing is…"

"We'll write it together." He paused. "After all, we are in this together. Aren't we, Matthew?"

THURSDAY

30

Bev was in the office, trying to decipher the handwriting on a note left overnight on her desk. She glanced up at a muffled fumble on the door. Mac appeared with a wide grin on his face. "See…I can knock, boss."

She frowned. God knows how. A bag with interesting-looking grease spots was tucked under an arm, both hands clutched polystyrene cups. "Come and have a look at this, mate."

Mac bummed the door closed, ambled over, deposited the coffees on the desk. She relieved him of the goody bag, handed him the scrap of paper. He had the same trouble; the scrawl was virtually illegible. Mac just had more patience. "Who's it from?" He quipped "Your doctor?"

She was poking doughnuts. "These raspberry?"

"No. Marmite. What d'you think they are?"

"Only asked." She took a bite. "It's from Bruce, the new SOCO." Doing her a favour. She'd asked for an early heads-up from the Graves's place. Shame she couldn't make head or tail of the bloody thing.

"The one as fancies you?" Mac waggled his eyebrows.

Thin smirk, smug nod. "Dead ringer for Donny Osmond."

"Jimmy," he corrected. "The fat one."

"You'd know, mate." She licked sugar from her lips.

"Anyway." He hoisted his jeans. "One of the Osmonds reckons he's got a match for prints they lifted from some crime scene at Handsworth Wood. Tudor Grange? Ring a bell?"

"Ping." She got a timely tongue to runny jam.

"Belong to a Caitlin Finney." Mac read. "Thirty-eight years

old. Address in Shirley. Shoplifting, speeding, contempt of court convictions. More bells?"

"Ish." She frowned trying to recall where she'd seen the name. Recently, she thought. "Anything else on there?"

He returned the note. "What more do you want. Kisses?"

"Jealous?"

"Ravenous." He grabbed the bag off her desk. "Why's he telling you anyway? Handsworth Wood's not our baby, is it?"

She gave him the condensed version: doctor's suicide, anonymous letters to the police and the widow, criminal damage at the family home. Small beer given how Operation Wolf was kicking off.

"Started off as a favour to Flint as it happens." She pulled her bottom lip, made a few mental notes: numbers to call, people to see.

Mac looked sheepish. "About that, boss." That Flint had chosen a newbie DC over Bev for a big interview.

"Not down to you, mate." She flapped a hand. "No worries."

"Yeah, well. Flint's going ballistic. No Wayne Pickering either."

The early brief was neither early nor brief. DCS Flint had put it back an hour and was still pontificating at half nine. Bev had just checked her watch. She sighed, couldn't be doing with time-wasting talk when there were actions to get stuck into. She'd spent the sixty minutes shoving inquiry irons in the fire; they'd need chasing on top of anything dished out now.

A quick glance round suggested the rest of the squad was equally keen to get going. Toes tapped, feet kicked, legs jigged; there was a buzz in the air. Flint had already run through top lines thrown up by the late shift diggers. Seemed to Bev they were now going over the same ground twice.

Much of the information was anecdotal, picked up by

questioning Pickering's neighbours. Apparently, he liked a tipple, and the booze loosened his tongue. Official checks were underway, but he'd told two drinking buddies that he came from a broken home, had spent much of his childhood in care in Burnley. The only family member he'd maintained contact with was the cousin, Eliza, who'd killed herself six months ago.

Bev crossed her legs, scowled when she spotted a ladder in her tights. What a bum hand those kids had been dealt. Wayne Pickering brought up by strangers in kids' homes, Eliza molested by a neighbour. The serial abuse had led her to self-harm, eventually to self-destruct. Eyes creased, as she recalled her first conversation with Eddie Scrivener. His daughter's story had parallels. Abuse that touched more than the victim's life, rippled on for years. She jotted Scrivener's name on a pad. He still hadn't surfaced, sightings had tailed off. The Pickering development had pushed everything else off the front page.

Flint's shoes squeaked as he paced the floor. "We know Pickering came to Birmingham in the summer. Took a short-term lease on the bedsit."

Positioning? Planning? Had his cousin's death been the trigger that launched a killing campaign? But why Birmingham? And what governed the choice of victim? Far as they could establish the hits had been random, the only criterion being each target had paedophile convictions.

She pursed her lips, had to admit that if Pickering wasn't the Disposer – he was a big fan. Last night, armed with a search warrant, a team had entered his pad in Acocks Green. Sparsely furnished, it was fastidiously neat – except for the newspapers: national, regional, local, redtop, broadsheet, every issue going back to the first murder victim were scattered around. Loose pages covered every surface, most of the floor. Every column inch, every picture, every reference to the killings had been hacked out, stuck on the walls.

Was Pickering the story – or a voyeur following it? He wasn't around to ask. Wayne Pickering was well and truly AWOL.

"No sightings, no steers, nothing." Flint's glare raked the troops as if it was their fault. "Where the hell's he gone?"

Not far, Bev reckoned. A new visual – a photograph – had now been released to the media, Pickering's details had been circulated to every police force in the country, ports and airports were on alert. Not that he had a passport with him. The search team had found it among other personal documents at the bedsit. Signs were that he'd not done a runner.

"Someone's harbouring Pickering," Flint said. "Got to be."

But was Wayne Pickering the real deal? Apart from the cuttings, there was no evidence linking him to the murders. So was he the Disposer? And had Doyle been on the hit list? Or was Pickering a copycat? The squad was taking its lead from Flint. The DCS wanted a collar, and seemed convinced it was round Wayne Pickering's neck.

Bev wasn't so sure. The MO – such as it was – didn't fit. She suspected Pickering was a freelancer who'd specifically targeted Roger Doyle. In which case, why tell the fat man he was the serial killer?

"What's Doyle saying?" Mac got the question in first.

"Nothing." Flint sniffed. "He took off last night for his sister's in Devon."

"Who says?" Bev asked.

"A neighbour, I think. Ian'll know. He was knocking doors." DS Ian Blunt on lates all week.

She frowned. "What've we got on Doyle? Apart from the convictions."

"Not a lot," Flint ceded. "He didn't leave any numbers."

"Sister's place? Sure about that?" Bev wasn't. "Doyle said he was estranged from his family. Claimed as far as they're concerned, he's a dead man."

Grim-faced, Flint tipped his head towards the door. Bev was already halfway there – just behind Mac.

Roger Doyle lay spread-eagled in a viscous lake of liver-coloured blood. The throat had been slashed; gore showed through the scrubby beard though fleshy chins covered most of the gash. Impossible to know at this stage whether death was down to the neck injury or the multiple stab wounds piercing, desecrating, the body. Bev bit her lip; Doyle put her in mind of a beached whale. She swallowed hard, noticed the ubiquitous dishcloth now stiff and brown lying just beyond his grasp. The kitchen he'd cleaned obsessively would always be stained.

Given the congealed nature of the blood, Doyle had almost certainly lain dying last night, his life draining even as DS Blunt and his partner hammered at the door, armed with questions that would now remain unanswered. By Doyle at any rate.

"It's an abattoir." Bev's breaths came in short gasps. Waves of nausea threatened to overwhelm her again. The sight, the stink, the shit, more than that: the sense of guilt. This butchery should not have happened. They should have known that while Pickering was at large, Doyle was at risk.

She inhaled slowly, deeply. She should have questioned Doyle more closely, elicited more background, confirmed the details, requested surveillance on the house. She should have done a proper job. And why hadn't she? Because the inquiry was over-stretched and under-resourced? Or because the fat man revolted her? Doyle certainly hadn't been given top billing. Mentally, she'd dismissed him as a flaky self-pitying shit. And now he lay rotting in his own faeces.

"Don't do it, boss." Mac wiped sweat from his forehead with an off-white hankie.

"What!" She spun round, immediately regretted it, felt dizzy, stomach lurched.

"Blame yourself."

"Bollocks. I didn't listen. Doyle was petrified. I should've seen it... should've stopped this..."

"Then so should I," Mac snapped. "And Ian Blunt. And Flint. He's the boss. He prioritises. The buck…"

"Fuck the buck." Flint hadn't talked to the fat man. She had. A lead detective's calls were based on information from his officers.

Mac put steadying hands on her arms. "Don't beat yourself up, Bev. You are not responsible." He pointed a toe towards the far wall. "He is."

In contrast, Wayne Pickering looked as if he was sleeping, curled on his side, slight smile curving his lips. Was Pickering at peace at last? An empty bottle of Bells lay close by used to down a cocktail of drugs. Bitter pills? Or happy release? He must have taken some satisfaction in killing the man who'd wrecked his childhood.

As they now knew, Eliza's recent suicide may have been the catalyst for the bloodletting here, but not the sole cause.

They ducked automatically as something dark crashed screeching into the window. Black wings flapped wildly against the glass before the stunned bird took off again. Looked like a crow or a raven. Magpie would have been even spookier.

As spooky as hearing voices from beyond the grave. Pickering had recorded the final scene, his vicious taunts, Doyle's pleas for mercy. Bev and Mac had only been able to listen to a few minutes. The tape was now bagged and tagged. It wasn't the only painful legacy Pickering had bestowed. A bloodstained letter – addressed to the police – fluttered in Bev's latex-gloved fingers. Confession? Catharsis? Both. Doyle's shaky signature was there too. With the soundtrack, it wasn't difficult to picture Pickering goading the fat man, forcing him at knifepoint to 'fess up to the years of abuse he'd committed as a carer in young Wayne's children's home. *Carer?* Bev snorted. What a joke. Doyle had certainly looked out for himself, fleeing before his crimes were discovered, changing his name. But despite the new-leaf-turned protestations the other day, he'd been unable to change his nature. If Doyle hadn't committed more offences, maybe Pickering wouldn't have been able to track him down.

Mixed emotions, complex thoughts, she shook her head. Doyle deserved punishment for what he'd done to young lads like Wayne Pickering, but not this.

"He should've left it to the courts." Mac echoed her thinking, doing quite a bit of that these days.

"Call it in, mate." She turned away, reached for her own phone.

Even though the sordid tableau told its own sorry story, the evidence still had to be collated. In less than an hour, the place would resemble a shoot from *The Bill*: white-suited SOCOs, steel cases, flash photography, pathologist putting in a guest appearance. Inquests would be held, outstanding inquiries would be made.

She glanced at the letter again. A posthumous postscript made one point crystal:

Wayne Pickering was no serial killer.

The Disposer's doing a good job. The man should get a medal for getting rid of filth.

"I'd best have a word with Flint." She grimaced, glanced at Mac. "Make his day this will."

At Highgate, DCS Kenny Flint's day was just about to be made. Leastways it was one he'd not forget any time soon: not so much red letter as black caps. Writing a report at his desk, the detective glanced up annoyed at the interruption as news bureau chief Bernie Flowers barged in and slammed the *Evening News* on a pile of files. Early edition. Flint couldn't see it getting any worse by the final. As it happened, it wouldn't take that long.

Bernie was too wired to sit, he hovered, polished his glasses with his tie. The outlook was still crap. "They're going ape shit, Kenny. The Beeb, ITV, Sky. The print guys as well. They all want interviews."

Flint was momentarily lost for words. The headline said it all.

SERIAL KILLER TAUNTS COPS

The detective's lips tightened further as he read the story.

A serial killer targeting Birmingham paedophiles claims West Midlands police are hunting a 'pathetic copycat'. In an exclusive interview with **Evening News** *Crime Correspondent Matt Snow, the self-styled Disposer is threatening to strike again to prove he's the murderer. "Unlike the police," the killer said. "I don't make mistakes."*

The man leading Operation Wolf, Detective Chief Superintendent Keith Flint, was unavailable for comment last night. Cont. page 3.

Not for Flint, he'd had a belly full. "This is crap, Bernie. It can't be true. Christ, they can't even get my name right."

"Not a main concern, Kenny." Flint read Bernie's cold stare, cool voice correctly.

The cops weren't just facing a bit of bad press. The media en masse would now be sniffing for a scalp. And if another paedophile died – forget scalps, they'd be after detached heads.

"Did Snow make an approach, ask you to comment?" Bernie asked casually, studied his fingernails.

"What do you think?" Flint snarled. Of course he hadn't. Because if Flint had caught wind of the story: a) he'd have done anything to prevent it appearing in print, and b) he'd have forced Snow to reveal where it came from. Tried to force Snow. They'd had nil success so far.

Bernie finally sat, took a biro from Flint's penholder. "I think we need to discuss strategy. How we handle the fallout. It's gone beyond damage limitation. We need to call a news conference, hang Snow out to dry." He nodded at the paper. "That's as irresponsible as it gets."

Flint nodded, snatched the phone before its second ring. "What?"

"Bev here, boss. We're still at Doyle's place. One thing's for sure – Wayne Pickering's not the Disposer."

"Tell me something I don't know. Got the story in front of me. I'm bringing Matt Snow in now."

"Snow?"

"Have you seen his latest offering? Get back soon as you can, sergeant."

"What about handing over? The crime team?"

"What crime team?" Flint's face drained of colour as she told him what they'd found. He hung up, stunned.

Bernie's pen was poised. "What is it, chief?"

Eyes closed, Flint massaged his temples. "You know when you think it can't get any worse…"

Even as Flint uttered the words, a fifteen-year-old terminal truant was studying a stiff on the Churchill estate. Steep learning curve for a kid who avoided lessons like the plague. Unlike the detective, Ryan Jackson was having a good day. Blue sky, sun shining, combats and hoodie pockets jammed with pickings: fags, crisps, Carling black label, Mars bars, mint Aeros, even a top shelf tit mag. Small shopkeepers on the estate were wise to Ryan, just not quick enough, and he'd had stacks of practice.

If bunking off was on the national curriculum, Ryan could give masterclasses. A short skinny target for bullies at Queen's Comprehensive, truancy was a form of survival. Ryan knew every scam in the book. Actually, given his reading age, not book. The only ABC he had a passing knowledge of was the acceptable behaviour contract he'd not been able to sign.

A few months back, his unemployed cokehead mother had been hauled before the courts for the umpteenth time because she couldn't get her little darling out of bed let alone the house. The family was well known to the cops; received wisdom at Highgate had it that Mona Jackson had spent more days in prison that term than her son had in class.

Though academically challenged, Ryan was streetwise, and like most kids, media savvy. Standing behind a tree, transfixed by the body in the distance, his first thought was: what's in for me? Second was: maybe he could flog a few pictures. Papers were always after photos. The telly even. *You've Been Framed*. Ryan scowled. Nah. Don't be stupid. No one'd die laughing at the sight of a bloke in front of a wheelie bin. This was serious, the sort of stuff he'd seen on the news. His weasel face lit up. Everyone knew the cops were after a psycho wasting kiddie fiddlers. What if…? And wasn't there a reward or something?

Eyes screwed, Ryan lined up a shot in his phone's viewfinder. Was the geezer even dead? Shit. Some dude was in the way, going through the pockets. Cheeky sod, getting in first like that. Ryan switched to video mode. Great timing: the scrawny dude looked up, glanced round.

Ugly git. Could turn nasty. Ryan legged it quick. Had he looked more closely, he might have noticed the graffiti spray-painted on the metal. Not that he could have read the word. Polysyllables didn't feature in Ryan's lexicon. *Disposed* wasn't a word that had hit his radar. Ryan was more interested in the action he'd captured on camera. He reckoned the cops would be too. When he reached the relative safety of his mate's dad's lock-up, he made a call.

Anna Kendall was on her mobile shouting over traffic noise. "I'm really sorry. I'd have told you sooner, but I've only just seen it myself."

"You and me both." Bev held the offending article at arm's length while Mac tried to nose the motor into a tight space back at the nick. After leaving Doyle's they'd nipped into a newsagent's, keen to catch up with what Flint had scathingly described as Snow's 'latest offering'.

"Serial killer taunts cops," Bev drawled. "Nice one. Not."

"The desk kept it under wraps till the last moment," Anna explained. "The editor's edgy. Probably scared of a leak, or something."

Something like an injunction. "Reckon it's pukka? Snow's not just making it up as he goes along?" The writer's reply was drowned by wailing police sirens. "Missed that," Bev said. "Say again."

"Sorry. I'm in Colmore Row. I didn't want to call from the newsroom. As to the story being genuine?" Slight pause. "I can't see how Matt got it past Rick if he couldn't stand it up."

"Rick?" New one on Bev.

"Rick Palmer. News editor. Sharp operator."

She made a mental note. "Is Snow there now?" There was barely space to open the door. She breathed in, squeezed out, threw Mac a scowl.

"No. He e-mailed the piece. The police have been here, but…"

Bev rolled her eyes. Presumably Mac had even less room to manoeuvre – the car was now in reverse. "Any idea where he is?"

"I've asked round," Anna said. "No one knows. Least, no one's saying."

Mac gave a sheepish grin. Bev's hand signal was neither helpful nor in the Highway Code. "Snow's in serious shit," she told Anna. "Facing charges now – not just questions. Obstructing an inquiry, perverting the course of justice. My boss is going ballistic. When Snow shows his face…"

"You'll be the first to know."

Smile in the voice. "Dandy." What the hell was Tyler playing at?

"Hey, Anna, we're done with Snow's notebooks. Any chance of another batch?"

The writer offered to bring in the next instalment when she got off work. Bev couldn't guarantee she'd be around, gave Carol Pemberton's name as backup. "Where you living, Anna? I could maybe drop round…?"

She gave the address. "I won't be in tonight, though. Actually, I'm out a lot in the evenings so give us a ring first. Save a wasted journey."

"Cheers. Catch you later." Lucky girl. Bev's social life was more washout than whirl. She pursed her lips, wondered if there was a lucky man around.

Certainly wasn't Mac. She shook her head. Three times he'd screwed the parking. Talk about pig's ear. She cut him a withering look as he finally clambered out clutching his booty from the newsagent's: Beano, Dandy, Dr Who comic, crisps, Smarties, sherbert dabs, diet coke.

"Seeing the kids at the weekend," he said, not meeting her eye.

Sceptical sniff. "Course you are, big boy."

Tall and tasty and lean and lovely, the fit guy chatting to Vince Hanlon at the front desk had to be Byford's son. In profile, his resemblance to the guv was striking. The likeness brought Bev up sharp as she strode through reception en route to audio. First stage of the Doyle/Pickering paperwork complete, she was dropping off the macabre death tape. Little detour wouldn't hurt. Combing her hair with her fingers, she advanced with intent, hoping her lippie was still intact. Not that she was out to make a mark or anything.

"Vince." Bright smile. Best side. "You called?"

"Did I?" Sergeant Hanlon's brow corrugated in a puzzled frown.

"Something about a package?" Like hell. She wanted a nose. Suss out the gene pool.

"Nothing's come by me, Bev. Hang on a bit. I'll have a butcher's." Hoisting voluminous trousers, he strolled over to the pigeon-holes.

"Bev Morriss?" Dark velvet voice, tad hesitant. Posher than his dad's.

"Sure is." She turned, surprised, as if she'd not already clocked him. It was uncanny, like seeing the guv airbrushed, computer-enhanced. No lines, wrinkle-free zone, grey hair back to black. Maybe not so much warmth in the grey eyes. Unless it was her imagination. "You must be…"

"Richard Byford." Thin smile as he shook her hand. "I've heard a lot about you."

Shoot. "All good, I hope." She tilted her head; he didn't elaborate. What had the big man told him? "You look just like your…"

"Old man. Yeah, I know." He flapped a dismissive hand. "Everyone says so."

She forced a smile. "Dead original, me." Awkward silence. Vibes were bad, distinct impression the guy didn't like her. Jealous? Resentful? Territorial? Get real. He couldn't know she wanted to jump his dad. Yet disapproval was coming off him in waves. If Byford had let anything slip, maybe junior didn't like the age gap? There was more than twenty years between her and the guv. Like she cared. No point responding in kind.

"How long you down for?"

He shrugged. "Haven't decided." Like it was any of her business.

Struggling for small talk now let alone common ground. "Vince looking after you?" Nice one, Bev. What a dumb question. Richard Byford didn't answer but the raised eyebrow was as eloquent as the guv's. Must be genetic.

"Look after everyone, me, Bev." Vince approached with an

envelope. "This it?"

She managed to mask her surprise, couldn't hide the shock when she recognised the handwriting. No stamp. Just her name. Personal delivery?

Footsteps behind, Byford approached, shucking into a trench coat. "Sorry to keep you, Rich." The guv had been grilling Joshua Connolly again, reckoned any connection between Connolly and the Disposer killings could be ruled out. Gut instinct wasn't always spot on. "You lunching, Bev? Welcome to join us."

Given baby Byford's churlish scowl, she almost agreed. "Up to here, guv." She swept a hand over her head. Had food for thought though. Her other hand clutched a letter from Oz.

32

Not that she had time to read it. Even before she'd parked her backside, an agitated Mac burst into her office. The fine white powder round his mouth meant he was either developing a nasty habit or he'd been at the sherbert. The line didn't go down well with her DC.

"We've got a body. Churchill estate. Just been called in."

She cast a rueful look at her desk. There was a shed-load on; messages were piling up, million calls to make. She grabbed her bag and bits. "I'll drive."

It'd be quicker.

Matt Snow reckoned he was on borrowed time. Soon as the early edition of the *News* hit the streets, he knew the cops would come running. Which was one reason he'd decided to go to them. Keeping a low profile in baseball cap and bomber jacket, the reporter was watching his flat from the lobby of the building opposite. He was keeping an eye open for the Bill. He wanted to get in, grab a few things, without getting nabbed. Look better if he turned up at Highgate off his own bat, and the more proof he could take, the easier it would be to persuade Flint he was telling the truth.

Jittery, nerves jangling, Snow had barely slept last night. Mind in turmoil, thoughts racing, he knew he couldn't take any more shit from the Disposer. He'd jumped his last hoop that morning. He shuddered, gagged when he recalled touching the body on the Churchill estate. He'd gone there expecting a meet with the killer – not to come face-to-face with a victim. Should've known it was more of the psycho's mind games. Yeah, well, no more Mr Nice Guy. Snow intended turning the Bad Guy over to the cops.

The reporter had no worries about his mother. She was on the way to her sister's place in Spain. A check with the airport confirmed she'd boarded the flight. As for his own back, Snow would ask for police protection until the mad bastard was under lock and key.

A limp cordon of police tape protected the Churchill crime scene. Not much was visible through clumps of sightseers. Residents were gathered on the patchy grass and crumbling asphalt at the rear of Asquith Tower. Smoke drifted from cigarettes and slack mouths as gossipers loitered. Focus appeared to be a line of wheelie bins. Several heads whipped round, briefly distracted by a screech of tyres. The Mäkinen manoeuvre provoked whoops and high-fives from a gang of youths.

Mac sniffed. "Very Sweeney."

Bev winked. "Showing your age, mate." Locking the motor, she addressed him over the roof. "Still owe me a fiver." She'd broken the eight-minute Highgate to Churchill police record.

"Get lost." Mac's remark was addressed to a dog with a lop-sided grin that was cocking its leg against the back tyre. Least she thought he was talking to the dog.

Even crisp sunlight couldn't put a sparkle on the estate. The back of the flats was the pits, a dumping ground for rusting bikes, burnt out cars, off-white fridges, tellies with shattered screens. Rotting leaves lay like drab moth-eaten carpets. Through aviator shades, Bev scanned the dreary surroundings for a uniform, spotted Steve Hawkins in the distance having words with a young lad.

"You're a bit late, sarge." Hawkeye's partner Ken Gibson had clocked the detectives. The constable rushed over, smoothing his hair. Tad breathless, they'd missed the excitement, he said. Air ambulance had just flown the body to the Accident and Emergency hospital.

"You'd not credit it, but the bloke still had a pulse." Gibson was firing on full cylinders. Must be a first – a helicopter landing on the Churchill. Sight more stirring than the usual vista of clapped-out Corsairs.

"Bad then?" Bev asked.

Gibbo nodded. "Pulped."

She exchanged glances with Mac. Déjà vu or what? It was Philip Goodie all over again. Only this time…

"Mate, we need a…"

"Police guard at the hospital. On to it, boss." He already had phone in hand, wandered off to make the call. The temperature dropped rapidly as the sun went behind a bank of cloud. Bev slipped the shades in a pocket, drew the coat tighter.

"What else we got, Gibbo?" ID. Witnesses. Murder weapon. Killer cuffed. Dream on, babe.

"Sarge!" The yell came from Hawkeye, dragging the now sullen kid towards them. "You need to hear this."

Short and skinny, the boy toed the ground, hands deep in pockets. The street gear all looked too big for him, the face he was putting on didn't fit either. "Cash up front, copper. Deal?"

"Shut it, Ryan," Bev drawled. She'd come across the lad in court; most cops had. She felt sorry for him more than anything: druggie mother who beat the shit out of him, feckless absentee father. Ryan had a touch of the Billy-no-mates. He wasn't cool enough to be in a gang let alone part of the culture.

"Or what?" Feisty little plucker though.

"Or you'll get a clip round the ear. From your ma. When I grass you up." Cruel but fair.

"Just tell her what you saw, Ryan," Hawkins prompted.

"What's it worth?" Jutting bottom lip.

She stepped forward, sank a hand in a combat pocket, pulled out a packet of fags. "Remind me, kid. What age are you?"

"They're me mam's."

"Yeah. And I'm your fairy godfather." She slipped the baccy into her bag.

"Hey!" he shrieked. "That's nickin', that is."

"Got that right, kid." She walked away. "Search him, officer."

Shocked silence, then Ryan spluttered. "There was this dude rifling the dead geezer's gear."

"What did you say?" The hairs rose on the back of her neck. She turned as slowly as she spoke. "If you're lying…" Her eyes narrowed as she advanced.

He thrust a mobile towards her. "Look if you don't believe me."

It was her own eyes she had trouble crediting. Christ on a bike. She reran the few seconds of footage. No wonder none of the patrols had picked up Matt Snow. They'd been looking in the wrong place. "Be hanging on to this for evidence, Ryan."

He gave a resigned nod.

"Hey, boss," Mac shouted. "Seen this?" Irritated at the distraction, she glanced across to the cordon. She couldn't make it out, but Mac was pointing at graffiti on one of the bins. She looked down at the screen, viewed the final frame, read the single word, Disposed.

"Snap," she muttered, reaching for her own mobile. Snow was toast.

Ryan tapped her on the arm. "Can I have me fags back, miss?"

"Let's think. No." She scowled. His face dropped. Relenting, she handed him a fiver. "You did good, kid. Don't spend it all at once."

He looked askance at the note, lip curled. "Sure you can spare it?"

"Now you come to mention it…" She snatched it back. "Sod off." She pocketed his Motorola as well. Assuming it was his. He'd probably nicked that too.

Matt Snow's flat looked as if it had been turned over. It had. Several times. A radiator was off the wall in the hall, kitchen and bedroom drawers had been pulled out, contents scattered around floors. The reporter's search had become increasingly desperate. Frantic now, he ran his hands through his hair, surveyed the mess, horrified at the possible fallout.

His insurance policy was missing. Insurance against a life sentence. Without the evidence he'd accrued, he couldn't prove the Disposer's existence. It was Snow's word against a man no one had heard or seen, and even Snow had only caught a glimpse of dark eyes in a driving mirror.

Wired and jumpy, he needed a drink. Where'd he left his glass? Couldn't be arsed to find it. Had to quit this place before the cops came calling. He took several slugs of Grouse from the bottle. Blunting the edges? Not even a dent. He'd thought he'd been so sharp, building up material that would support his story, secreting it in various places around the apartment. Now everything had gone: his laptop, the photographs and notes sent by the Disposer, the last two conversations Snow had recorded with the psycho. Even the naffing pay-as-you-go had gone. He patted his breast pocket again. Knew it had been there earlier when he was on the Churchill. It had been an unwanted umbilical cord these last few days. Snow had long wanted to cut the connection. Now it looked as if the Disposer had got in first; this break-in had to be down to him. Not that he believed the killer's intention was to cut him loose.

Snow pinched the bridge of his nose. Think, man, think. He had another drink, then another. Even with the pay-as-you-go, the cops might not believe a word he said. But without it he hadn't a leg to stagger on. Maybe if he went back to the estate, tried to locate it? Yes. Nice one, Snowie. He weaved a path to the bedroom, the unsteady gait exacerbated by mounds of clutter. The weekend bag was on top of the wardrobe. He blew off a layer of dust, threw in a change of clothes, few toiletries. If he couldn't locate the mobile he'd just have to bail out for a few days. Till the heat died down.

Five minutes later he was stowing the bag in the boot of the Fiesta. The tap on the shoulder came from behind. Hard to tell from which cop. The one with the bull neck spoke first: "Going somewhere, Mr Snow?"

News of Matt Snow's arrest broke in the nick of time. An increasingly hostile press conference was underway at Highgate. DCS Flint was feeling the heat, cold sweat trickled down his spine as he wiped his face with an already moist handkerchief. He leaned to his right, muttered in Bernie Flowers's ear: "Bloody Jerry Springer show in here."

The boardroom did resemble televised bearbaiting. It was the only space big enough to accommodate the media turnout, let alone the cameras, mics, tripods. The fourth estate was in communal maul-mode. Most reporters carried copies of the *Evening News*, pointedly and prominently displaying the Serial Killer Taunts Cops headline. That, and the Disposer's threat to strike again had brought the journos here in force. And they hadn't heard the full story yet.

When Flint released details of the latest attack on the Churchill estate, the noise level rocketed. Journalists shouted over each other, fired questions like arrows. Poisoned.

"Is this another police failure?"

"Are you considering your position?"

"How many more mistakes?"

"Will you resign over this?"

"Will there be more killings?"

"Have you been in contact with the Disposer?"

"Are you liaising with Matt Snow?"

Even now they hadn't been given the complete picture. Flint

was withholding the fact that Snow had been filmed at the crime scene, that every cop in the city was hunting him. Questions were still being thrown. Flint raised a hand to quell the flow. It didn't. The door opening had more effect. There was a brief lull as DC Darren New strode in, headed for the top table, whispered a few words to Flint.

The detective got to his feet. Hacks sensed the story was moving too. Lenses focused, lights flashed, cameras rolled. Flint took a few sips of water, before speaking. He must've lost a litre in perspiration. "A man's been detained following an attack earlier today on the Churchill estate in Ladywood. While in custody, he'll also be questioned about the recent killings of paedophiles in the city. At this stage, we're not looking for anyone else in connection with the inquiry."

Which as everyone in the room knew was police-speak for we've got the bastard

Matt Snow had sweated two hours in a police cell before being escorted to Interview Room 2 where he was left alone for a further sixty minutes. Solitary confinement could work wonders getting suspects to open up. When Bev and Flint joined the reporter just after four o'clock, it was like walking into a distiller's. Whisky fumes clung to Snow's unwashed clothes, emanated from his stale breath. He was sober now, sober and subdued. His brief was stuck in court in Manchester; Snow just wanted to get on with it. Bev thought he was off his head not to wait.

"Give me a chance to explain." The reporter tugged at his fringe. "It's not how it looks."

"From where I sit," Flint said, "it can't look any worse."

Far as the DCS was concerned, Snow was in the frame for four murders, one attempted. They had a search team at his flat; Flint was convinced Ryan's movie would turn out to be the tip of the evidence iceberg. Snow was going down. Flint had no doubt. If the chief was right, neither did Bev.

She took Flint's cue to press buttons, ran through the spiel for audio and video recordings. Given the scale of the inquiry, Christ knew where he'd start.

"Where were you today between ten a m and twelve noon?" Confident, casual, Flint lounged back, legs crossed at the ankle.

Snow frowned. "Hold on. Just trying to think."

Flint tapped a slow beat on the table. "If this is you explaining…"

"Whatever I say'll sound bad." Snow would pull the fringe out if he didn't stop messing with it.

"It is bad," Flint told him. "We have film of you on the Churchill estate. You and a man who's now on life support. You going through his…"

"Wrong." Snow tightened his mouth, shook his head. "I was checking…"

"Checking what? Another story?" The explanation for his premature presence at crime scenes was wearing thin.

"Checking for a pulse, Mr Flint. The guy was in a bad way."

"Still is." The unidentified victim was actually off the danger list and out of intensive care. Flint saw no reason to share the news with Snow.

"It wasn't down to me. Not this morning. Not any of it. I've not killed anyone. I've been stitched up from the word go. Only thing I'm guilty of is being a complete dummy." Convincing. Calm. Contrite. If Bev didn't know better she'd believe him.

"That why you were doing a runner?" She sniffed. His packed bag was with the custody sergeant.

"I was on my way here. I was going to ask for police protection."

"You taking the piss?" Bev asked.

"Protection?" Flint laughed out loud. "Who from?"

"The psycho who says he's the Disposer." Calm? Rational?

Clinical? Calculating?

"Would that be the invisible psycho?" Flint sneered. "The psycho with the juicy exclusives? The psycho who selected Matt Snow from every hack in the country to write about his so-called mission?" Flint shot forward, raised his voice. "The psycho who's killed four people?"

"God, this is what I was scared of." He rubbed both hands over his face. "I had evidence, Mr Flint. In case I was being set up. Photographs he sent, e-mails, notes, tapes."

"Course you did," Flint drawled. "It's over, Snow. Admit it. It's pure invention. The Disposer only exists in your sick head. You're going down…"

"I swear…"

"Had?" Bev narrowed her eyes. "You said 'had' evidence."

"It's all gone. He broke into my place. Took everything."

Tap on the door. Mac popped his head round. "Chief? A word?"

Something afoot. Mac had that look. She rose, paused the recordings. "Tea, coffee, anything to eat?" Regulations. Had to ask. Could do with a drink herself.

He shook his head. "D'you think I'm lying, Bev?"

"Four people are dead, Snow. Let's say it's not down to you – why'd you go along with the guy?" Had to be something in it for the reporter.

He outlined the Disposer's proposition, the promises, the film, the book. Christ, she thought, it'd be the sodding t-shirt next. If Snow was telling the truth – what a plonker. "I'm not stupid, Bev. I thought the bastard might not deliver. But I never suspected for a minute I was being set up to take the rap for the killings."

She studied her nails. "Why didn't you come to us? I warned you about playing with fire."

"It wasn't just me he was threatening to burn." He explained about the photographs: his mother stepping out of the shower, the shot of Snow and Anna Kendall in a bar. Pictures now conveniently disappeared. "He said he'd kill them too. He's insane, Bev."

Or Snow was. Every syllable could be a lie. And if Snow was the psycho, that meant he'd not only killed four times but concocted the Disposer to big up the story, aggrandise his career. Weirder shit happened. Without evidence, there wasn't enough proof either way.

She turned her mouth down. "Why'd he come to you?"

Snow hunched forward, elbows on knees. "Said he liked my stuff. Thought I'd do him a good job."

Yeah. Dirty work. She got up, stretched her legs. "What do you know about him?"

He told her about the time the Disposer had lain in wait in the motor. The abused childhood he'd talked about. How he loathed paedophiles. That he'd threatened to kill himself when the mission was complete.

"Names, places, dates?" It was all fairy stories without facts.

Snow shook his head. "You're a reporter – didn't you ask?"

"With a knife at my throat?"

Bev shrugged. Saw a neck on the block. The door almost hit her when Flint re-entered. The DCS had a similar look on his face to Mac's minutes ago.

"Sergeant?" Flint pointedly ignored the reporter. "I'm terminating the interview until the search at Mr Snow's flat is complete. Given the initial findings, it'll save time."

Snow frowned. "What findings?"

"Enough to send you down for life," Flint snarled. "When we resume, I seriously suggest you start telling the truth."

33

"No one can argue with evidence." Which was Flint's way of telling Bev to back off, not rock the police boat. She'd not said anything to make waves; maybe he'd read the scepticism in her face. Either way, it had been the chief's parting shot before heading to the Prince where he was getting in the drinks. Most of the squad including Mac was there to celebrate – bar the shouting – the end of the case. Bev had declined. Partly because her desk had been hit by another paper avalanche, partly because there was a niggle in her head that wouldn't go away. If Snow was innocent, the real killer would go free.

She was in the murder room now. Empty and dark apart from moonlight, it seemed otherworldly, an alien landscape, silver, cold, deserted. The line of whiteboards with its grisly displays was silhouetted against the windows. She didn't need light to see the images; they were imprinted on her brain: grey ghostly features, dead unseeing eyes.

She reached for a copy of the search team's findings, flicked on a desk lamp. She'd read it twice already, still reckoned it needed further illumination. Especially as Snow would face charges first thing on the strength of the contents. They were a forensic guy's wet dream: bloodstained clothes at the bottom of a laundry basket, the victims' photographs taped to drawer undersides, aerosol paint cans on a shelf in the garage. And a cushion stuffed under a wardrobe. Bev had gone to exhibits to check it out, confirmed it was Gladys Marsden's. Snow might as well have left big red arrows saying Here I am; come and get me.

Knackered, she perched on the desk, massaged her bump. She'd felt the odd twinge during the last couple of hours. Felt another when she recalled her last sighting of Snow when he was led to the cells, drawn, haggard, protesting his innocence. Whatever doubts she had about the reporter, she knew he wasn't stupid. Who in their right mind would leave incriminating stuff around the place? Assuming he wasn't mental. When confronted with the findings, Snow claimed they'd been planted, again insisted he was being framed by the psycho.

Flint agreed. Only in his version, Snow was the psycho. The Disposer had never existed. The proof hadn't been stolen, as the reporter claimed, because it had never existed in the first place. Snow had staged the frantic search of his flat to back up his make-believe.

Bev tapped fingers on her thigh. It didn't add up. When Snow took the place apart, why hadn't he come across the incriminating items? Surely he'd have got rid of everything? Flint argued that Snow thought he was so far ahead of the police he'd no idea they were on to him. But what if the items hadn't been there during Snow's search? What if they'd been planted after his arrest? By a killer who'd coolly entered the flat and hidden enough evidence to see Snow behind bars for the rest of his life. That was revenge so cold it was dry ice. So who'd Snow pissed off big time?

Ears pricked, she heard her phone ring, dashed back to the office. Too late. Missed it. She sighed, reckoned she'd make a couple of calls, see off a bit of admin, then head for home. She shuffled papers as she listened to the dial tone, half-expecting Anna Kendall's answerphone to kick in. She wanted to let the writer know what was happening with Snow. Off the record. After half a dozen rings a man answered with the number and a jokey: "Ms Kendall's residence. How may I help?"

Bev raised an amused eyebrow, cut the connection. The news could wait, it sounded as if Anna was in line for a good night. She frowned. The voice was vaguely familiar. Where'd she heard it before? She racked her brain trying to place it.

Knew it was in there somewhere. Couldn't call it up, talk about information overload.

Fidgety fingers now played with a note from a mate at Handsworth nick. Bev had asked to be kept in the loop on Caitlin Finney whose prints had been lifted at the Graves's place. The name meant nothing to Madeleine. Least, that's what the widow had said earlier when Bev phoned with the development. Bev sat back, recalled the slashed portrait, the canvas covered in red paint. Hard to believe Finney had targeted the family at random. She wasn't around to ask. Neighbours hadn't seen her, and she'd not been in work for several days.

Fingers tapped the door. Carol Pemberton popped her head round smiling. "Not coming out to play, sarge?"

"Nah. Look at this." Every inch of the desktop was covered in paperwork.

"Least we won't need any more of these." Pembers strolled in, plonked half a dozen shorthand notebooks on the floor. "Tell you what, Bev, by the time I finished this lot, I was seeing double."

Snow's shorthand books. Bev narrowed her eyes. Of course. That was where she'd seen Finney's name before; one of the few bits of scribble she'd been able to make out in the first batch. So why had Matt Snow been in contact with Caitlin Finney?

"Going through these, Caz." Bev pointed a toe at the pile of books. "Come across the name Graves?"

She nodded. "Adam Graves. Mean anything to you?"

34

Matt Snow had been sniffing round Adam Graves after Caitlin Finney approached the *Evening News* with a string of sexual allegations against the doctor. Accusations that could destroy a career, wreck a life. And drive a man to suicide? Snow's short-hand hadn't given much away, but news editor Rick Palmer was currently on the phone filling in some of the gaps.

Before leaving the nick, Bev had tried calling Anna Kendall to see if the writer could shed light on the Snow-Graves-Finney triangle. Left a message on the third attempt. Palmer had been next on the list. The news desk wouldn't give his number, said they'd get him to call. Bev had been home enough time to demolish a plate of the absent Frankie's lasagne when Palmer rang back. Initially reluctant to divulge detail, the dealmaker was an undertaking from Bev that when the time was right the *News* would get the inside track. Like that was going to happen.

She sat at the kitchen table making notes as Palmer talked. "Finney alleged Graves had drugged her and repeatedly raped her. Claimed she wasn't the only one, the guy had knocked up some kid young enough to be his daughter. Big story if it panned out. Matt put the allegations to Graves. The doc denied the whole thing. Said the woman was a pain in the backside. She was obsessed with him, apparently. Followed him round, bombarded him with letters, e-mails, phone calls. Touch of the stalkers, you know?"

More than a touch, given the heavy-handed vandalism to the portrait. On the other hand… Bev sniffed. "Graves would say that, wouldn't he?"

She heard the rasp of a match. Palmer was having a baccy. "Yeah, well, we did a load of background checks. Discovered

Finney had been in and out of psychiatric hospitals, made two false rape allegations when she was in her teens. Woman's a flake."

"And?" Bev prompted. He inhaled before answering. She sucked her pen, swallowed a craving.

"It didn't stand up, did it? No way could we run a story like that. Matt did the decent thing. Told Graves we were dropping it, he had nothing to worry about."

Yet Graves had still topped himself. "How'd he react?"

"Have to ask Matt. All I know's the threat of legal action went away."

"Legal action?" Ryan's contraband was still in her bag. Her fingers fumbled for the pack.

"Yeah, from the family."

"The family?" Fucking high-pitched echo in here. Where were the ciggies? She needed a smoke to help her think.

"Graves was up front about it. Wasn't the first time a woman patient had made allegations. Occupational hazard, I guess. The wife knew we were investigating the claims. She rang the editor gave him a right rocket."

Her hand stilled. That'd be the same wife who'd looked Bev in the eye and lied through her root canal work. Furious, she upended the bag, pictured Madeleine, and the protective son, lippie Lucas. What was it the snide sod had said in his lah-di-dah voice? "It's her job to upset you?"

"Stone me." The hairs rose on the back of her neck. The voice. It was the same drawl she'd heard on Anna Kendall's phone.

"You all right, love?"

"Peachy." Like hell she was. She lit an Embassy, took a deep draw; it'd take more than a pack of twenty to sort the jumble of thoughts spinning round her head. The Graveses had cause to hate Snow. But what, if anything, did it have to do with the killings?

"Mr Palmer, this nutter, the Disposer? You ever seen him? Spoke to him?"

Long pause. Enough to hear the telly in the background: advert for Gillette. "Not as such."

"That a no?" Palmer's minced words meant the paper had published stories from a decidedly dodgy source.

"Matt's a sharp operator." Palmer was clearly on the same page.

"Not the question."

"If you're asking do I think Matt made the whole thing up – the answer's no. There's a killer out there, love. I never doubted it for an instant."

"Ta, Mr Palmer. Gotta fly."

"Come on… you said…"

She cut the connection, narrowed her eyes, one small part of the puzzle beginning to take shape. She could be way off beam, but she had the faintest glimmering of an idea. She needed to see it again: the photograph Byford had shown her after the first abortive visit to Tudor Grange. A happy snap showing mums and kids on a school trip. Bev pursed her lips, realised she'd jumped to a couple of conclusions that evening which didn't now stack up. Lucas Graves couldn't have been in the line-up. He was way too young. The guv's boys were a good seven or eight years older. She'd assumed Madeleine only had one kid. What if…?

She checked the time. Bit late to call the guv. Tough. She needed to ask a favour, run a few points past him. Best stub out the baccy; Byford had the hearing of a bat colony. She hit a fast-dial button, tapped impatient fingers, groaned when a recorded voice told her no one was in to take her call. Yeah yeah. Message left, she slung the mobile on the table. It rang before she lit another cigarette. Guv must've decided to pick up after all.

"Screening your calls now, guv?" Coy tease.

"Where were you?" Bev's blush started at the neck. It wasn't the big man. It was Oz Khan.

35

For once, Bev was lost for a comeback, though the lasagne threatened an encore as it lurched in her stomach. Thank God Oz was on the end of a line. Least he couldn't see the state she was in. The call must have something to do with the letter. With so much kicking off she'd not given it a second thought. She clocked the envelope now, almost hidden under the fridge. It must've slipped out when she tipped the bag to get the baccy. She sidled over to retrieve it.

"How you doing, mate?" Casual. Neutral. Like her heart wasn't doing a ton. She stooped, slid a finger under the flap, scanned the few lines. Bugger. He'd been waiting at the Hard Rock. Asked her to call if she couldn't make it. Wanted a talk.

"You didn't answer the question. Where were you?"

"Couldn't get away. Sorry, mate."

"Come on, Bev. You could've given me a bell. I've been hanging round since nine."

She grimaced. Cooker clock read 23.02. "Hell of a day, Oz. Anyway, I'm all ears. Shoot."

"Open the door then."

That had to be a joke. She froze, eyes wide. "What?"

"I'm at the front."

She crossed her legs. "Love to, mate." No effing way. She looked crap, hair a mess, button off her trousers, big toe poking through her tights. "I'm tucked up for the night. Early shout and all that. Y'know how it is."

"Sure do. So the sooner you let me in."

Khanie was a bloody-minded sod. Just like her. So much for the attraction of opposites. She shook her head, knew she'd have to relent, let him in, break the baby news. Babies. She'd run this scene a million times in her head, lain awake at night inventing different dialogue and denouements. Her emotions fluctuated daily, hourly; she'd no idea how he'd feel. The next few minutes could determine years of their lives. No pressure then.

She pinched her cheeks, smoothed her hair, opened the door, stepped aside.

"Sleep in your clothes nowadays?" Oz's top lip barely twitched.

"Nightcap? Cuppa cocoa?" Weak smile. She followed as he made for the kitchen. Neat bum, tailored trousers, tight t-shirt, leather blouson slung over a shoulder. He knew his man-in-black look turned her on. She frowned. Best not be expecting any action.

She watched as he filled a glass from the tap, took a few sips. The black hair suited him a tad longer. She liked the way it curved at the neck. As for the cheekbones, she'd give her eye teeth for bone structure like that. She'd forgotten how beautiful he was, licked her lips.

"So." Hands in pockets, straight-faced stare at her bump. "When were you going to tell me?"

Of all the scenarios she'd envisaged, this wasn't one of them. Muffled guffaws through the wall broke the silence: neighbours watching comedy? This was no barrel of laughs, more kitchen-sink drama. From an angry young man? Her mouth opened a few times before she found words. "Who told you?" And how was he taking it? Furious? Disappointed? Hurt? She couldn't read the face she thought she knew.

He was in Birmingham for a few days on a Met inquiry, popped into Highgate yesterday, knew the minute he saw her. With two sisters who'd both had babies it wasn't rocket science. Patronising scowl.

Cocky git. "Why didn't you say anything?" She tapped a foot until she spotted the peeping toe. It lacked gravitas.

He raised an eyebrow. "That's rich coming from you. Anyway,

the cop shop's hardly the best place to talk, and besides…I needed time to think."

"'Bout?"

Pregnant pause. "You. Me. The baby."

"Babies."

His Adam's apple took a dive. "You're expecting twins?"

Expecting? "Came as a bit of a shock actually."

He pushed himself up from the sink, sat next to her at the table. "Two babies?"

"One each." She nicked Frankie's line, folded defensive arms. "Obviously don't run in the Khan family or you'd have clocked that too." His lips tightened. She softened. He deserved more than weak one-liners. She gave him chapter and verse from the first day she found out about the pregnancy to the scan.

"Why didn't you tell me, Bev?"

Hardest part. Fudge it? No point. "I didn't want to keep it – till I found out there were two."

"And now?"

She shrugged. "Manage somehow."

No hesitation. Not a heartbeat. "We'll manage." Gently he unfolded her arms, closed his hands round hers. "Get a transfer, Bev. Come to London. We can get a place together. Be a family." His gaze searched her face. She didn't know what love looked like, but his expression seemed to cover it. What a star. What an offer. Mighty tempting.

She bit her lip. "Wanna make an honest woman out of me?"

"I'm no miracle worker." Suspicious sniff. "You still smoking?"

"Nah, mate. That'd be Frankie. Anyway…" She flashed a grin, sucker-punched his arm, spoke from the heart. "I'm hugely flattered by the invitation, Oz, enormously pleased…"

"I hate it when you talk like that."

Warmest smile this time. "You're the nicest man I know…"

Withering look. "Nice?"

"Y'know what I mean." Like she knew he'd always loved her. One of the reasons he'd moved on was because she couldn't commit, wouldn't let him close. Close to tears now, she couldn't even meet his eyes. For a bloke, he picked up on it quick.

"There's a 'but' in there somewhere?"

She nodded, eyes still cast down. "I can't do it, Oz. You know that." Her mum and gran were here, Frankie, her home.

"Your folks?" Oz knew all about family pressure. He tilted her chin, stroked her cheek with a thumb. "Thing is, Bev, you'll soon have two more people to think about. What's best for them? Have you thrown that in the equation?"

Little people. He was right. But she'd only just seen the figures. So focused on her present, she'd not fully considered their future. She was always banging on about kids needing two parents, preferably one of each gender. Oz would make a great dad. She loved the guy. But did she love him enough? And what about the unfinished business with the guv? It was late, she was knackered, mixed up, pissed off.

"Can't get my head round this tonight, Oz. Let me think about it, yeah?"

"That's all I'm asking, Bev." He kissed her gently, took his leave, turned at the door. "Just don't keep it to yourself this time."

When he'd gone, she reached for a smoke. "Tea-leaf," she muttered with a wry smile. The pack had gone too.

FRIDAY

36

Highgate. Seven a m. Good on you, guv. Byford had responded
to the message she'd left on his answerphone. The photograph
of the school trip was on Bev's desk. It was the first thing she saw
through admittedly bleary eyes. The blurred vision was down to
an almost sleepless night. She'd thrown on her sharpest Prussian
blue suit and boots in sartorial compensation. Bag dumped on
the floor, coat slung on a hook, she picked up the snap for a
closer look. The big man had stuck a post-it note on the back,
indicating where the kid was in the line-up. Shame she'd missed
the guv. He must've been in at the crack of dawn; maybe he'd
had a crap night as well.

Wasn't just Oz's bolt from the cobalt that had left her tossing
and turning, thoughts on the case had been – still were – in
overdrive. Shots in the dark? Flashes of inspiration? Or so off-
field she was out of the game?

She chewed the inside of her cheek, turned the snap over, ran
her gaze along the smiley gap-toothed kids. And focused. One
notion had hit the mark. She'd been right about Madeleine Graves
having an older child. A daughter. Was she also right about who
that daughter was? Bev studied the little girl's face. Couldn't tell
from this. The image was too small, taken too long ago.

She reached for the phone, dialled the imaging unit. "Al, I've
got a favour to ask."

"So what's new?"

Mac was in the canteen, ploughing through a full English. Bev
pulled up a chair, straddled it, legs jigging.

"How's it going, Mac?" Disarmingly sweet smile.

He stared open-mouthed for a few seconds before answering. "Off to babysit. Thought I'd stoke up first."

Plate like that he'd be in charge of a crèche. "Oh?" She twirled a spoon between her fingers.

He told her Flint wanted him down at the Accident and Emergency hospital. Yesterday's attack victim was compos mentis, might be up for questioning some time that day. If the man could identify Snow as his assailant, they'd have eyewitness evidence on top of the forensic. Enough to throw away several keys.

"Enjoy the bash last night?" Her fingers drummed the table, legs still pumped.

"Flint's do?" Mac burst egg yolk with a crust. "I wasn't there."

Great. Might be easier if he shared reservations. "Reckon he's counting chickens...?"

"Doubt it." He shrugged. "I couldn't go... I was looking at houses."

"Course you were." She should've remembered; he'd told her often enough he wanted out of that bedsit.

Mac raised an eyebrow. "Why you asking about Flint?" Her nonchalant shrug didn't go with the tapping foot, drumming fingers, darting glance. "Come on, boss. Out with it."

"What?"

"Either you're working up to something, or you're sat on an ants' nest."

Quick calculation: the guv was otherwise engaged, she needed a sounding board, might as well take the plunge. Hunched forward, she lowered her voice. "I don't buy Snow as the killer." She outlined what bits of theory she'd come up with, the rest was too sketchy to share. She told Mac she believed the Graves family held Matt Snow accountable for Adam Graves's death. That the doc had been so scared of bad press he'd topped himself. That his wife and son had set up the reporter to take the rap for the murders. "Revenge pure and simple. What you reckon?"

"I reckon you're sat on an ants' nest. Where's the evidence?"

She snorted. "With exhibits." All the items the Graves had planted in Snow's place. "Thing is Mac, the story'd been spiked anyway. Snow couldn't stand it up. The doc's suicide wasn't down to Tintin."

"I'll say it again: where's the evidence?"

She flapped a hand. "It's a family affair, Mac. Don't know the detail, who did what, when, but they're in this together. Heartless arrogant bastards. Wasting what they see as a few losers to trap a fall guy like Snow." Both fists were tight now. "Think they're so smart they'll get away with it. And if we don't do something…"

He studied her face for a second or two. "You're out of your tiny."

"It makes sense, mate. We always believed there had to be more than one killer." She held his gaze. "I think it's three."

He pushed his plate away. "You can't go flinging wild accusations round, boss. Not without…"

"Evidence." She tightened her lips. "I know. I'm working on it."

"What's Flint say?"

She shrugged. "He's got his killer."

"What you going to do?"

"Working on that as well." Thin smile. "Might need a favour…"

Seemed to Bev her office clock was on go-slow. Probably because she'd asked Al Copley for a rush job. Bev didn't do patient. With endless paperwork and phone calls, the morning had dragged interminably, her brain the only thing on fast-forward. One minute the Graves scenario was sound as a bell, the next it had more holes than a sieve shop.

The twenty-minute break around midday had been for fresh air as much as food. No one at the nick to play with anyway: Mac still at the hospital, Byford at the magistrates' court for the Joshua Connolly remand. At a pinch, Powell could've filled the social gap but the DI had swanned off to Brighton on a few days' leave. That and the blue sky made her realise how much she needed a break. Most of the people she'd passed on the streets round Highgate looked as if they were on a permanent breather. Youths hanging round offies, single mothers pushing double buggies. Bev didn't go down that mental path, concentrated instead on where the Graves connection was going. One solid link was all she needed.

She fancied running a few points past Snow, but Flint had left her out of the latest interview. Didn't think she had the right attitude. Mid-afternoon now, and the chief was still in Interview 2; Carol Pemberton was sidekick. Bev'd sneaked several butchers' through the spy hole during the day. Every time she looked, Snow was slumped further in the chair. Sullen-faced, tight-lipped, it looked as if the reporter was letting his brief do most of the talking. Wise move.

She stifled a yawn, ambled to the window, spotted the guv walking to his motor. Actually, rewind. On second glance, it was Byford junior. She'd made that mistake before. She breathed on the glass a few times, drew a smiley face, stepped back, head cocked, to admire the handiwork.

"Busy day then?" Al Copley. Imaging unit's Picasso-man. He put Bev in mind of Harry Potter on stilts.

"Stops RSI, this, mate." She winked. "Think of the money I'm saving the brass."

He raised an eyebrow, stepped in carrying an A4 envelope. "There's a point in there somewhere?"

"Bashing that keyboard for hours on end?" She nodded at the desk. "Ever know me slap in an industrial injury claim?"

He rolled his eyes. "I'm sure the brass'll be jolly touched."

She almost snatched the envelope from his hand. He pushed his glasses up his forehead. "With a bit more time, Bev…"

Al had worked magic anyway. She'd asked for a rush job, and he'd delivered. Seeing Richard Byford that first time – that airbrushed computer-enhanced version of his dad – had given her the idea. Only she'd asked Al to do the opposite. In seven hours, he'd added twenty years to the little girl in the school photograph. And she'd grown into Anna Kendall.

37

"I'm going out there. Tudor Grange." Bev was parked at the back of Highgate in the MG talking to Mac on the phone. He was up to speed though still stuck at the hospital. Her thinking was that Madeleine was the easy first target, the family's soft underbelly.

"You're not." Adamant. "Not on your own."

"Do me a favour." Like she'd go in without backup. "When can you get away?"

The eye roll was audible. "Tell Flint. See what he says."

"Tell him what, Mac?" Her hand gripped the wheel. "There isn't enough to go on." All day she'd speculated with ideas, possible scenarios. "I need to get her talking."

"Have you spoken to Kendall?"

"Yeah, sure. Hey, honey. Guess what? You're nicked." Despite the scorn, she'd lifted the phone seven or eight times to call the cow before deciding against. Tips-offs were more Kendall's baby than Bev's. She'd given Rick Palmer a bell though, discovered among other things that Kendall was out on a job. Business as usual then.

Waves of fury had washed over Bev, as she'd taken on board the full depth of Kendall's duplicity. Reckoned she could drown in Embarrassment Ocean. "Needs a face-to-face, Mac."

"And if you're wrong?"

"I'm wrong."

Rustle on the line. "It's six o'clock now." Checking his watch. "Flint's sending a replacement any time. I'll call soon as…"

"Meet you there."

"No, boss."

"Place needs an eye on it." Her biggest fear was that they'd do a flit. Then again, they were so effing cocky they probably thought they could walk the Channel.

"Don't go in on your own."

"As if."

Bev had no intention of going in on her own. She was getting the lie of the land. Through the sitting room window, she spotted two liars softly lit by lamps, chatting, drinking red wine. Very cosy. Mother and son reunion. She scowled: as if Lucas Graves had ever gone away. Snide sod's hair still looked as if it had been dipped in red paint.

Bev felt like a theatregoer watching a play. Instead of the stalls, she was keeping a low profile from the Midget.

Parked opposite – the profile wasn't that low. Deliberate? Maybe.

Twenty minutes on, it started tipping down. Rain hammered the soft top, ran down the windscreen. She watched through a soft focus waterfall, as Madeleine drifted to the window, drew the curtains. End of act one

Bev flicked the wipers, wished she'd brought something for the interval. Could be some time… There were only two cars on the drive. Probably meant no one else was in there. Shame. She itched to confront La Kendall; she smacked her palm against the wheel. More she thought about it, stronger the mortification. She'd been jerked round by the same puppet masters as Snow. How dumb can you get? She hadn't been stringing Kendall along at all. Kendall had wanted to get near the inquiry, engineered it herself. And Bev had swallowed the arse-licking lies, hook line and sodding sinker: *Oh Bev, you're a great role model. Oh Bev, I hope the head start helps. Oh Bev, you'd be ace. Sergeant Morriss! Are you asking me to be your snout?* She groaned. Fuck's sake. She'd even let the frigging woman have a nose round the incident room. She dropped her head in her hands.

And almost missed Lucas Graves's exit.

DC Mac Tyler pulled out of the hospital just gone seven. Shucking into his coat, he ran towards the car park, hit fast dial on reaching the Vauxhall. The boss would think she had a heavy breather on the line. He gave a grim smile: the quick dash wasn't entirely down to the cloudburst.

Mac had finally been given the medical green light to talk to the Churchill estate attack victim. He'd spent the last twenty minutes interviewing the thirty-year-old who'd been left for dead. Paddy Jarvis had revealed more than his own identity.

PJ had been a fighter, he told Mac. Literally. Won medals as an amateur boxer; knew how to roll with the punches, how to land a few. During an almighty struggle, Jarvis had whacked his attacker in the face, not sure exactly where because he'd worn a hood. Fired and furious Jarvis had yanked it off for a closer look. It was at that instant a syringe was plunged into Jarvis's arm. But the glimpse he'd caught of his assailant before hitting the ground was enough.

Whatever crimes Matt Snow may have committed, he hadn't attacked Paddy Jarvis. Not unless the reporter dressed like a member of the Adams family.

"Come on, boss," he muttered. "Pick up will you?"

The sound of crunching gravel alerted Bev. She lifted her head to catch Lucas Graves, dandy-strutting in a long dark coat, towards the silver BMW. Nasty bruise on his cheek. Good. She hoped he'd walked into a wall. Madeleine, framed in the heavy oak door, blew kisses as he got into the car. Bev curled a lip, felt like spitting. She watched as the taillights disappeared, tapped tetchy fingers on the gear stick. Couple minutes later, a light came on upstairs. Madeleine again. Was she alone in the house?

Bev snatched the phone on the first ring, listened as Mac filled her in on the development. Paddy Jarvis's description of the

261

attacker fitted Lucas Graves in every detail, even without the clincher bruise. She felt her palms tingle. It had been worth freezing her ass off. If nothing else, Lucas Graves could be brought in for questioning. She'd pass the BMW's registration to Highgate control; Graves wouldn't get far.

"Have a word with Flint, will you, mate? Fill him in on what's going on." Mac was always on at her to delegate more.

"Gee thanks, boss." Short straw in poisoned chalice.

Bev checked the clock on the dash: 7.10. "How long'll you be?"

"Ten mins max. Boss… don't go in…"

"Mac. I know."

Meant it too – had Madeleine Graves not emerged minutes later with a Louis Vuitton in one hand, car keys in the other.

38

The gravel did its early warning act again. Madeleine Graves spun round on kitten heels before Bev was in spitting distance. She registered the flash of contempt in the widow's face before the practised warm smile was smoothed on. Unlike the patchy heavy-handed make-up.

"Sergeant." Arms wide. "As you can see, I'm on…"

Slow head shake. "I'd like a word, Mrs Graves. Got some news."

Peachy lips tightened. "It's really not convenient."

"Wet out here." Bev's flat palm underlined the rain check.

Without speaking, the widow stowed the cases in the Audi's boot, nodded towards the house as she stormed past. Bev brought up the rear, tugged her forelock. Inside, she noted the huge gilt mirror replacing Adam Graves's damaged portrait. Madeleine gazed at her own reflection; droplets of rain fell on the tiles as she ran a hand through her hair. Eye contact with Bev in the glass was fleeting and hostile. "News, you said?"

"Not here." Not in the hall where Bev had left the door slightly ajar. The widow had no choice, followed Bev to the sitting room. Virgin territory to Bev. Her quick glance took in dark woods, deep reds, tapestries, tassels. She perched on the edge of a chesterfield opposite a fireplace big enough to burn tree trunks. Madeleine Graves, still wearing a navy swing coat, posed in front of it.

Grandfather clock ticked, rain needled windowpanes. "Caitlin Finney," Bev began.

Deep sigh. "I told you on the phone I've never heard of the wom…."

"Bollocks." Time for faffing round had long gone. These people had plotted meticulously, executed ruthlessly, presumably had an exit strategy in place; some sort of confession was needed. From a woman who dished out lies as easily as she took breaths. And a woman Bev believed had blood on her hands. Figurative if not actual.

"How dare you." Hard face. Clipped voice.

Easy shrug. "Finney was a threat to your husband; she went to the press."

The eyes darkened. "Don't be absurd."

"All those allegations. Nasty." Bev pursed disapproving lips, shook her head. "'Nough to get him struck off."

"This is outrageous." Madeleine bit her lip, a quivering hand went to her throat. Maybe lying was second nature. "Adam was the most… wonderful man…" Except where her husband was concerned. She'd protect his memory at any cost.

"Phoned the editor just for a chinwag, did you?"

The widow's foot stopped tapping. She loosened her coat. "Editor? I… don't…"

"Heard you gave him a right rocket." Car engine? Bev pricked her ears. "All those smears, accusations." She turned her mouth down. "They'd have destroyed your old man. Know what they say? No smoke…"

Madeleine clamped her hands over her ears. "Stop it." If the widow had an Achilles heel it was called Adam.

"You stop it, lady," Bev hissed. Time she heard some home truths. "Stop lying through your teeth. Stop the charade. Stop…"

"All right! I phoned the editor." She swallowed, cooled it. "So what? I had every right. The exposure would've ruined Adam. Ruined us. There wasn't a single word of truth in what that cheap trollop was saying. Yet still that muck-spreader kept digging for sleaze that didn't exist."

Bev creased her eyes. She'd not heard, then. Didn't know the paper had dropped the story. That Snow had told Adam Graves they'd not run with it. Think. Feet. On. What did it mean? Didn't know yet. She sniffed. Casual. "Whose idea was it?"

"What?"

"To stitch up Matt Snow. Make him pay. Bump off a few paedo-losers along the way."

"I have no idea what you're talking about." But she did. The warm brown eyes held chips of ice.

Bev shrugged. "No one gives a toss anyway. Scum of the earth." The widow kept shtum. "Who came up with the Disposer? Good game, eh? That down to Anna, was it? Her and Lucas do the strong-arming? You a dab hand with the needle, are you, Maddie?"

Flared nostrils, tight fists. "You know nothing."

"I know this, lady." Straight delivery. "You're going down."

"Wrong again, ace detective." Condescending drawl. "Isn't she, Mummy?"

Heavier the rain, slower the traffic. Slick roads, slack driving. Mac reckoned it was closer to twenty minutes by the time he turned into Tudor Grange. Peering through the screen, wipers on max, he spotted the Midget two-thirds the way down. Couldn't see the silhouette of a driver. He drove past slowly. Where the hell was she?

He parked the Vauxhall behind the MG, tapped his fingers on the wheel. Impatient, pig-headed, bolshie, Bev was all that. But she'd not have gone in without good cause. Maybe she wasn't inside at all? Just taking a closer look from the street? Yeah. Right. In this pissy weather.

Resigned, he got out, locked up, wandered towards the house. Eyes peeled, ears pricked, he walked on by the first time, dodged spray when a passing car hit a puddle. On the second pass he registered the tiny line of light where the door wasn't flush. That settled it then. His duty as a cop to tell the householder, wasn't it?

The boss had been right about the gravel. Dead noisy? Too noisy? Frowning, he turned his head. Just a fraction too late.

Bev didn't react, continued talking as if Anna Kendall had been there since the get-go. The devious cow would never wrong-foot her again. Bev thought she might have heard the cavalry approaching as well. The gravel was better than a burglar alarm.

"See, I know this is a family affair," she said. "But I can't work out who did what when."

"Never were much of a cop." Kendall sauntered in wearing frock coat, slouch boots, elitist sneer. She dropped a peck on her mother's cheek, lowered herself into a leather armchair. "Hannah York, by the way. Anna Kendall's my professional name."

Bev so wanted to slap off the smirk. She unclenched tight fists. Woman had a point though. Bev should've seen a lot of things sooner. Eyes were beginning to open now, pieces slotting into place. Kendall was the only member of the Graves family who could've known Matt Snow was no longer a threat. Why maintain the delusion? Unless it served her self-interest.

"Help me out here." Bev spread her hands. "Who wrote the note?"

"What note?" Madeleine asked. Bev sensed Kendall, York, whatever the hell her name was, watching closely.

"The suicide note, lady. The one you destroyed."

Exasperated, Madeleine showed plump empty hands. "There was no…"

"Let's think, what would it say?" Bev cocked her head like she was working on a form of words. "Something like: I can't stand the pressure? I'm being hounded? Matt Snow's destroying me?"

"Guttersnipe with his tawdry accusations." The widow's face twisted in ugly hatred. Bev had hit the true colours button. "That pathetic little man drove Adam to his death. What my husband did, he did out of love for his family to save us the shame, the…"

"Pile of shite. Your old man wasn't under pressure from Matt

Snow. The guy couldn't stand the story up. The paper was never going to run with it."

"But... Adam..." Bemused frown.

"Knew all about it. Soon's Snow found out it was a no-no he did the decent thing. Told your old man he had no worries." She turned to the woman she still thought of as Kendall. "But he did, didn't he, love?"

Kendall yawned. "Sorry. Did you say something?"

The interchange had gone over Madeleine's head. Mind on recall. "But the note... Adam was afraid..."

Yes! Bev hid her elation. Little more than inspired conjecture had just been confirmed. Stack more needed verifying. "The note was written by someone else, Mrs Graves." She paused to let it sink in. "Cause it sure as hell wasn't the one your old man left."

Madeleine frowned, whispered, "What?"

Kendall casually adjusted a boot. "We're really not interested in your infantile suppositions."

"She didn't mention it then, Mrs Graves? The real note." Wing. Prayer. Busk.

"You bitch," Kendall hissed. "Shut your stupid mouth."

Bev dived at the last minute; knew she should've kept her eyes on the younger woman. She dodged the blow's full force. Frigging lucky, that. Kendall hadn't lashed out with a fist. The black-handled knife had come from her pocket, maybe a boot. The blade had ripped into Bev's sleeve, nicked the upper arm. It'd sting like crazy later but the adrenalin kicked in same time as the training.

Bev aimed just above the wrist, heard the crack as her foot made contact with the bone; the knife flew across the room. Kendall screamed, clutched the wrist close to her body. Bev grabbed the injured arm, twisted it up Kendall's back. Twisted it higher. Kendall gasped in pain. "Don't fuck with me, love."

Bev had taken more self-defence courses than Bruce Lee.

Without a weapon, Kendall stood no chance. Bev stood behind Kendall, positioned her so she faced her mother, still holding the injured limb in a vice-like grip. "Go on, love. Talk to Mummy. Tell her the truth."

Mac didn't see what hit him. Heard the sickening crunch as a missile whacked his right temple. He caught fleeting movement in the corner of his eye, sensed a dark form in the shadows behind. Angry accusing noises were coming from the house. Pain was so bad it hurt to think. Knew he only had seconds to make a move. Dizzy and nauseous, he sank to his knees. He covered his face with his hands, not sure how long he could keep it together. Please God, let the bastard show himself soon.

The split second the figure emerged Mac hurled a fistful of gravel at the guy. Paddy Jarvis's description had been spot on. Lucas Graves. The movement sent shock waves through Mac's head, spasm after spasm of pain. Police sirens in the distance undoubtedly saved him. Lucas Graves snarled, aimed a last vicious kick at Mac's face then fled. The backup Mac had called was closer. Not close enough. Slowly, wincing with every move, Mac staggered to his feet, inched forward, felled once more by waves of sickness.

The piercing scream from inside drowned the sirens' wail. Mac forced himself to stand again, lurched forward, arms flailed for balance. Blood ran from his nostrils, streamed from the head wound. Swollen eyes were almost closed by the time he reached Bev. It was too late then anyway.

Madeleine Graves was like a marble statue. "Tell me what, Hannah?"

"Don't listen to her, Mummy. She's…" The words were lost in a scream as Bev ratcheted the arm.

"Tell her, Kendall. Tell her about the note her old man really wrote. The one you found and thieved." The writer struggled; Bev tightened her grip. "Cause if your ma found it – she'd have known, wouldn't she?"

"Known what?" Madeleine asked. Cool.

"Killed to stop it getting out, didn't you?" She gave the arm a vicious twist.

"Stop what getting out, sergeant?" The widow couldn't have known, or she'd not have gone along with the murders. The paedophiles had been wasted so Snow would get life. Madeleine wanted him behind bars because she believed he'd as good as killed her husband. But the reporter had no longer been a threat to Adam Graves's precious reputation. The threat was closer to home.

"The secret of their sordid affair," Bev sneered. Shame she was holding Kendall from behind, she'd like to see the cow's face. "Shagging your mum's old man, weren't you, love?" Bev narrowed her eyes. Something Rick Palmer said sprang to mind. Conjecture took a leap in the dark. "Got you knocked up, didn't he? You're having his kid. See, lady, your precious husband was screwing a girl young enough to be his daughter. His fucking stepdaughter. That's why he topped himself."

Preternaturally calm, the widow stared into space: the sham of the past, shame of the present.

"Tip him over the edge, did you, love. Threaten to tell the old lady if he didn't leave her? Set up with his bit on the side?"

Police sirens. Guttural roar. It was over in seconds. The widow's arctic eyes had calculated the distance between hand, knife, Kendall's distended belly. Course was set, momentum unstoppable. Light flashed on the blade as Madeleine swung it over her head, charged.

Scalp tingled, heart raced, Bev screamed at the widow to stop. Futile. The weapon was trained on Kendall, the unborn baby. Bev still held the writer shield-like from behind. She had to release her. Had to push her away. Had to protect her. Had to get out of the…

Bev barely felt the blade enter her body, caught a glimpse of Mac as she passed out. Poor sod looked in a bad way.

39

Groggy when she came round after surgery, the guv's grave face had told Bev the only thing she wanted to know. What she considered trivia had filtered out during his visits over the ensuing days. Numb, listless, she didn't give a toss that the Graveses were in custody, that her instincts had been right. That SOCOs had uncovered enough evidence at the house and outbuildings to nail the murdering bastards and secure Snow's release. She couldn't even get worked up that Byford was arriving any time to drive her back to his place. They'd take it easy; see how things worked out a day at a time. Few months back, she'd have been delirious at the prospect. Now?

Ten days she'd lain here surrounded by the sunflowers he'd brought, the books and mags she hadn't read, music she couldn't listen to. She'd been weighing up the personal cost, the price she'd paid. Reckoned her account was in the red, couldn't envisage clearing the debt any time soon.

Professional losses too? There was bound to be a disciplinary; surely she'd lose her rank? She'd endangered her partner's life as well as her own. Mac said he'd speak up for her at any hearing. But could she face another? Did she care? Mac was currently blue-eyed boy; he'd had the nous to call control who'd sent in backup. Not that she begrudged him. Last time he'd popped in to try cheering her up, his eyes were more damson than blue.

Her jacket was on the back of the chair. She slipped it on. Street clothes felt strange: denims, Docs. She checked her watch. Grimaced. Wandered to the window. Brave-face time. She was mildly surprised her reflection was unchanged, given her insides were shattered. Only Byford knew about the night terrors, the damp pillow every morning, the interminable fury, frustration.

She scrabbled in her bag for a bit of lippie. Waste of time; her hand shook too much to put it on straight.

What had the guv said? "You saved two lives, Bev. Hold on to that."

Saved two. Lost two. Easy come. So not easy go. She closed her eyes, gasped at the ache in her soul. The good dreams were even harder to bear. In those she held the twins in her arms. They hadn't been butchered by a mad bitch.

Except Madeleine Graves wasn't insane. Nor were her evil lying kids. For different self-serving motives they'd conspired in a monstrous plot. The arrogance was breath-taking. Waste a few paedos? The Graveses didn't give a rat's arse. Soon as Snow was in custody, they were bailing out.

She'd gone over the case time and again, tiny detail to final frame. Tortured herself with thoughts of *what if...*? Could she have spotted the Kendall-Graves connection earlier? Should she have cottoned on to the fact that the glitzy girlie tops in the widow's bin liners could never have belonged to Madeleine? Shouldn't Kendall's fawning and flattery have rung alarm bells? Taken for a ride? Nah. World cruise.

Seeing something wasn't always enough – it had to be interpreted properly. With hindsight, Caitlin Finney's anonymous note hadn't been questioning the fact Adam Graves committed suicide. Finney had wanted them to investigate the reason why. Why couldn't she have just said so? Saved them all a...

She dug her nails into the palms of her hand. Finney was damaged goods too; back in psychiatric care. Eddie Scrivener as well. He'd never recovered from – in effect – losing his daughter, Tanya. Recent events had brought it flooding back. He'd had a breakdown, been found sleeping on the streets in Walsall.

All those people. All that pain.

Far as Bev could see, the only winner was Matt Snow. The

reporter was writing a book: *Death Sentences*. Insensitive moron had asked her for input. She'd given him two words – one of which was 'off'.

She groaned. How the hell was she going to get through this? Sobbing, she dropped her head in her hands, didn't hear the door. Hands massaged her shoulders, smoothed the knots from her neck. She hated the guv to see her cry. Head down, she surreptitiously wiped away the tears, mustered a weak smile, then turned to face him. "What the hell are you doing here?"

"Nice to see you too." She'd not let Oz visit, couldn't stand to see his pain as well.

"How are you, Bev?"

"Peachy, me, mate."

Sceptical eyebrow. "Yeah, I can see that." He took her hands. "Bev, I can't say how sor..."

She snatched them back. "Don't, then."

Tender smile; he knew gentle words choked her. "I'm up visiting the folks... heading back south this afternoon. I just want you to know... I still think we could make a go of it. If you're interested... the offer stands."

Could they? Was she? Clean break. New start. Maybe that's what she needed. She saw her own reflection in his eyes, reached a hand to stroke his face.

Both turned at a tap on the door. The guv popped his head round, gave an uncertain smile. "When you're ready... Bev?"

Author's note:

What's in a name…?

During the writing of each Bev book, I've experienced one of those extraordinary coincidences that really send the hair on the nape rising. *Bad Press* was no exception – this one still amazes me.

Like many authors, I often find it difficult to come up with names for characters. They have to be just right and I can agonise for hours before finally deciding. For *Bad Press*, I created a news editor. I could see him in my mind's eye, hear his voice even, but what was I going to call him? After much metaphorical pen-chewing, I recalled a couple of reporters I'd worked with in the early days of BRMB radio. I borrowed one's first name and combined it with the other's last. Perfect. I was writing Rick Palmer's first appearance when I decided to check my e-mails. When I saw the inbox I gasped. One of those erstwhile colleagues had just sent a message. Was I surprised? You bet. It was the first time I'd heard from either of them in nearly thirty years.

Heaven, Earth, Horatio… as Bev might say.

Maureen Carter
April 2008